THE GODS OF WAR

Copyright © 2014 Graham Brown
All rights reserved.

ISBN 13: 9781939398185
ISBN 10: 1939398185

Also by Graham Brown and Spencer J. Andrews

Shadows of the Midnight Sun
(Book 1 of the Shadows Trilogy)

Shadows of the Dark Star
(Book 2 of the Shadows Trilogy)
Coming August 2014

The Gods of War: Redemption
(Book 2 of The Gods of War Series)
Coming November 2014

Other novels by Graham Brown
Black Rain
Black Sun
The Eden Prophecy

Co-authored with Clive Cussler
Devil's Gate
The Storm
Zero Hour
Ghost Ship

THE GODS OF WAR

GRAHAM BROWN & SPENCER J. ANDREWS

STEALTH BOOKS

THE GODS OF WAR
Copyright © 2014 by Graham Brown and Spencer J. Andrews
All rights reserved. No part of this book may be used or reproduced by any means, graphic, electronic, or mechanical, including photocopying, recording, taping or by any information storage retrieval system without the written permission of the authors or publisher, except in the case of brief quotations embodied in critical articles and reviews.
Stealth Books
www.stealthbooks.com
ISBN-13: 978-1-939398-18-5 (Paperback Edition)
ISBN-13: 978-1-939398-19-2 (Kindle Edition)
ISBN-13: 978-1-939398-21-5 (ePub Edition)
Published in the United States of America

Dedication

Every story draws inspiration from a thousand sources, be it a snippet of conversation overheard in a restaurant or a street sign emblazoned with an odd sounding name that somehow becomes a character. And above all, from those who support and encourage.

For this story two people in particular stand out and we wanted to say thanks. To Michael Palmieri, who gave us direction when we were lost in the labyrinth of too many plots, and to John Soriano who taught us to re-write and refine until the job was done, no matter how long it took. In effect, to never give up, or give in.

Prologue

August 2137

"The Earth is dying."

These words were spoken by Lucien Rex from his position at the head of the long conference table. "And there is nothing we can do to save it."

Tall, lean and imposing. Lucien stood in a dimly lit room, reserved for the powerful. Around him, pinpoint spotlights illuminated twelve men and women who sat at the table. They were the members of the Cartel, those who'd risen above all others. So wealthy and powerful that their voices mattered more than the billions who lived in the filth beneath their feet.

They stared at Lucien as if confused by what he'd said.

"Let me clarify," he said. "This planet is already dead. We are merely living off its last gasping breaths."

He spoke to them without pity or fear or remorse in his voice. As if there were nothing to be mourned in the loss of humanity's home. He spoke to them as subordinates or perhaps students.

Despite the grave words, they sat like statues, these twelve pillars of power. They were accustomed to such predictions. The prophets of doom had not been silent all these years. But in the enclaves of the wealthy, where all things were plentiful, the misery of a decaying planet, endless war and the suffering of twenty billion people in a constant struggle to survive simply did not register. Private armies and fortress-like compounds saw to that.

Finally, a rotund man at the far end of the table cleared his throat. "Not like you to play the part, Lucien. The sky falls on others, not on us. What's your angle here? Are you trying to scare up more money for President Collins and his efforts?"

"And where is Collins?" another voice asked. "Why isn't he here?"

Lucien almost smiled. "Our President for Life and Leader of the Military Executive was not invited to this session, because he is not aware of the true gravity of the situation."

"How could he not be aware?" one of the Cartel asked. "These are his studies."

"I have my ways," Lucien replied without elaborating. "I assure you the data sent to government offices has been altered."

"For what purpose?"

"To keep the president believing his own foolish hope: that this planet has a future. To keep him passive while we act."

Lucien reached forward and pressed a switch. A holographic image appeared in the center of the table, displaying a graph. Various lines crossed it, moving from the bottom left to the upper right. The scale of years was marked across the bottom.

"We've crossed the threshold," Lucien said. "The glaciers are long gone, the ice caps have melted. And now, the seas are beginning to boil. In the next twelve months they will release more carbon and methane than man has released in the last hundred years. No amount of human engineering can possibly counteract what the Earth is giving off in her dying gasps."

"Are you sure?" one of them asked.

"How do you know this for certain?"

They were leaning forward now. Concerned with what Lucien might say next. He was not some environmental do-gooder, nor a politician or preacher. He was one of them. The richest and most powerful of them. He was the unspoken head of the Cartel. He might have been the president in Collins's place, had Collins not controlled the military with an iron fist.

"Beyond a doubt," Lucien replied.

"What will happen?"

"In six months the dark clouds that never part will become so thick that even genetically engineered plants and algae will no longer produce meaningful amounts of photosynthesis. The food chain will collapse and the twenty billion inhabitants of this planet will go from wretched and sedentary to starving and desperate. So many of them at once will be starving and angry that neither our forces or the armies Collins commands will be able to stop them."

The suggestions began to fly.

"We'll have to convince Collins of a greater solution," one the twelve said. "A purge. A culling of the herd. If we reduce the population drastically, culling ninety percent of humanity, the rest would survive. Those who are spared might even thank us."

"Yes," another voice said.

"It's time. We've all known this day would come," another called out.

Lucien sat down, rested his arms on the edge of the table and tented his hands together. He'd considered such an option himself, years ago. He'd never suggested it aloud because President Collins and his armies saw themselves as defenders of the downtrodden. Or perhaps guardians of the collective human soul, if there was one. They would never allow it.

Humanity must rise or fall together. The president's favorite quote. How wrong he was.

"You misunderstand the nature of our peril," Lucien said, returning his attention to the Cartel. "We've passed the point of no return. The world will continue to get darker and hotter. The seas will boil dry and skies will become thick with poison, too heavy to breathe, too dark to see through. This planet will die whether we exterminate the masses or not. Killing them to the last will only mean we die here alone."

"So what can we do?"

"The solution is simple," Lucien told them. "If all who remain here are going to die, then we have no choice but *to leave.*"

"And go where?"

"To Mars," Lucien said bluntly. "Our president's other pet project."

The group fell silent, perhaps appreciating the irony of the situation. Collins had forced them, under the gravest of threats, to contribute massive levels of funding to the Terra-forming of Mars.

New technologies had been developed; a fleet of massive transports larger than the great tankers that plied the ocean had been built in orbit. New fuels and engines designed and tested, to allow faster transits. Even the development of a rudimentary artificial gravity system.

The costs had been astronomical, most of it borne by those who could pay. In other words, the families represented at this table.

Lucien had been the easiest to persuade because his corporations were given many of the contracts, but the others gave in only kicking and screaming. Now, the very project they railed against would be their lifeboat, their salvation.

Lucien tapped the screen in front of him and the holographic image of the graph vanished. It was replaced by a spherical image in red, partially see-through and marked by a great canyon, several large volcanoes and a smattering of craters.

"Mars was supposed to be an agricultural colony," Lucien said. "Supposed to feed half of the earth's population in twenty years. A wildly optimistic dream of our glassy-eyed president, of course, but at the very least it will be self-sustaining. It will survive even as the Earth goes dark. And we will survive on it: the pinnacle of humanity, leaving the dregs of society behind."

"I'm not interested in living in a hole in the ground," one of them said.

"Cities are being built," Lucien insisted. "Crops are being harvested. Livestock raised."

"My people tell me the whole project is way behind schedule," another one said.

"It is," Lucien admitted. "There have been difficulties. Primarily the president's mismanagement of the project and the fine dust of Mars that destroys machinery without mercy. But I've found a solution to get things back on track and even speed up the timetable. It's already in place."

They sat back quietly contemplating the scenario. "How much time do we have?" one of them asked.

"Less than a year."

They took a collective breath. Lucien understood. It was a dark reality. One not easily faced by those used to getting their way.

"What do you need?" the rotund man offered.

"Very little," Lucien replied. "Unity among us… and Collins out of the way."

This was a dangerous request. Each of them would have killed Collins a dozen times if they could have guaranteed that Collins would go quietly and that his military would not turn on them in a violent response. But Collins was a career soldier. Unlike previous generals, he'd protected the military from being used wastefully. He'd cultivated an esprit de corps and an almost cult like following among those in armed forces. If there was a hierarchy on Earth, and there certainly was, the Cartel and their family members topped it, but the military came in just below them, a place of honor and of special rights. And while the masses despised both organizations, the Cartel was hated more passionately. As such Collins couldn't be deposed easily.

"You'd better have a good plan," the rotund man said, speaking for the rest. "If you fail Collins will show no mercy."

"I'm aware of the risk," Lucien said. "You should have more faith. When have I ever steered you wrong?"

Lucien looked around, his eyes traveling from one face to the next, staring at each of them until they nodded their agreement.

"Mars was meant to be a giant bread basket," a silver haired woman noted. "A new start for humanity."

"And so it shall be," Lucien replied. "For us."

Chapter 1

Central United States, 2137

Dark clouds churned above the barren, dusty plain, mixing together in a colored pallet of purple and yellow like a painful, fading bruise.

Far below, Major James Collins stood on the bulwark of a steel-reinforced battlement. Sweat, grime and three days of stubble covered his face. He wore dusty, camouflaged fatigues with a simple flak jacket over the top. His wavy black hair was uncovered but mussed from the helmet he'd discarded earlier, and his brown eyes were hidden by the reflective orange shield of the blade-like sunglasses he wore.

A well-worn patch on his shoulder displayed a giant, metallic claw grasping three lightning bolts. Writing beneath the powerful image read: *41st Armored, Numquam Numquam Cedere. Never, never, surrender.*

At thirty-seven, Major Collins had spent more than half his life in the military. Scars on his face, chest and back attested to that. He'd spilled blood on every continent around the globe in battles no monument had ever been erected to. In a way he was like every other lifer in the military, and yet he was also the only surviving child of President Jackson Collins, a designation that had always bothered him.

Barred from entering the military because his older sister and brother had been killed in the War of Unification, James had run away from home and enlisted in the military under an assumed name at age seventeen. He'd come up through the ranks starting as a grunt like everyone else. He'd fought in two long campaigns, earning a sleeve full of medals, before the brass actually figured out who he was.

By that point, battlefield promotions had him in charge of a full company at age twenty, and despite expecting he'd end up in the stockade or at least be drummed out of the service, he was promoted to lieutenant and allowed to stay. Far from pissing the old man off, it seemed like the only thing he'd ever done that made his father proud. Eleven years on he was still in the service. He carried a colonel's responsibility, commanding the 41st, but his rank never rose above major as he rejected every cushy promotion that he'd been offered.

Many in the unit and across the military admired his choices. Most of the military billets were filled by those from the lower classes, who saw it as a way out. They signed ten-year contracts and their families had a chance to move from utter poverty to something resembling normal living.

James obviously didn't need that, and was often asked: *What the hell he was doing here?*

He never answered. Just smiled and laughed. Maybe he didn't know. Maybe the reasons changed. But as he stared out at the current surroundings, the question seemed more valid than ever.

They were in the middle of nowhere, a section of the old United States that had been written off after waves of nuclear fallout. When illegal squatters set up shop and found a way to survive, someone up high thought it must be time to reclaim the land. Millions of legitimate settlers were relocated to the plains only to have their numbers decimated year after year by disease, terrorist raids and radiation poisoning.

The only hope was to find clean water, and to that end James and part of his brigade were watching over a sprawling complex built to bring water from one of the deepest aquifers ever found and bring life to a choking land. The only problem was they hadn't found any yet.

As the drilling went on and the water hid from them, a crowd began to gather and watch. Each day there were more of them. Each day they seemed to grow more restless. As James looked out over the crowd from behind the orange shield of his sunglasses, he saw thousands, tens of thousands. They now surrounded the complex in a crowd twenty or thirty deep, lining the concrete walls and electric fencing that surrounded the installation. More could be seen approaching, trudging across the wasteland like long streams of ants.

He noticed their faces were gaunt and thin, their eyes no longer held hope but anger.

Some of them had begun to chant. "Water…water."

It was little more than a quiet murmur, but James had no doubt the chant would grow. Trouble was coming. If they didn't find water soon, they'd have a rebellion on their hands.

With that thought in mind, James turned his back on the crowd and stepped toward the men running one of the huge drilling rigs.

The grinding noise of the drill was as monotonous as the crowd's chanting.

"How far down are you?"

"Eighteen thousand feet," the man replied.

"Anything?"

The driller shook his head. "The studies say it's down there, but all I'm finding is rock."

"Great," James uttered sarcastically.

He looked up at the churning sky. The driller's gaze followed. "Maybe the rains will come back," the driller suggested.

"Poisoned rain isn't going to help these people," James replied. "Keep drilling."

"How far do you want me to go?"

"As deep as you can. In fact, drill until you run out of pipe. And then you fake it until we get more. These people find out we've hit a dry well, and we're gonna have a damned riot."

The driller glanced nervously at the crowd and then nodded. As he went back to work, Collins hopped off the rig and strode across the dusty ground to where two of his men stood, Captain Leonardo Perrera and Lieutenant William Bryant.

Perrera was dressed in grungy fatigues, smoking a cigarette with one hand and holding the heavy ZR-94 pulse rifle lazily in the other. He'd been with the 41st for almost as long as James.

Bryant was new. Straight from the war collage. He was done up in full battle gear, armored up like a damn crusader: helmet on, body armor strapped tight, leg and arm protectors in place. He held his own rifle across his body and down at a forty-five degree angle as if he might need it any second. He looked nervous. "What do you think Major?"

James gave him the once over. "I think, Bryant" he began, "that you must be insane to wear all that gear in this heat. On the other hand…you may finally end up needing it today."

Bryant didn't get the joke; he was always in full armor. Perrera, on the other hand, chuckled, took another drag on the cigarette and then flicked it to the ground.

"Any word out of the insurgent we captured?" Collins asked.

"Nope," Perrera said. "He was definitely Black Death."

Black Death. The leading terrorist group of the day. After the last war, a new type of insurgent had begun to feed on the decay. They wanted radical change, more radical than anything before. Their desired goal was the destruction of their own kind. Only with humankind gone, they reasoned, did the planet stand any chance of survival. They hoped to cause the mass starvation and worldwide pandemic the government was fighting so hard to prevent.

"You think the Black Death care about something this small?" Collins asked.

"Nope," Perrera said. "I don't. I think they know *you're* here. Like it or not, you're a target."

"Someone should tell them that killing me would do my father a favor. They might stop trying so hard."

Perrera laughed. Bryant looked on nervously, not sure if he should laugh or protest.

"You know this wouldn't be a problem if we had our heavy armor," Pererra said. "We look vulnerable with just a few rigs. Any word from Lieutenant Dyson?"

Dyson was one of the company commanders. He was supposed to be bringing in a full squadron of heavy armor. But for reasons no one had seen fit to tell them, he'd been delayed incommunicado for nearly three weeks now. Every time Collins asked he was simply told that Dyson and the big rigs were en-route.

"Not a damn word," James said.

Out beyond the fence the chanting had begun to grow louder. The gaps were filling in, and James could see the crowd growing deeper all along the fence. "Armor or not, we need to back these people off the gate. Get the MRVs up here and move the rest of your men into position. We need a show of force before they do something stupid."

Perrera tossed the cigarette to the ground and grabbed his radio. But Bryant hesitated.

"Problem with my order lieutenant?"

Bryant shifted his weight. "With all due respect, Major, I'm not sure we need to threaten these people. They're just worried. There's a rumor going around that we're stealing the water for ourselves. I think if we talk to them, explain what we're doing…"

Collins smiled. Bryant didn't understand what they were dealing with out here in the settlements. The very people they were trying to save hated them and blamed them for everything. It didn't take much to fire them up. And if the Black Death were swirling around, they'd be damn sure to play on that fear.

"By all means," Collins suggested. "You go talk to them, lieutenant. I'll bring up the big guns just in case they don't like what you have to say."

James smiled as he spoke; he figured this would be a valuable lesson for the newly minted lieutenant.

For his part, Bryant didn't seem to know what to make of the offer, but he hopped down off the battlement and hiked toward the main gate. As he went forward, Perrera and Collins ordered the men into position.

With quiet efficiency, the reserves began streaming forward. While from the far side of the complex, a heavy thudding sound could be heard as three MRVs (Mechanized Robotic Vehicles) came forward.

Like giant walking tanks, the MRVs stood three stories tall. The main cab housed three men and swiveled like a turret. Each side bristled with rotary cannons, rocket launchers and high power plasma cannons. They took up positions around the main drilling rig in a triangular formation.

As the forces took up the defensive positions, James joined Lt. Bryant.

"Please," Lt. Bryant was saying. "Please listen to me. We're trying to help you. We haven't found water yet, but we will."

"Military filth!" someone shouted. "You sent us here to die."

Another voice shouted from a different section. "They're taking the water for themselves. Stealing it!"

As a clod of dirt was hurled into Bryant's face, James sidled up next to him. "Still think you can make them love us?"

As Bryant swept the dirt from his uniform, someone at the front of the crowd began banging a pipe against the iron gate. "Water, water!"

The others joined in, and the chanting and banging grew louder and louder until it was echoing across the vast complex.

It was all too perfect, James thought. Too choreographed. He began to think it was a distraction. His ignored the chanting crowd and the banging pipes and began scanning for signs of different activity.

It didn't take long before he spotted a group of men moving oddly, sliding through the crowd but not chanting or raising their arms and pumping their fists. They were hauling something.

He put the radio to his mouth. "Eagle One, scan sector two immediately. Possible terrorists."

One of the big MRVs took a step forward and pivoted to the right.

The men had dropped out of sight, crouched down behind the crowd. James clutched his rifle and began moving that way.

"Guard the rig!" he said to Bryant. "Perrera, you're with me."

"Where are you going?" Bryant asked.

"We've got bigger problems than an angry crowd."

James began to run forward, but it was too late. Explosives went off behind the crowd. The startled members of the crowd realized they were in trouble. They surged forward into the gates and the electric fencing. Sparks shot across it, and screams of pain went up as a second wave of explosives went off behind them.

"Get away from the gate!" Bryant was shouting. "Please back away!"

At the same moment, a new threat appeared as several off road vehicles came racing over a hill trailing clouds of dust. They opened fire on the crowd members who were trying to flee, forcing them to turn back toward the gate.

Even as the MRVs locked in on the speeding trucks and opened fire, another series of explosions thundered, and the crowd surged forward again.

This time they crashed the gate in an unstoppable panic, a mass of humanity shorting out the fence, bending and breaking the heavy gate and pouring through like water from a collapsed dam.

Hidden in that crowd would be dozens of terrorists with explosives strapped to their bodies.

"God no!" James shouted. "Eagle One, drop the hammer!"

He took cover in a ditch as the MRVs opened fire on the crowd. Thousands would die, but they had to protect the drilling rig, or a hundred times that many would die out in the settlements.

The MRVs tilted their cabs toward the crowd and opened fire with their rotary cannons. Thousands of shells screamed overhead, laying waste to the stampeding crowd like a forest being cut down.

Only now did the terrorists show their hand. From positions behind the scattering crowd, missiles came screaming forth. Two of them hit the lead MRV engulfing it in a ball of flame. A third hit upper reaches of the main drilling rig, while others hit among the men of the 41st.

The crowd began to scatter, but several dozen terrorists continued to fight. Collins saw the MRVs swing into action and begin a quick eradication of the foes, but they were just part of the cover. He finally spotted what he feared. Three men were running directly toward the drilling platform.

He took aim and fired, hitting the first man, who fell and then exploded in a fireball two stories high and fifty feet across. But he missed the other two, as civilians crossing in front of him took the next two shots.

"Damn it!"

James took off running, forcing his way through the crowd. Pushing people out of the way.

"Get down!" he shouted, raising the rifle. He pulled the trigger winging the second terrorist, but he was too late to get the third. The man reached the drilling rig and threw a satchel into the works. An ear-shattering explosion followed. The rig was blown completely apart, the mangled metal toppling over to the sides.

Despite being a hundred feet away, James was thrown backwards by the blast. He landed on the ground stunned and woozy.

Seconds later someone was pulling him to his feet. It was Lt. Bryant.

"Major? Are you alright?"

James saw Bryant's mouth moving but his ears were ringing and he heard nothing. He got to his feet. In one direction the mangled wreckage of the drilling rig was burning. In the other, the suicide bomber he'd winged was slowly getting to his feet.

Without acknowledging Bryant, Collins raced toward the man, tackled him and knocked the detonator out of his hand. As the terrorist stretched for it, James hammered the man across the face with the butt of his rifle.

"You son of a bitch!" he shouted.

The terrorist looked up at James, his face bloody and covered with grime.

"The end of man is near," the man said. "Even you can't stop it."

With fury burning in his heart, James raised the rifle above his head intending to smash the bastard's skull.

"Major!" Bryant yelled, grabbing his arm.

A new wave of cannon fire from the MRVs burned the air above them. James looked around. The crowd was dispersing, fleeing from the onslaught. The off road vehicles were getting picked off one by one as they raced for the horizon.

He grabbed his radio as the last of them was obliterated by a missile from Eagle Three. "Hold your fire!" he ordered. "I repeat, stand down and hold your fire!"

Across from him, the MRVs ceased firing almost instantly. Their rotary cannons whirled to a stop, the tips glowing red from the heat and smoke pouring from the barrels. They turned from quadrant to quadrant but the crowd and the terrorists hidden among it were racing headlong into the distance.

James looked down and ripped a black band from the terrorist's arm.

"Who sent you?" James demanded. "Who's your leader?"

The man did not reply; instead, a strange froth appeared on his lips. James grabbed the man's throat to stop whatever poison he'd taken from being swallowed, but it was too late. Slimy, white foam began pouring from the man's mouth as he choked and coughed and convulsed into death spasms.

"Cyanide," Bryant said.

Disgusted, James released the man. He stood slowly, holding the armband.

"Black Death?" Bryant asked.

"Yeah," James replied. "And they certainly weren't after me."

He threw the armband down and turned. Bodies lay all around them: soldiers, civilians, terrorists. Among them Lieutenant Perrera laid awkwardly, his eyes open, his body riddled with shrapnel, his blood staining the soil beneath him.

A look of anguish settled over James. He stared for a moment—as a medic tried to help—but it was clearly too late. Perrera was already dead.

With a feeling of despair that he could hardly contain, James looked up at the poisoned sky and took a deep breath. Then he turned to Bryant. "Gather up our dead, Lieutenant."

"And the civilians? What should I do with their bodies?"

James hesitated. They didn't have time to bury a thousand civilians. "Burn them."

Bryant hesitated for a moment and then went to work. His armor was dirty now. Charred and scuffed. His soul would soon follow.

As Bryant moved off, another group of soldiers stepped forward to re-secure the main gate if they could. A weathered sign above it read: *Prairie View, Kansas, USA.*

Chapter 2

Isidris Basin, Mars

Hannah Ankaris sat in the passenger seat of a huge ten-wheeled vehicle, known as a Deca-Trac, as it trundled across the red surface of Mars. The big machine moved slowly, more like a monstrous caterpillar than an off road vehicle out on the plains.

Thirty-one years old, with straight black hair, olive skin and green eyes, Hannah was attractive enough to most men, but more stern and standoffish than they seemed to like. She was tough, thick skinned and decisive, traits that made for a better friend than lover.

Not that it mattered, she thought. With life a constant struggle for most, love and passion seemed little more than a selfish lie. Human existence was fairly desolate, though at least tinged with hope like the planet around her.

After decades of work, a colony was growing on Mars. A city, named Olympia, had been built, protected by an artificial magnetic field and surrounded by a hundred square miles of green fields and cropland. But beyond the protection of Olympia's shadow, the world was still mostly inhospitable to mankind.

One cog in the effort to change lay to their right, where the ugly tower of an atmosphere processing unit belched clouds of black smoke and grey steam.

The ungainly collection of rigging, steel plates and high-pressure tubing looked something like an oversized oil rig. One of nearly a thousand that dotted the planet, they were designed to burrow into the crust, extract, grind up and then melt the rocks and soil, ejecting the molten remnants in a volcanic stream, and releasing prodigious amounts of sulfur, nitrogen and oxygen in the process.

Ugly enough to begin with, the plants quickly became encrusted with black soot and surrounded by piles of slag a hundred feet high and stretching ten city blocks in every direction. When they had exhausted a particular extraction site, the plants pulled up stakes and moved to a new spot, crawling at the break-neck pace of one mile per day before settling down and digging in once again.

After years of effort, the atmosphere of Mars had reached a density almost half as thick as Earth's, and the planet itself had gained a collection of long, dark scars. Seen from space, it looked as if the planet was being stitched together in some great medical experiment.

As Hannah studied the atmospheric plant, Alvin Davis drove the big rig. He was a friend and an ally, and also a member of the tech squads that maintained everything on the colony. "How close to you want me to get?" he asked.

Hannah checked the coordinates she'd been given. Their goal lay well beyond the plant, but the plant would give them some cover.

"Take us in onto the access ramp and then around the back," she said. "From there resume our course."

Davis nodded and turned the Deca-Trac.

"Once we've pulled in behind it," she added, "set our status to indicate arrival and maintenance, and then switch off internal tracking. If anyone's watching us on the board they'll have to assume the plant is blocking our signal."

Davis nodded and did as ordered. "Better hope no one comes out to lend a hand."

Hannah doubted that would happen. No one liked to leave the Green Zone if they didn't have to. Fewer still liked working on the modification plants.

"If they do, I'll come up with some excuse," she said. "Or have them committed to the psych ward and sedated."

"So being the chief medical officer comes with a few perks after all," Davis replied.

Hannah laughed. She was in charge of three doctors, a nursing staff and two labs. Her group was kept busy by an endless string of testing, injuries and strange maladies that cropped up among the colonists. Just keeping on top of the work kept her constantly on the move. A privilege that helped with her second, covert occupation. Still, she would be hard pressed to explain what she was doing out here at an un-manned plant.

Before long, they'd put the processing unit behind them, and rolled out onto the vast empty plains. Hannah looked to the west. Low on the horizon and ready to set, the sun was a ball of orange in the darkening sky. To the east, a second source of light beamed down on them. Hazy and scattered like headlights in fog, this source of light came from a massive collection of orbiting mirrors, called the Solaris Array.

It had taken a decade to build and launch the array, which was made up of fifty thousand computer controlled reflective panels, each the size of a ten-story building. But the effort had been worth it. This second *sun* added another twenty percent to the incoming heat. Most of it aimed at a band along the equator. The combined efforts of the Solaris Array and the atmospheric modification plants had raised the average temperatures on the planet by forty degrees. But with the atmosphere still so thin it was like the harshest of deserts, broiling in the day and cold to the point of frost at night.

Further north or south the temps dropped dramatically, but if the progress continued, in another ten years or so half the planet would be habitable without environmental suits.

The future was bright, Hannah thought to herself, bright and warm. But there was no guarantee any of them would live to see it.

The Deca-Trac continued to rumble forward, shuddering slightly as the wind buffeted the vehicle's side. With heat and thicker atmosphere came weather. Wind was becoming a problem, mostly because it whipped up the ultrafine dust blanketing the surface.

Hannah could hear it sand-blasting the side of the truck. The curved Plexiglas windshield was already hazy after less than a month of exposure. In another month it would be opaque and need replacing.

"The forecast didn't mention these winds," Davis said, slowing.

"They'll probably die down after sunset," she replied.

"And if they don't and we get caught in a dust storm?"

There was no need to answer. If that happened they would most certainly die.

"Keep going," she said. "We have a mission to finish."

Davis stared at her for a minute, and then reluctantly nudged the throttle forward. "We get caught out here, the dust will clog all the filters and kill the engine. We can't walk in it, we can't breathe in it, and we sure as hell can't call for help if we need it."

He was right about that. Hard to call for help when you were crossing a zone you weren't supposed to be in in the first place. "Trust me," she said. "We'll be okay."

They continued on, traveling another five miles, closing in on the coordinates she'd been given. After rolling over a small ridge, they came down a sandy hill and passed a rocky out cropping. On the far side they came upon a sight neither of them had expected.

Another Deca-Trac similar to their own lay there, half buried in the sand. Thirty yards away a huge, tracked vehicle called a rock hauler sat buried up to the chassis in the soft sand. Only the cab and the very top of the four tracks it rode on remained visible.

Its mammoth size and derelict appearance brought to mind a shipwreck on a deserted coastline.

"Well, I'll be damned," Davis said. "Someone has been out here after all."

"We knew that already," she replied. "The question is why? What the hell were they doing out here?"

"I'll circle the rigs," he said.

She nodded. "Watch out for soft spots. Don't want to end up stuck like them."

"Will do," Davis replied.

It was nearly dark. The sun had gone down an hour ago, and the last portion of the sparkling Solaris Array was dropping below the horizon. The landscape had turned the dark maroon of dried blood, but soon it would be too dark to see.

In response Davis reached for the headlight switch. Hannah stopped him.

"Wait till we're certain there's no one else out here."

They'd circled both vehicles, confirmed that they were empty and scanned the surrounding area.

"Nothing on the horizon," Davis said.

"Put us next to the hauler," Hannah said.

As they pulled in front of the rock hauler and parked, Hannah pulled on a helmet. It wasn't pressurized, but it would seal out the dust and a micro filter would allow her to breathe.

Davis did the same and with Hannah's blessing flipped on the exterior lights. The ground around the Deca-Trac and the long flank of the rock hauler was instantly bathed in a warm glow, accentuated by the pink and red soil of the planet.

Hannah reached for the door, opened it and stepped through. As she and Davis approached the abandoned rig with flashlights in hand, their boots left two-inch deep boot prints in the sand as if it were red snow.

Hannah stepped up on a rail and pulled open the rock hauler's main door. "Give me a hand," she said.

Davis grabbed the handle and the two of them pulled in unison. The door creaked and then swung open. Reddish sand flowed out. Half the cab had been filled with it. As she looked around, Hannah saw where it had come in. Several holes had been punched in the windshield. They were bullet holes from some large caliber weapon. What looked like dried blood was all over the cab.

"Whoever was driving this didn't get out alive," she said.

"We should have brought a few rifles," Davis announced, his voice tinny and monotone over the helmet speaker.

"No one here to shoot us now," Hannah replied. "But that doesn't explain what happened."

"You hear of any gunshot wounds down at the hospital?"

Keeping up with injuries was part of her official job. And every week brought a litany of new ones as the breakneck pace of construction caused accidents and incidents. She'd definitely have heard if someone had been shot, especially since possession of weapons on Mars was strictly forbidden except for the security teams.

"No," she replied. "But I doubt these people made it to the hospital. You have any reports of missing persons?"

"No," he said. "I checked with admin this morning. Everyone is accounted for."

That was a bad sign. It meant someone was lying. Or worse.

"I'll check the other rig," Davis said.

Hannah nodded. As Davis moved off, she stepped out in front of the abandoned rock hauler. Playing her light across the red soil, she spotted other equipment nearby. She crouched beside one piece and began to clear the sand away. It looked like an oxygen generator.

"Hannah!"

She turned. Davis was waving her over.

"Come here. Look at this."

She dropped the oxygen generator and ran over to where he was. Even in the bulky outfit the light gravity of Mars made it easy to move quickly.

"What is it?" she asked, stopping next to him.

"Look."

He pointed the flashlight into the space between the hauler's front and rear tracks. The wind was tunneling underneath the machine, peeling back the fine sand in layers. The scouring effect had exposed something sinister: human bodies half buried in the sand.

At least a dozen were clearly visible. They seemed emaciated, but they weren't skeletons. With the bacterial loads on Mars so low and the insect populations limited to those the settlers had brought and genetically engineered to help with pollination, the bodies hadn't decayed, they'd just desiccated in the arid air, drying out until they looked like mummies from an ancient time.

"Get the shovels," she ordered.

An hour of digging would reveal other bodies. She couldn't even guess how many remained buried underneath or who they were. None of them had identification or even proper uniforms. Some carried bullet wounds; others showed signs of plasma burns.

"We're looking at a crime scene," she said. "Someone covered this up and hoped the wasteland would finish the job of hiding it."

"Should we bring the bodies in?" Davis asked. "As evidence?"

"Against who?"

He turned her way and offered a sarcastic look. "I think we can both guess the answer to that."

"No," she said. "We're not here to *guess* or to tip our hand at the first sign of trouble. Leave them for now. They're not going anywhere. We need to head back and get this information off to Earth."

Chapter 3

New York City, 2137

The Fortress was the colloquial name given to the most imposing of the mega-structures that sprouted from various spots on Manhattan Island. One hundred and ninety stories tall, its base spread out across mid-town Manhattan: a giant footprint in the world's most powerful city. It tapered as it rose, like a narrow pyramid, with protruding sky ports and landing pads sticking out from the sides at the seventy-first floor and the one hundred twentieth. The defensive missile systems and countermeasures bristled from nodes on all sides every ten stories or so.

Ninety thousand people lived in the Fortress. During the day another forty thousand came to work there. Most of them worked on the lower levels, where the government offices were staffed with the most basic civil servants. They came and went from a terminal on the fourth floor using busses and mag-lev trains like the office workers had in the big city's heyday.

The more important players never touched the ground, using the sky-ports to jet in and out, traveling back and forth to their enclaves and other areas reserved and protected for the wealthy.

But even among the wealthy there were few who ever made it to the top floors where the upper crust of the world's government lived and worked, enjoying huge arboretums pumped full of artificial sunlight, pools and spas and other touches that allowed them to soak up the illusion of a world like it once was.

Strangely enough, the most important voice among all those who lived at the top of the pyramid, shunned such indulgences. President Jackson Collins, leader of the United World Government and Commander in Chief of the World Military Forces preferred the gritty reality of the world as it was. Otherwise, he thought, it would be too easy not to work for the change that was needed.

Standing on the rooftop amid a spitting rain, he watched an angular shaped hover-jet with glowing engines and quadruple tails thunder across the dark sky towards the fortress. Crimson flares trailed out behind it, launched at precise intervals to ward off missile attacks, should the Black Death or any other group of insurgents try to take the hover jet down.

Collins watched as they fell slowly, tiny points of burning light dropping beneath the ever-present clouds and toward a darker swath of the city below.

From this height much of the city looked like a wasteland. Most of the buildings were dark and filthy, coated with carbon and scarred by the acid rain. Many of them were no longer electrified, though they were inhabited and indeed overpopulated. On the streets below, fires were always burning. No one bothered to put them out; the surface dwellers would just light them up again.

Much like the flares from the hover jet, the fires were there to ward something off. *Hopelessness and utter darkness*, Collins thought to himself. Something he sought to avoid as well.

"Mr. President," a man said reverently from behind him.

President Collins turned. Arthur Inyo was coming toward him from the rooftop shelter a few yards back. With one hand he gripped a file, with the other he held his suit jacket closed as if it might blow open and drag into the air like a kite.

Arthur Inyo was thin, well into his mid-fifties and almost completely bald. He'd been Jackson's friend and confidant for twenty years, all through the Fall of the Nation States and the War of Unification. He was the bureaucrat who made things mesh together; Jackson was the warrior who forced the issue when they didn't. In the complicated government structure, Inyo held the title of Prime Minister.

"I wish you wouldn't stand out here in the rain like this," Inyo said. "You know what this stuff does to your skin? You look old enough already."

Collins glanced over at Inyo. The heat in the city was ever-present now, even in winter it rarely got below eighty degrees, but half a mile up in the misty rain it was quite cool.

"Your concern for my physical appearance is duly noted," Collins said with a grin.

The hover jet had finally swung onto an approach course, escorted by two smaller, more lethal looking military craft.

Inyo glanced at his watch; the hover jet was late. Thirty minutes overdue. "It's wrong for them to make you wait like this," he said. "You're only the leader of the damned world."

Collins nodded and offered a sad smile at Inyo's unfortunate choice of words. *The damned world indeed.*

"That they come at all surprises me, Arthur. In truth it's a bad sign. It means they no longer fear us. They no longer feel the need to hide."

"Are we really going to blame them for what's happening on Mars?"

"Among other things," Collins replied.

Inyo shook his head. It was a clash a long time coming. A clash he'd warned Collins about years before. "You shouldn't have brought them into this," he said. "Partnering with them in the first place was like making a deal with the devil."

Collins had done terrible things in the name of peace and stability. Ordering massacres and assassinations. Sending his armies to lay waste to regions that harbored the enemies of unity. It had been his goal to make war so terrible that those who wanted it would finally have their voices drowned out by those who wanted it to end. Partnering with Lucien Rex and the twelve oligarchs of the Cartel had secured that peace, but at a terrible cost.

"I had no choice," Collins replied. "Look around you, Arthur. God doesn't live here anymore."

Inyo nodded sadly and both men watched as the hover jet eased across the threshold of the building, deployed its landing gear and dropped slowly toward the pad. Over the whine of the engines he shouted to Inyo, "Have them checked for weapons, and then send them inside."

Twenty minutes later, in the shelter of the building, Jackson Collins waited at his desk for Lucien Rex and whomever he'd brought with him to enter. When the door was finally opened, Collins was surprised to see Lucien enter on his own with only a bodyguard behind him.

"You wanted to see me," Lucien said with obvious disdain.

"Where are the others?" Collins asked. "The rest of your Cartel."

"We speak with one voice now," Lucien said. "Mine."

Collins nodded. He was not surprised. "If you speak for them, then you'll answer for their crimes as well."

"Is there such a thing anymore?" Lucien said, taking a seat across from Collins.

Collins ignored the statement, though it might have been the crux of the difference between the two men.

"You're being paid to send men and equipment to Mars, to speed up the Terra-forming and the cultivation efforts. My people have been waiting for months on your heavy machinery. Now I find out, you're not sending equipment at all. You're sending slaves by the thousands."

"I don't know what you're talking about," Lucien replied.

Collins stood. "We've found bodies out in the wastes. Hundreds of them. Buried where you or your people thought no one would ever look. And from what I understand that's just the tip of the iceberg."

For the first time in the president's memory, Lucien Rex looked surprised. He said nothing. He just sat and seethed.

Collins smiled. "That's right Lucien. Someone leaked your little secret. It seems that some of your people have a conscience."

Still Lucien remained silent, and for a moment, Collins thought he'd knocked Lucien back on his heels. But whatever sense of contrition Lucien Rex had, it vanished quickly.

"Laborers," he spat. "That's all they are. Laborers sent to do the job you wanted done."

"Slaves," Collins shot back.

"If you want to call them that."

"Why, Lucien? What's the point?"

"To save the machines," Lucien replied.

Collins was stunned. "What are you talking about?"

"Mars and its fine red dust," Lucien said. "Ten times finer than anything found here on Earth. It gets in everything, the gearing, the engines, all the systems. It wears them to pieces. A rig that might last thirty years on Earth won't make it six months on Mars. Less, if it gets caught in one of the sand storms. But those laborers—these slaves as you called them – they can last for years. And when they succumb you can use them for fertilizer."

Collins's fury burned, he slammed his fist on the table. "Money? This is about money? I'm talking about fundamental human rights here! There haven't been slaves on Earth for almost three hundred years."

Lucien's ire rose in response to the president's. "Are you sure about that, Mr. President? Who do you think built these cities? The canals and tunnels that that bring the fresh water in and the walls that keep the sea out?"

"Engineers and workers."

"Who were paid almost nothing."

"There is a difference, Lucien. They were free to leave at any time."

"And go where?"

"Anywhere they thought might be better," Collins snapped. "The people you've been abducting and shipping to Mars have no hope of survival. In fact from what I've been shown, those who've tried to leave have been killed to keep your secret hidden."

"I have no information about that," Lucien said. "What I do know is that trillions have been wasted both here and on Mars. Between the wars, the reclamation of useless, dead land and the Terra-forming effort, our resources are strained to the breaking point. Money, equipment and time, all these things are in short supply. The only thing that isn't, is the mass of humanity beneath our feet. And unlike you, I'm not afraid to use them."

"Human lives are not a resource," Collins said bluntly.

"Oh yes, Mr. President, they most certainly are. You above all others should know that. You've spilt more blood than the rest of us combined."

The two men glared at each other coldly, titans who could no longer exist in the same space. The time for cooperation was over. One must rise and one must fall.

"Where did they come from?" Collins demanded.

"Does it matter?"

"I've been hearing of mass abductions in certain cities, including this one. If I find out you've been rounding up people and sending them to Mars…"

"You'll do what?" Lucien snapped. "Are we really going to fight a war over the worthless lives of the untouchables?"

Collins took a breath. Lines were about to be crossed; the falsehood of the alliance between the government and the Cartel was about to be stripped bare. Collins knew that, but if he didn't rein Lucien and the others in now there would be no legitimacy left.

"There will be no slaves on Mars," he said. "Or anywhere else for that matter." "You will obey my directive, whether you agree with it or not, or I will seize your factories, your homes, your compounds. I will destroy you, imprison your family to the last man, woman and child and obliterate your hated name from the face of the Earth."

Lucien sat unmoving, his jaw clenched as if he were calculating the amount of truth in the president's threat. Finally, a wry smile formed on his face. "You should have done that when you had the chance, Mr. President. We have our own armies now."

Without another word, Lucien stood, turned his back on Collins and walked out of the room.

Chapter 4

New Amsterdam Burial Complex, 2137

James Collins stood in the dimly lit space beneath a sprawling canopy of glass. The soft patter of rain could be heard tapping away at the clear roof, but looking up, he could see only heavy clouds and the night sky.

New Amsterdam Cemetery was a military only facility. Each of its four sections, designed like giant greenhouses, covered a full square mile. But instead of nourishing food or hothouse flowers, it held only cold granite tombs and marble vaults, as long furrows of the dead ran in straight lines from wall to distant wall.

At an hour well past midnight, the facility was empty and was supposed to be closed. But the caretakers had let James in. Maybe they knew who he was, or maybe they did it for every soldier who'd just buried a friend. Either way James was grateful.

He stood in front of a freshly sealed crypt. Freshly engraved letters on it read:

Lieutenant Leonardo M. Perrera, 2105-2137
United World Forces, 41st Armored Division

As James stared at the name, he tried to guess the number of brothers in arms he'd buried over the years. In the big war, the War of Unification, there had been far too many to count and in fact far too many to actually bury. Lists of the dead were read off each night. Drinks were raised to their memories and bitter curses spat out toward them for cutting to the front of the line and heading off to a better place before the rest of the group.

And then the drinks were knocked down, one after the other until the bars ran dry. All save one, a single glass that went untouched no matter how bad the night got.

Since the unification, things had become more formal. With more time on their hands, real burials and cremations had become the norm, official ceremonies with crying and weeping and strained attempts to explain what it meant to live and die.

In all honesty, James preferred the old way.

"I don't know if you've found peace my friend," he said. "But in case you haven't."

He pulled a small bottle of scotch and two shot glasses from his coat pocket. He set the glasses on top of Lt. Perrera's crypt and began to pour the scotch.

"One for the living…" he said, filling his glass to the rim. "And one…one for the dead."

With both glasses topped up, he put the bottle down and picked up his shot. "You're nothing but a low-life bastard for leaving us behind," he muttered. "But damn, I'm gonna miss you, brother."

With a lump in his throat that he could hardly choke back, James held the shot up high and then knocked it down in one gulp.

As the fiery liquor burned away the emotion welling up inside him, James placed the empty glass beside the full one and stared up through the rain-streaked panes above them. Skittering around up there was a small bird that had found its way into the building and now couldn't find its way out. Endlessly it searched without rest. Like a soul trying to escape to the heavens.

It occurred to James that the bird might be better off in the quiet and shelter of the cemetery than out in the endless rain. It didn't take long for him to realize that he felt the same.

He sat back on a small bench, his shoulders slumping, his mind so numb it didn't even wander. He'd been there for quite some time when the sound of a heavy door opening and then closing again echoed from the end of the path.

In its wake the sound of footsteps coming his way were easy to make out.

James listened to them intently. Every man walked differently. Some light on their feet and quick, squirrels skittering from tree to tree; others were ponderous and slow, like big animals grazing in the field. The steps he heard now were measured and steady, heavy and precise. Military steps he thought. Those of a man in control.

He figured someone other than the caretakers had come to see him off.

"Looks like I have to go," he said toward Perrera's crypt. "Tell the boys, I'm sure I'll see them soon."

As he stood a voice called out.

"The dead should be cremated," it insisted. "Burial is a waste of valuable land. I thought that's one thing we agreed on, at least."

James held his ground as President Jackson Collins emerged from the shadows. Further down, he could see a group of bodyguards keeping a respectful distance. No doubt there were other security measures in place, both in the building and outside.

"We do agree on that," James replied. "Perrera's family felt otherwise. He served fifteen years. He earned the right."

In a time of constant war, there were a myriad of rights those in the military could accrue that were not bestowed upon regular civilians. They were earned with time and pain. And the right to come mourn the dead was among them, at least it was for those who'd served a decade or more.

President Collins knew that. He nodded slowly. "That he has."

An awkward silence followed and James blurted out the first thought that came to mind, just to end it.

"What are you doing here?" he asked. "I didn't think you left the Fortress much these days."

"I came to find you," his father said, a hint of disgust in his voice. "You've been in the city for ten days and you haven't made an appearance yet. From what I heard you haven't even checked in at the base."

"I've been a little busy," James said.

His father glanced at the bottle and then back to James. "If by busy, you mean drinking and letting yourself go, then yes, I can see that you have been."

James knew he looked like hell. He hadn't shaved in a week. His uniform was grungy. He'd barely been eating.

He couldn't explain why, but this time, after so many rounds and so many body blows, he was having a hard time getting up off the mat. That was only half the reason he hadn't gone home yet; his father knew the rest.

"I thought you might want to court martial me," James said flippantly. "Not only did we lose the drilling rig, but we failed to protect the civilians. In fact we shot them up by the hundreds. That can't have looked good."

"You can't take that on yourself," his father said.

"Then who takes it?" James asked. "Or do all those dead citizens just roll off the ledger somehow."

"I read the report. You did everything you could have."

"I could have done more if I had some armor with me," James said. "We all knew the Black Death were targeting those rigs, and yet someone took our heavy equipment away and sent us out there with a skeleton force. If we had a full brigade, those cowards would have never risked setting foot on that base."

"So blame it on me then," the president said. "The units were diverted on my orders."

James had already guessed that answer. Being the president's son was a pain in the ass, but it usually meant his requisitions got answered without much delay. When the armor was diverted over his strenuous objections, and no answers as to why were forthcoming, he guessed the order came from the top.

"Why?" he demanded.

"I needed it sent elsewhere," the president said bluntly.

"Where?"

The president eyed his son harshly. "To the Olympia colony on Mars."

James was stunned into silence for a moment. "What? Why?"

"We're dealing with a threat out there," the president said. "One we never expected to face."

"And you had to send my unit? My armor?"

"I chose them for a reason. And now I need you to join them."

James found himself baffled. He'd never heard of any threats to Mars. The distance alone kept them safe. Not to mention the fact that every colonist and worker sent there was handpicked, screened and checked by the government's best thought police to make sure no one dangerous slipped through. Even if a few bad eggs did make it there, it seemed absurd to think an entire armored brigade would be needed to deal with them.

"It's the Cartel," his father said.

"The Cartel?" In some ways this made less sense than anything else. The Cartel and the military had been thick as thieves for the past thirty years. That very alliance had put Collins in power. And it was the forces at the president's disposal that kept the hordes of humanity from overrunning the wealthy and devouring them.

"You'll have to forgive me for sounding shocked," he said, "But I thought we were on the same side."

"We were," the president replied, "while it suited their purposes."

James shook his head in disgust. "Imagine that. Thirty years of war and all we've managed to do is make another enemy."

"They've become our enemy because they no longer share our goals. They no longer believe Earth can be saved."

"Maybe they're right about that."

"They're not," the president insisted. "But without Mars to feed us, billions here will starve and the fragile order we've constructed will be shattered once again. With it goes any hope of healing our planet."

James just stared. Personally he hated the arrogance of the Cartel, hated it almost as much as he hated the Black Death and their gleeful murder. But the regular people, the ones his father wanted so desperately to save, were not much better. Easily swayed to one side or another, they were as much an impediment to peace as they were the victims of its absence.

It was a never-ending cycle, a spiral that seemed impossible to break.

"Do you have any idea who it is you're trying to save?" James whispered. "Have you seen these people? Do you ever come down from the mountain and walk around with them? Of course you don't. Half of them would rip your throat out if they could get to you. The other half would watch and cheer them on. They hate you. They hate us all."

"Only because they don't understand," his father said.

"Or maybe they're just pissed off about all the things we've done in the name of saving them," James said.

"Like in Kansas," his father guessed.

"And a hundred other places."

The president exhaled. James wasn't sure if it was a sigh of disappointment or a hint of understanding.

"Listen to me, James. We do what we have to, because there's no other choice. At the end of the day we have to forgive ourselves for that. They feel as they do because their emotions control them and because they're ignorant or misled or unable to see the bigger picture. We have to forgive them for that.

"But none of it gets any better if we don't keep fighting. We have to carry on. Even if it takes everything we have, every day of our lives and our very last breath, we have to keep going. Whatever it costs, we have to take the pain and carry on."

For some reason hearing this brought a new wave of grief to James. *How much more pain could any of them stand?*

"Mom died twenty years ago," he said. "And then Ben and then Kelly. And a thousand other friends since. How much blood do we have to shed before it's enough?"

"Your mother died in the plague."

"The plague that came from the first war."

"Exactly," the president said, as if that proved his point somehow. "And your brother and sister died fighting to stop civilization from collapsing in the aftermath of that plague. You owe it to them to keep -"

Something in James snapped and he stepped toward his father menacingly. From the corner of his eye he saw the bodyguards react. "I don't owe anybody a god-damned thing," James snapped. "I've done my time. More than both of them combined before they were killed."

The statement came from James with a great deal of emotion but it provoked little from his father. The old man just stared at him. Sometimes James wondered if he felt anything at all.

To the relief of the bodyguards, James stepped back and leaned against the stone crypt. The silence was so complete he could hear the rain falling again; the rain that never seemed to stop, just like the wars out there in the world and the one between him and his father.

"Maybe I don't want to do this anymore," he said with a weary voice. "Maybe I've had enough."

The president remained silent for a moment. In all their arguments this was something he'd never heard. "You can't just turn away. Like it or not, this is our burden."

"No," James said. "It's your burden. I didn't choose this. You're the one who decided to pick up the world and carry it on your shoulders. Maybe I don't want that for myself. Maybe I want to feel some of the good things in life before I die and turn to dust."

James knew his father wouldn't like hearing that. The career military man expected his son to fight to the end. James had no problem with that plan, except he was pretty sure *there would never be an end*. One war finished and another began. One enemy destroyed brought two more out of the woodwork. This news about the Cartel was only the latest proof.

"Indulge yourself?" the president said with revulsion. "Is that what you'd choose?"

"Why not?" James shouted. "I have as much right to it as anyone else."

As his father took this in, the disgust was so evident on his face that James had to turn away.

"So you live while others die," his father said. "You enjoy *a taste of life* while others starve. And then what? How long do you think it will last? How long till death and destruction find you anyway? Can you really be that naïve, James? Do you really think you can save just yourself?"

It was a rhetorical question of course. The main plank in everything President Collins did and felt and thought. The core of his beliefs. Either we all live or we all die, but humanity would rise or fall together. James had always accepted it as truth. But recently he'd begun to wonder—not whether his father was right or wrong—but whether they might be asking the wrong question all together.

"I think it's open for debate," he said, "as to whether any of us are even worth saving," he said. "Least of all, you and I, Mr. President."

At this, the president's back stiffened. He stared down at his son; angry leader and frustrated father all wrapped up in one. The disappointment in his eyes quickly changed to anger. Most likely because James now sounded like the real enemy, like the nihilists of the Black Death who considered mankind the scourge of the Earth, who wanted a catastrophe that would eliminate most, if not all, humans on the planet and leave the Earth to recover or die on its own.

"Then I won't ask you," the president said bluntly. "You're still in the service. You'll damn well do as your told. The next transport for Mars leaves in three days. You will be on it, or I'll throw your ass in the worst stockade I can find. Maybe rotting away in some deeper, darker hell will help you understand why this society—as bad as it may be —is still worth fighting for."

The president didn't wait around for an answer, he turned and stormed off and James remained where he was, listening to the sound of the slamming door and then the silence that followed.

Chapter 5

Lucien Rex stood in a garden, bathed in brilliant daylight. Green grass, trees and scented flowers surrounded a small lake. White clouds floated in a sky of brilliant blue.

"The resolution of the sky is excellent," a voice said. "I can even feel heat from the sun."

Lucien turned to see Arthur Inyo standing in a doorway.

"Infrared emitters hidden in the screens," Lucien said. "We even have a UV version in case you want to get a tan."

Inyo came forward. "Next time I'll bring sunglasses," he said. "Assuming I can find any."

"Antique stores are full of them," Lucien said, then tilted his head a little. "System off," he called out.

Somewhere in the ceiling a heavy switch disengaged and the sky above faded to grey. The warmth vanished with the light, while the lake and distant trees disappeared, replaced by a curved wall.

An area of one acre remained. Real grass, real plants, real trees.

"One day we won't need these anymore," Lucien said. "I understand that the soil on Mars and the low gravity environment promotes phenomenal vegetative growth."

"Only where we've blocked the UV rays," Inyo corrected him. "The rest of the planet is sterile. Outside the protected zones, the solar radiation is still deadly during the day. A few hours in the sunlight are all a man can take."

"Yes I know," Lucien said cryptically. "That's why they work at night. But don't worry, over time the safe zones will grow, and you and I will enjoy them before too long."

"Not if you keep pushing Collins, we won't," Inyo said. "You know he's sent more units to Mars."

"An inconvenience. We have more men in place than you might think."

"It won't be enough," Inyo insisted. "Collins has sent in heavy equipment. Part of the 26th Armored Division and half of the 41st. Your forces—our forces—won't stand a chance."

Lucien wasn't surprised. In fact, he'd expected some push back from Collins. In some ways it fit into his plan.

"It takes thirty days for the fastest transport to reach Mars," he reminded Inyo. "By the time they land we'll already be in control. When the ships touch down, we'll take them by force. The MRVs and all the heavy weapons will be buttoned up for travel. Locked down and secured. Our men will swoop in and secure them like so many birthday presents. There will be some bloodshed of course, but I assure you it will be minimal."

Lucien smiled wickedly at the thought, but Inyo did not join him.

"You misunderstand me," Inyo said. "The units are already there. They landed this morning."

"That can't be." Lucien said. "I only argued with him a few days ago."

Inyo didn't flinch. "I warned you not to underestimate him, Lucien. He didn't get where he is by chance. He must have discovered what was going on and kept it quiet. Getting these two divisions in place before he decided to confront you."

Lucien buried the anger down deep inside. Anger with himself. Once again Collins had blocked him. Lucien had been putting mercenary forces on Mars for months, slowly, methodically. Half the machines he was supposed to deliver for the Terra-forming had been replaced with modified versions of the military MRVs. They were hidden in warehouses and other temporary structures on the outskirts of the habitable zones waiting for his orders. Had he moved a month ago, his forces would have made quick work of the militias and official security teams on Mars, but this was more than they could handle.

"Damn it!" Lucien said finally. "We'll have to act here, first."

"To what end?"

"A coup," Lucien said. "Our only hope is to take control of the military. Those units will follow orders. Your orders."

Inyo looked shocked and ill at the same time. "My orders? Are you insane?"

Lucien shook his head. "We've already been prepping for this, Inyo. We're set to move against Collins and certain high-ranking officials who are extremely loyal to him. It will look like the work of the Black Death. In the aftermath, you'll assume the president's role as provided for in the new constitution. You'll vow to stamp out the terrorists once and for all, and send the military on the rampage. It'll be search and destroy."

Inyo hesitated. "You're asking for chaos."

"The more the merrier," Lucien said. "It will give us cover to depart under. No one will be watching the skies when enemies are lurking around every corner. You don't know this, but we've provided weapons and intel to the terrorists through back channels. They will prove to be more difficult to eradicate than anyone expects. With the military engaged and bogged down, we'll finish the Mars operation and begin to transfer those of our choosing. As we leave, a false flag government will preside over the fall of man, and this world will collapse and consume itself while we rebuild on the red planet."

Inyo looked pale. A man too small for the moment, Lucien judged. "It'll never work," he whispered to himself.

"What was that?" Lucien asked.

"It'll never work," Inyo repeated more firmly.

"Why not?"

"I've never served," Inyo said, "never held a rank. Neither have you. The military will never trust either one of us. For the last fifty years only those who've lived and breathed the service have been allowed to give orders. Even before Collins united the civilian leadership and the military command under one banner, civilian orders were basically treated as requests. If the military thought them unworthy or counter-productive they were simply rejected or ignored. You or I trying to change that won't do anything but get us both killed."

"But the constitution-"

"It's just a piece of paper," Inyo said, not even letting Lucien finish. "It's only four years old and no one gives a damn about it except Collins. The man you're about to kill."

"We have to act," Lucien said. "We can't pull back now."

"Then you'll have to find someone on the inside," Inyo said. "Someone they trust."

Lucien shook his head. "All those in positions of power are loyal to Collins. He's seen to that."

"Not all of them," Inyo said coldly.

Lucien studied the little man. He knew Inyo was far more shrewd than he ever appeared to be. A quality the president had failed to discover. "You have someone in mind?"

"James," Inyo said. "James Collins. He would be the perfect choice."

Lucien's eyebrows went up. "The president's son?"

"He's highly respected in the military," Inyo said. "He's got the name they all trust. And he's been in combat since he was seventeen. No pretender to the throne there."

"He's only a major, if I recall correctly."

Inyo nodded. "By his choice. He's turned down every promotion that would take him away from the field. Nothing carries more weight with the rank and file than that. Nothing. They know he's not a bureaucrat, they know he doesn't want power, and for those reasons they would follow him, just like they've followed his father."

Lucien considered what Inyo was saying. It fit almost perfectly, except... "Why would he help us?"

Inyo smiled. "Because he's been at war with his father even longer than he's been fighting on the battlefield. There is nothing but distance and anger between them."

Lucien hadn't heard this, but Inyo was closer to the Collins clan than anyone. He was like family. And family knew the secrets. "Do you think you can turn him?"

Inyo nodded confidently. "It will require some finesse," he said. "Despite their animosity James would never betray his father to us. But if it seemed more like he was saving the president from his own mistakes…well that has all kinds of appeal to an angry young man."

Lucien smiled. "He would get to rescue his father and prove himself wiser and better all at the same time."

Inyo nodded. "Exactly."

Lucien had to consider the possibility of Inyo failing, no matter how finely he crafted his plea. There would be contingencies, but he would put them in place on his own.

"Track James down," he said. "But understand this. If he won't come on board, he dies like his father, you take over and do the best you can."

Inyo didn't seem to like that idea, but Lucien didn't care. There was no more time for discussion.

Chapter 6

James Collins drove along one of the elevated roads that crisscrossed Manhattan, keeping the wealthy above the fray of the surface streets while they traveled between the various mega-buildings and government stations.

From up on the highway, things didn't look too bad. But to reach any other location in the city that was not served by the highways, one had to brave the old surface roads down below. They weren't always dangerous, millions upon millions used them daily—mostly on foot or using small carts, bicycles or mopeds—but they were filthy, in utter disrepair, and teeming with beggars or worse. Most who didn't need to see that part of the world avoided it. James didn't really blame them.

He continued south along the west side transect. From here he could see the Hudson River and the huge sea wall that ringed the island. It stood eighty feet high and sixty feet thick. Overly large because the storms that came each winter had fifty-foot surges and seventy-foot waves.

Along the wall, battlements and guard posts marked every hundred yards or so. Though it was designed to hold back the rising seas, the wall gave Manhattan the look of a citadel island, a castle in the middle of the sea. Because no similar wall had been built on the Jersey or Brooklyn sides, those shorelines were now several miles away.

James turned his attention back to the road, veered around a pair of heavy trucks and guided the car toward the exit. It took him down toward the southern tip of Manhattan and into the huge military base that occupied the entire bottom end of the island. Officially it was the Battery Park Military Staging Complex, but everyone called it The Arsenal.

Now on a military only road, James slowed for the curves. He pulled up to the gate. Steel barriers the size of small trucks blocked any further progress. Eyes watched from the control center behind them, while armed guards waited in a small shack out front.

James stopped beside the shack, lowering his window as one of the guards stepped from the shack.

"ID," the guard said.

James handed over his credentials "Major James Collins," he said. "41st Armored Division. Serial number Alpha, 420-7797."

The guard took his ID and scanned it while a red electron beam scanned the car from nose to tail. A green light flashed on the scanning device.

The guard spoke into a radio. "ID confirmed. No contraband detected."

"Roger that," a voice replied from somewhere up in the control building. "Proceed."

The guard handed James his ID back and then saluted. "You're cleared sir."

Accompanied by the sound of whining machinery, the huge metal gate began to rise. James took his ID and drove through. A few minutes later he'd parked and made his way to the secondary officers' club on the seventh floor of the main building.

He stepped inside. Music played loudly in one section accompanied by flashing laser lights. A packed floor had men and women dancing, looking for a hook up that might make the night pass easier. Others sat at spacious booths and drank. Laughing loudly or even arguing. James passed them by and headed for the bar.

He took a seat. The bartender paused. "What can I get you, Major?"

"What do you have?"

The bartender looked glum. "Only the synthetic crap."

No surprise, James thought. "Then it doesn't really matter does it? Just make it a double."

"Whiskey?"

James nodded and the bartender grabbed a glass and poured it over some ice. James picked it up and took a sip. It tasted like jet fuel.

He put the glass down and contemplated the future. *Mars or a military prison somewhere.* There was no middle ground. Jackson Collins didn't get to be where he was by bending. Once he'd made the threat, he'd follow through.

"Hell of a choice," he muttered to himself.

James raised the glass to his lips. The synthetic whiskey was strong, strong enough that he could knock down a few more tumblers, get blind drunk and start a fight without really remembering it. If he was going to be thrown into the stockade...

"Care for some company, Major?" a voice said from behind him.

James turned his head. Prime Minister Inyo stood behind him with a smile on his face. James began to stand but Inyo waved him back into his seat. "We're not in chambers here."

James smiled. He'd always liked Inyo. Sometimes when James and his father were at their worst, Arthur Inyo had been the only link between the two of them who'd seemed willing to listen without taking a side.

"I guess my father sent you," James said.

"Not exactly," Inyo replied. "But in a strange way I'm here on his behalf."

That sounded odd. "Can I get you a drink?" James asked, holding up his glass. "The worst stuff money can buy."

"No," Inyo replied. "But finish yours. Then we need to talk."

There was a dark tone in Inyo's voice. James didn't like it. He took a look at the tumbler, then put it down and stood. "Let's talk."

To escape all the noise and commotion, the two men went outside and up a flight of stairs onto a section of the roof that doubled as a balcony. James stepped toward the low wall. From here, he could see the whole military yard: weapons and munitions stacked in holding grids several stories high, armored vehicles and machines everywhere. A maintenance yard to the left was lit up with acetylene torches where a dozen MRVs were being repaired or rebuilt. Across the way, a lighted landing pad on the far side was busy launching a squadron of hover jets for a night patrol.

All things considered, it wasn't a bad night. No rain for once and the ever-present clouds painted a dull orange color by the city lights.

Inyo looked out over the complex before speaking. "We have two or three bases like this in every major city in the world," he said. "And still the insurgency goes on."

James turned. "We could have ten bases in every city, Arthur. It wouldn't make a damn bit of difference."

Inyo cocked his head. "Why do you say that?"

James wondered where this was headed. "We're too passive. Everything is based on defending. We're prisoners in these cities. Just like the kings of old trapped behind their castle walls."

"So we should go out and attack," Inyo said. "Take the battle to the enemy? Is that what you would do?"

James narrowed his gaze. "What's this all about, Arthur? Why are you asking me these questions?"

The prime minister paused and then exhaled deeply. "People are losing faith in your father," he said.

"You mean the Cartel is losing faith in him."

"Of course," Inyo said. "They feel he's lost his way. No longer willing to do the things that are necessary. No longer willing to act as decisively as he did during the war."

James almost laughed. "Jackson Collins has gone soft? Is that what they think?"

Inyo didn't respond immediately and James got the feeling he was being measured, felt out.

"They have a point," Inyo finally added. "Your father refuses to see the truth. He refuses to understand that there is an *us* and a *them*. And if he won't see that, then he risks dividing the coalition."

James felt his thoughts flashing back to the conversation with his father at the cemetery. He felt a rage of defensive anger growing inside him. "I don't know what you're after, Arthur, but you're barking up the wrong tree. You of all people know my father won't take advice from me, so if that's what you want you're wasting your time. And if those sons of bitches in the Cartel think my father has gone soft…tell 'em to take a swing at him and find out for themselves. I promise you there's more fight in that old man than any ten of them, or us for that matter. Now if you don't mind, I have a drink to finish."

James went to push past Inyo, but the prime minister grabbed his arm. James shook loose and in the process shoved Inyo backward. The prime minister tripped over his feet and landed on his backside. In response, Inyo's security team came rushing out of the woodwork. Three men, holding compact weapons.

James stepped back.

"It's alright," Inyo said to them, holding up a hand. "I tripped. I'm clumsy."

They held back, but the weapons stayed in plain sight.

"I came here as a friend," Inyo said as he got to his feet. "Things are in motion. Things I have no control over, nor any power to hold back."

James was up against the ledge, only the seven-story drop behind him. Inyo was in front of him, the security team twenty paces beyond. James focused on the prime minister. "What the hell are you talking about?"

"A move is going to be made against your father tonight. The Cartel is no longer willing to support him."

James stepped toward Inyo. "You traitorous son of a bitch!"

"He can still be saved," Inyo insisted. "I've made a deal on his behalf. A bargain to avoid another civil war."

"What kind of bargain?"

Inyo spoke quickly—as if time were of the essence. "Your father will be removed and exiled. House arrest, somewhere far from here, somewhere he can actually enjoy the rest of his life. And you, James, *you* will be put in his place."

"Me?" James could not measure how stunned he was to hear this. "Have you lost your mind? You honestly think I would--"

"You'll have to do as we direct you to," Inyo said, butting in. "You'll be a figurehead. I'm not going to lie. But if I know you, your views on this disgusting planet are similar to ours. You've buried enough friends in the last few years to know we'll never win the battle against these insects if we don't eradicate the nests. The new orders will be to hunt the Black Death, to attack and hound them to ends of the Earth. If their leaders hide in a town or village, we'll obliterate those settlements. If a province tries to support them, that entire section of the map will be laid waste too. Collateral damage will not be considered in the equation and any uprisings will be crushed with unmitigated force. And then finally, at long last we will have peace. Real peace."

James glanced past Inyo to the security men, eyeing them up. "And if I don't agree?"

The prime minister opened his jacket. James noticed a pistol in his shoulder holster, but Inyo reached for a hand held transmitter instead.

"One call is going to be made from this phone," the prime minister said. "If I make it, your father and his supporters will die and the Earth will most likely descend into a new bloodbath."

He paused and took a deep breath.

"But, if you make it, James. If you make the call, your father lives and the reins of power pass calmly to you. And millions if not billions of lives will be spared."

James listened intently, but his mind was on the night before and the argument he'd had with his father at the cemetery.

Inyo held the phone in one hand and offered the other for James to shake and seal the deal.

James hesitated.

"You know what you have to do," Inyo urged.

Still James held back.

"Fine," Inyo said, moving the phone toward his mouth.

"Wait."

Inyo paused and slowly, reluctantly, James nodded.

The prime minister offered his hand and James clasped it, holding it firmly, looking Inyo in the eye. And then he began crushing it with an ever-tightening grip, pulling the prime minster closer.

"My father was right. Our enemies are all around us."

With a snap of the wrist, James twisted Inyo's arm and reached in and snatched the pistol from Inyo's shoulder holster.

"James. No!"

Still holding the prime minister, James began firing, shooting through the back of Inyo's long coat.

His first two shots dropped two of the guards. But the third began to return fire. James pulled the prime minster in front of the blast, using him as a shield. Inyo's body shook as the first of several shells hit him. His legs buckled. But James held him up and kept firing until he'd blasted the third member of the security team to the ground.

With his forearm around Inyo's neck, James pulled him in close. "Call it off," he demanded.

Inyo held up the phone, one of the slugs had gone right through it. He dropped the shattered device. "It's too late," he said weakly. "You should have… listened. I did this for you."

James knew a lie when he heard it.

"You did this for yourself," he growled.

With that, James spun, throwing Inyo over the edge of the building. The prime minister fell, flailing for several seconds, his coat opening like a cape until he hit the dark concrete below with a sickening crack.

James never saw the impact; he was off and running. Running for his life, and the lives of countless others.

Chapter 7

At a landing pad by the waterfront, a few miles from the Arsenal Military Complex, a pair of civilian hover jets waited, engines running and ready to go. Despite their civilian status, these vehicles bristled with weaponry like their military counterparts. They belonged to Lucien Rex, part of his security service.

Thirty feet away, a vicious looking man stood at a monitor. Magnus Gault had a narrow, craggy face, marked on one side by a jagged scar that ran diagonally from the bridge of his nose back across one ear and into his hairline. On the other side, a series of precise parallel marks looked like horizontal lines but were actually tattoos of micro text. They designated his allegiance to Lucien's band of mercenaries and his rank, so to speak, among that group. Other tattoos hidden by his clothing would show the battles he'd fought in and the kills he'd racked up. After a dozen years in Lucien's service, Gault wore plenty of mercenary ink.

"What happened? Gault, do you read? What happened?"

Lucien Rex sounded small and distant on the tiny speaker, at least compared to the whining engines of the hover jets behind Gault.

Gault was studying a feed from a small camera installed in Prime Minister Inyo's coat. He'd seen the confrontation begin and then nothing but shaking and static. The feed was finally coming back. All he could see was Inyo's hand laying on the ground and blood pooling around it.

He flipped a switch and spoke into a microphone. "I think we have a problem, sir."

"What kind of problem?"

"Well," Gault said. "For one thing, you're going to need a new prime minister."

"*What are you talking about?*" Lucien asked.

"Collins tossed him off the roof," Gault said. "An interesting way of turning down your proposal. No grey area in that."

Lucien was silent for a moment. "*Where is he now?*"

Gault flicked a switch. A tracking device installed on Collins's vehicle was moving. "He's on the run."

"*So be it,*" Lucien said. "*Take him out.*"

"With pleasure."

Gault signed off, holstered his pistol and began walking toward the first of the two hover jets. He held up one hand and made a twirling motion. "Spool 'em up," he shouted. "We're rolling."

The pilots went to work, and by the time Gault climbed onto the skid of the first jet the whine of the engines had risen to fever pitch.

Gault had once been in the military, but a court martial and a dishonorable discharge left him with a bad taste in his mouth for the entire military order, especially Collins and his kind with their high and mighty attitude.

Years later, an explosion that had sliced the huge scar into his face had only hardened Gault's anger, as the blast was caused by substandard munitions the mercenaries were forced to use because the military wouldn't release the grade A munitions.

In his mind, Gault had plenty to blame the military for. Tonight's festivities would be a little bit of payback, a tiny step in evening the score.

⋏

James had made it through the officers' club and down to the main floor before the commotion really hit. The gunfire on the rooftop had been muted and masked by all the noise in the club and on the base in general. The prime minister's body landing in the main yard was a different story. Several people had seen him fall. Despite the damage done by the impact, they'd quickly realized who Inyo was, that he was dead, and that he'd been shot before falling from the roof.

James was in the main lot when the alarms began sounding.

He climbed into his car, gunned the throttle and spun the tires as he raced out onto the access road. In thirty seconds the whole base would be locked down. He had to be out of there before then or he and his father would be dead men.

In seconds, he was approaching the perimeter, but the exit gate was locking down into place.

Red lights were spinning on top of the control shack. "Halt your vehicle!" a voice yelled over the loud speakers.

James stood on the gas, and the car shot forward. Even as he did, he could see the exit gate dropping; he'd never make it. He swerved left. A small convoy of supply trucks were coming in the entry side. That gate couldn't be closed.

Gunfire rang out from the tower and tracer fire cut across his path. He narrowly avoided the first truck, split the gap between the second truck and the edge of the wall, and shot out onto the road.

He was a fugitive now. He would be linked to the prime minister's death, labeled an assassin or a terrorist, but it didn't matter. All that mattered was reaching his father before Lucien made his next move.

He sped up the access road and turned onto the elevated track of the upper highway. There were few cars and he could just about fly.

He swerved around a bit of slower traffic and then spoke aloud to the car's computer. "Emergency contact: Jackson Collins, direct line."

A screen on the dash cycled. *"Requested line inactive,"* the computerized voice said.

"Contact Presidential Security Team," he said. "Authorization, Collins James; alpha, seven, seven, nine, seven, three."

The screen cycled and then flashed red. *"Request denied. Authorization invalid."*

James slammed his fist into the dashboard and stepped harder on the accelerator, whipping around a curve barely in control. He thought of one more option.

"Emergency call," he grunted as he fought to keep the vehicle from tumbling off the highway and dropping a hundred feet to the surface streets far below. "Terrorist action imminent."

This was the equivalent of a 911 call to the military controllers. It was supposed to get priority and put him in touch with the local defense force no matter what his other status might be. *"Request denied. Account no longer connected to Unified Signal."*

They'd cut him off completely. That was a bad sign. Before he could come up with another plan, a wave of gunfire cut across his path. It came from above.

James cut to the left as twin streams of rapid-fire plasma melted sections of the guardrail and obliterated a small delivery van.

The explosion and flash of orange covered the highway ahead of him, but James raced through it.

"Damn!" he shouted as a second burst pelted his car with chunks of the roadway.

The next curve took him between a pair of burned out skyscrapers that were linked together by a dozen makeshift bridges. The hover jets chasing him peeled off, high and right. But on the far side, they quickly dropped back into position again.

James killed his lights, took an exit and swerved onto a ramp that took him to a lower roadway. This one cut across the city diagonally. It was still sixty feet above the surface, but it ducked under the main highways, and that would give him some cover.

"Where the hell did he go?" Gault yelled from the gunner's position at the side door.

"Lost him," the pilot said.

Gault pressed the comm switch. "Falcon Two, do you see him?"

Hesitation and then, *"We've got him. He's dropped a level and turned east. He's gone dark by the looks of it. Switching to infrared."*

Out the side door, Gault watched as Falcon Two peeled off to the right.

"Stay with him," he ordered.

He gripped the door as his own craft banked into a turn, and as they straightened out, Gault switched his sighting mechanism to infrared.

James knew the capabilities of the craft following him. He knew they'd find him quickly, even in the dark, but racing at breakneck speed on this lower level might give him a chance. He was only a few minutes from the Fortress. Even if he crashed onto the steps, his father's most loyal men would be there, and whoever the hell was following him wouldn't stand much chance.

He went around another turn, sideswiped one vehicle and then scraped the guardrail for fifty feet before he got control back again. A long straight away lay up ahead, crisscrossed by so many cables and bridges that it was almost tunnel like. He shot down it, raced out into the open again and immediately came under fire.

The first blast missed to the right, but the second rocked the back of the car. The rear window blew out. The wind howled through the car and the flames whipped forward, licking at the back of James's neck.

He fought to control the car, kept the accelerator floored and looked forward. The Fortress was dead ahead. Its towering, almost volcanic shape looming in the distance like a beacon.

And then there was a flash, bright enough to illuminate the entire city in false daylight for a second or two. The blinding glare faded, replaced by a fireball hundreds of feet across. It lit up the top third of the Fortress and billowed outward spewing black smoke, orange flame and streams of molten debris like a starburst.

James had no time to exclaim. No moment to process the realization, or even to feel anger or remorse. The shock wave from the burst hit him at almost the same instant that another storm of gunfire tore the side of his car.

The sheet metal was ripped apart and both wheels on the right side were blasted free. The car went airborne, came down on the guardrail, sliding along it at the same breakneck pace which James had been driving and then flipped and tumbled over the edge.

The car flipped as it fell, doing a complete roll before hitting one of the slag heaps that piled up against the pillars of the highway like sand dunes. Still moving forward, the car slid down the slope and across a small open lot, trailing sparks and flames. The gas tank separated and exploded, and the body of the car slammed into a wall under the recessed overhang of a blacked out fifty story apartment building.

▲

Gault saw the hit. Saw the car go over the rail and caught sight of the gas tank explosion from the corner of his eye as the two jets raced past. They shot the gap between the next group of buildings and climbed out over the city.

As they pulled up, he could see the top third of the government building burning in the distance. The explosion had been massive—probably a thermofusion bomb. He'd been worried about the military units intervening in his pursuit of Collins, but Lucien had insisted they'd have other things to deal with. This was more than Gault had expected.

He tapped the comm switch, transmitting to Lucien. "Target's down," he said. "I repeat. The target is down."

A long moment of silence followed, and Gault wondered if the huge explosion had somehow effected communications.

Finally, Lucien's voice came back through the speakers. "We need confirmation."

"ATC is ordering all civilian craft to land," the pilot called out. "We have to get out of here. This city is going into lockdown."

That didn't surprise Gault. With the explosion at the Fortress the military would be out in moments. Shooting first and asking questions later. He relayed the message to Lucien.

"I need you to make sure James Collins is dead," Lucien replied without hesitation.

"We blew him off the damn highway," Gault replied. "He's on the surface level in a fireball."

"I don't care where he ended up. Unless you saw him take his last breath in person, you go find him and make sure he didn't survive."

Gault knew better than to cross Lucien. He looked to the pilot. "Take us back around. Make it quick."

Chapter 8

James opened his eyes to the smell of burning fuel and the sight of shattered glass. The windshield of his vehicle was a super polymer so it didn't break or crumble, but there were so many cracks and fractures crisscrossing it that it was almost white instead of clear.

Somehow he was alive—the vehicle's airbags and a type of instant restraint system that locked him into place had seen to that—but he was disoriented. For a minute he had no idea where he was.

As the airbags deflated, James looked around. The vehicle had spun around during its fall and slammed backwards into the walled exterior of a large building, which overhung it by at least twenty feet. The nose of the car, or what was left of it, now pointed back the way he'd come.

Through the cracked windscreen, James could see fire flickering in the distance. Debris and junk littered the open space. He saw the base line of another building across a small plaza and the slag heaps of junk and debris piled up around the pillars of the highway's support system.

He was down on the ground level. And if he was right about where he'd landed, this was not a spot he wanted to end up in, not in a rich boy's, fancy car. Not in the middle of the night.

As if to prove the point, he saw shadows moving towards him in the flickering light. They emerged from under the highway and climbed out through the empty window frames of the other darkened buildings.

James knew he was in trouble, even if the attacking jets didn't come back. A car like his, even a wrecked one, had value down here. Easily stripped parts could be sold for months of food. The frame and sheet metal could be melted down or sold for scrap. His clothes, his money, his personal effects, all of it held the same kind of value. Even his life could be ransomed.

He felt around for the gun he'd taken off the prime minister. He couldn't find it. He tried to move but the belts of the instant restraint system held him. He reached for the release and punched it. The belts retracted enough for him to squirm free.

He searched for the gun once again but to no avail. He reached for a locked compartment in which his own side arm was hidden, but without power to the car, he couldn't open it. He yanked on the handle as the first shadows reached the car.

Grubby hands appeared around the doorframe and pulled in unison. The door was bent and wedged tight, but the combined power of several people began to bend it back.

James yanked the handle of the weapons compartment. It wouldn't budge. He slammed his fist into it, denting the metal.

Guttural shouts outside the car rang out. A few people jumped on the remnants of the hood. The car began rocking back and forth as the mob pulled and released and pulled in unison.

James yanked on the dented weapons compartment again. It moved but not enough. He slammed his fist into it once more bending the metal further as someone smashed a pipe into the windshield. New cracks spread in a circular pattern.

The door was bent further. A dirty, bearded face appeared in the gap between it and the frame. A hand reached in and grabbed James's collar. He yanked free and pounded the weapons compartment repeatedly. It flicked open just as the door was pulled wide.

Three sets of arms grabbed him, as he shoved his hand into the gap and grasped his sidearm. He was yanked out of the car and pulled into the mob of people.

He shook free of the first group of hands, but others grabbed him, grabbing for his dog tags and pulling at his coat. All James cared about was the weapon.

As the coat was pulled off one arm, he slipped free from the other. A second later his ID packet fell from the pocket. Half the group lunged for the contents, fighting over it like pigeons in the park. Still others fought their way onto the car, while others were grabbing at James, trying to dig anything they could out of his pockets.

"Get the hell off me!" he shouted. He elbowed one guy in the face, slugged another, and shoved a third derelict away before getting enough space to fire a shot into the air.

"Back off!"

The crowd spread out and James found some breathing room. Half of them looked to the car, but the pecking order there had already been established. If they wanted anything out of this, they would have to get it from the man with the gun.

A good dozen of them tried to encircle him.

James waved the gun around, keeping them away. Limping and covered in blood from a gash in his forehead, he edged his way toward a graffiti covered concrete wall.

One guy whipped out a knife, but James blasted him in the leg. He dropped in pain and the crowd stepped back. James released his watch and tossed it into the crowd. He did the same with some tokens from his pocket. A new fight broke out, and James got clear of them.

He backed away, checking behind him and waving the gun back and forth to keep the crowd at bay.

Without warning, all the activity stopped. A few of the scavengers looked up into the night sky.

James heard the hollow sound of whining turbine engines and spotted a pair of shadows cutting across the dimly lit sky.

"Street-sweepers!" someone yelled, using a slang term for the crowd control version of the heavily armed hover jets, which were commonly deployed against riots and demonstrations.

The people broke in all directions, most running for cover. Some making last, desperate attempts to remove a part from the wrecked car. James got caught in the stampede. Hobbling on an injured leg and watching as the rag-tag group of surface dwellers scattered in all directions.

Some went for the broken windows they'd come out of, others raced into dark alleys and recesses between the buildings. No way in hell he was following them into either.

He made for a ditch twenty yards away and hurdled the small pile of rubble in front of it, only to find it wasn't a ditch but the entrance to a sloping tunnel. He slid down, missing the make shift ladder and tumbling out into darkness twenty feet below.

The howl of the street-sweepers and the roar of gunfire reverberated in the tunnel as the hover jets made a pass, laying waste to all those who'd run for cover too late.

The sound of people running echoed down the tunnel. Footsteps disappearing into distant darkness.

James turned the other way and began to climb up the rickety ladder. Halfway up he stopped. The jets were coming back around again. Slower this time.

The sound of rockets screaming came next. A series of heavy concussions followed. One of them must have hit near the tunnel's entrance because James was thrown back again. Dirt and dust swept over him, and when James looked up, the source of light was gone. The entrance to the tunnel had been caved in.

Chapter 9

Gault stared from the gunner's position on the side of the hover jet as the last of the explosions faded.

"Plaza looks clear," the pilot called out. "No movement whatsoever."

Gault was pleased. He had no desire to get swamped by a group of shadow dwellers. "Falcon Two, you ride cover," he ordered.

"Roger that."

"Set us down in an open spot," he said to the pilot.

The pilot slowed the jet further and landed in an open spot a hundred yards from the wrecked car, which lay wedged under an overhang from one of the buildings.

Gault unlatched his safety cable and hopped out. As he set foot on the ground, one of the injured shadow dwellers grabbed at his leg. Gault shook him off and fired a shot into the man's skull, putting him down without a second thought.

Getting a better look at the position of the mangled car caused Gault to pause. It was a long way back into the darkened section. Even with Falcon Two covering them, it was not a place to be on foot for long.

He reached back into the hover jet and pulled a rocket launcher from the weapons rack. The T-7 could take out a small tank. It would make quick work of the mangled car.

Stepping away from the hover jet, Gault raised the launcher up onto his shoulder, and zeroed in on the car. Through the infrared scope, he could see a human shape moving around in the vehicle. Switching to standard visual sighting, he caught sight of Collins's military shoulder patch.

"Time to die, Collins."

Gault pulled the trigger, and the missile lit forth from the launcher like a screaming banshee. It hit the mangled sports car and obliterated it, blasting what was left of the vehicle apart at the seams. Bricks and mortar and other debris from the overhanging building flew in all directions, and chunks of flaming metal rained down all around them.

It was a little bit of overkill, Gault thought. But it got the job done.

Without much delay, he stepped back onto the hover jet's skid, placed the empty launch tube back into the rack and shouted to the pilot, "We're done here. Let's go!"

The idling jet spooled up and lifted off quickly, rising straight up almost a hundred feet before it began to move forward.

As the jet began to accelerate, Gault looked into the distance. Military jets were now streaking across the sky toward the Fortress. A dozen or so were already buzzing around it like angry bees defending the hive.

If all had gone according to plan, they were too late. The president and most of his staff were dead. Not to mention all the other advisors and power brokers who lived in the upper third of the huge building. The military-industrial machine had been grievously wounded, but it would strike back without delay. If Gault was right, the response was likely to be massive, and with no clear enemy to hit at, it would lash out blindly at anyone and anything that seemed even slightly suspicious. They needed to get on the ground safely before that act went into full swing.

"Radio base," Gault shouted above the noise. "Tell Lucien we have his precious confirmation. And let's hope he knows what the hell he's doing."

Far behind them, James Collins remained crouched in the darkened tunnel, trying not to choke on the dust. He listened as the latest explosion died away and the muted whistle of the hover jets faded.

In their wake, the tunnel went silent. James crawled forward and began to dig at the rubble that had poured in after the rocket impact. He was able to move some loose debris and gravel, but he soon came up against heavier obstructions. Huge sections of blacktop and concrete blocked him. He strained and pulled until his fingers bled but couldn't even budge them.

He was cut off from the surface, trapped in the only place worse than the burned out neighborhoods up above. This was an entrance to the sub levels, the vast warren of tunnels underpinning the grand old city. Old subway lines and sewer tunnels for the most part, though stories of the underground dwellers and their endless burrowing suggested the tunnels had been added to over the years.

Rumor had it a million people lived down here. A city below the city. A lawless place rife with gangs and cannibalism and who knew what else.

James had no idea if the rumors were true, nor did he care to find out. He checked his pistol, raised and clicked on the pin-point light that was attached beneath the barrel, and stared into the depths. The stark white beam pierced the darkness, illuminating curtains of dust.

The tunnel was roughhewn, carved out of the earth. It ran straight for a hundred feet before some kind of turn or drop. It also angled down.

"Great," James muttered.

He had no real choice; he had to head in deeper in hopes of finding an exit. With little hesitation, he began walking.

Chapter 10

Lucien Rex was well versed in moving against those who stood in his way. Thirty years before, he had been one of the Cartel's junior members, but through manipulation and treachery he'd slowly risen to dominate it. The most important thing he'd learned along the way was to make sure it looked as if someone else had committed the deed. There was an art to it. It was not something to be done quickly.

For the last six months, he'd been setting up a rumor of the Black Death going after the House of Collins. The activity in Kansas was part of this, but there had been other attempts and even the capture of a Black Death member who held an encrypted drive, listing the Collins family as first and foremost on an assassination hit list.

This and other false information fed to military intelligence sources would confirm the Black Death's hand in the events of the evening. It would redirect any suspicion that might have come Lucien's way. To make sure of it, he'd had his own compound attacked simultaneously with the Fortress, obliterating his home and pristine grounds with a similar device, even taking with it a few relatives whom he'd never really liked.

Fortunately, he'd been elsewhere at the time.

He was now meeting with the ranking members of the military and some of the surviving government officials. They were in shock, and Lucien played to their fears.

"Martial law," he demanded. "Nothing short of that will stabilize things now."

"Who will run the government?" one general asked.

"You will," Lucien insisted. "All major decisions will be made by this council until we can safely gather the surviving senators and the international parliament."

Those around the table nodded. Their biggest fear wasn't war; it was chaos, the total loss of control. Riots, civil war, other sections of the world breaking away. Undoing the work of the past twenty years.

"I suggest we tell the world that Collins survived," Lucien added. "That will stabilize things even more and give us breathing room. All orders and directives should seem as if they're coming from him, until we're ready to announce a change."

"What about economic pull back?" another asked.

"I'll see to it that the Cartel pumps cash into the system. We'll find a way to increase food distribution now, even if it causes more pain later on. We'll order our companies to go on a hiring spree. People getting new jobs has a way of calming things."

The military men nodded. The surviving parliamentarians, most of who were Lucien's friends spoke up to reinforce these ideas.

"That's good for the long term," a ranking senator noted, "but we have more immediate problems. We're already hearing of riots here in the city. There have been explosions on the east side, and other issues in mid-town. It almost seems as if the Black Death are concentrating their efforts here, to destabilize the seat of power."

This was enough to get one of the generals riled up. "We'll deal with that after we've hunted down the insurgents," a military aide suggested.

"This island has been rocked to the core," the senator replied. "This is not a time to show weakness."

"I have security forces at my disposal," Lucien told them. "I can put them into action."

"Mercenaries," one of the generals noted.

"Para-military units," Lucien replied. "Not as efficient or powerful as your forces, but they can do the dirty work of securing the city while your men take out the known and suspected terrorist strongholds."

"He has a point," another of the generals said. "If our men get bogged down in civil unrest performing crowd control, it'll keep us from hitting back as quickly as we like."

"Okay," the first general agreed. "Draw up your plans, Lucien. But keep your people out of our way so they don't get hurt. We'll be taking action immediately."

Lucien nodded. At this point, he'd heard all he needed to hear.

Chapter 11

Olympia Settlement, Mars

Hannah Ankaris was in the council room in the city of Olympia when the news hit. She watched a video feed along with the rest of the council, the elected group chosen to manage local affairs among the settlers and Terra-formers of Mars. As the report detailed violence spiraling out of control on Earth, the chamber fell into a stunned silence.

"I would never have believed the terrorists to have such reach," one of the councilwomen said.

Hannah could only agree. As she stared with her mouth agape, video of the Fortress in flames played and a huge section of the burning structure detached from the frame of the building. It slid off and tumbled to the ground, damaging the lower half of the sloped building on the way down.

Moments later, an aide walked in and handed a print out to the head of the council, an older man with tanned skin and white hair whose name was Aaron.

Aaron read the paper and his hands began to tremble.

"What is it?" Hannah asked.

"It's from the military high command," he said. "New intelligence, gleaned from captured terrorists confirms they have sleeper cells in place, here on Mars," he said. "An attack is believed to be imminent."

Gasps came from the council.

"That can't be," Hannah said, finding it hard to believe what she was hearing, and fearing what it might mean if the intel was right.

"What if it's true? What if there are members of the Black Death here?" someone else asked. "We've had so many equipment failures. Some of the workers have become convinced that it's sabotage."

"The mechanical failures have been explained. It's not sabotage. It's the dust and the harsh environment."

"If the main shielding array was destroyed," another person pointed out, "everything we've done would come to a halt. The crops would burn up and die under the ultraviolet radiation. The soil would be sterilized once again, like it was when we first arrived. All our work would be for nothing."

"That's right," a few of the members agreed.

"Not to mention the Core Unit," another said. "At its heart, it's a fusion reactor. If they overloaded the system, it would go off like a bomb. Olympia would be vaporized. And without us, the Earth would starve. That's what they want right?"

"Hold on a second," Hannah shouted. "You're getting yourselves worked into a panic. This is fear. This is paranoia. We've vetted every single person brought here."

"I'm sure those with access to the Fortress were vetted too," someone pointed out. "But the president's building was obliterated all the same."

"We have to do something."

A sigh and a shake of the head came from Aaron. "I'm afraid there's nothing left for us to do," he said continuing to read from the order. "All facilities are being ordered into an immediate lock down. Martial law is being declared, and operations of the council are suspended until further notice. Military units will be directed to guard all vital facilities. Internal matters will be handled by the additional security forces."

Hannah felt her world spinning. "What additional security forces?"

Even as she spoke the words, the door swung open behind her and a group of armed men came in. They spread quickly around the room. Hannah recognized them as contractors. They worked for one of the Cartel's construction firms.

One of them spoke. "*We* are the additional security forces."

"And who the hell are you?" another councilman asked.

"My name is Cassini," the man replied, handing over another official looking piece of paper. "As per the emergency order of President Jackson Collins, I'll be acting as executive governor of this colony, beginning immediately."

"What?" one of the councilmen shouted.

"Governor?"

"This is outrageous," another councilman said. He stood as if to emphasize the point, but was grabbed and slammed face first onto the table in front of him and held there with his arm twisted up behind his back.

"*You* would think so, Councilman Sullivan," Cassini said. "After all, your name is on the list."

"What list?" Sullivan grunted.

For reasons unknown, Cassini handed a flat sheet of clear glass to Hannah. Maybe he chose her because she wasn't an official member of the council, or maybe just because she was the closest to him at the time.

The thin sheet of glass was actually a hand held display linked to the city's mainframe. Hannah looked it over. A list of names was written on it, cross-referenced with ID numbers and work locations. They came under several headings beginning with the term *Suspected Dissidents*.

She scrolled down. The list had hundreds of names on it.

"What is this?" she asked.

"There are subversive elements among us," Cassini replied. "Councilman Sullivan and Quorum Leader Aaron are both considered to be suspects. They are to be detained for questioning."

Gasps came from around the room. Two of the armed thugs headed for Aaron.

"This is insanity," Aaron shouted, backing up and trying to fend them off. "I've been a loyal member of the government for fifty years."

"Apparently, the president and the intelligence services think otherwise."

With that Aaron was cuffed and dragged out. Sullivan was removed shortly after. Two others were taken from their chambers.

Hannah watched in horror. Her mind was racing. How could these orders come from Jackson Collins? Could the events on Earth have really scared him that badly?

"You will help us find the rest of the people on this list," Cassini told her.

"Why me?"

A grin of such malevolent evil crossed Cassini's face that Hannah felt a chill run down her spine. "Because, I chose you to do the job," he replied. "And because as chief medical officer, you have familiarity with most of those on the list."

She hesitated, staring back at him. Cassini released the catch on his holster and put a hand on his side arm. "Maybe you don't agree with the new protocol?"

Something very wrong was going on, she knew that for certain, but there was nothing she could do about it if she was dead or imprisoned.

"No," she said. "I'm just…in shock." She took a deep breath and recovered her wits. "You're right, of course. We can't be too careful. I'll help you find them. But you must promise me they'll be treated well."

Cassini nodded, and pointed toward the door. "You have my word," he said. "Now lead on."

⋏

Ten miles out from the city of Olympia, two squadrons of MRVs were guarding the northern power array. Each of the twenty-four vehicles carried the makings of the 41st Armored Division.

A three-man crew in the lead MRV was augmented by the presence of Lieutenant Jeremy Dyson. He stood behind the systems officer and the MRV's pilot, who were seated at the control console. All three of them were studying the image displayed on the MRV's long-range camera. It revealed a large group of armored machines spreading out across the streets of Olympia. Some of the machines took high ground positions from which they could cover the rest; others stomped around into the city squares, setting up shop in front of various structures.

"What the hell are they doing?" the pilot mumbled. "We get any deployment orders you forgot to tell us about, Lieutenant?"

"Nope," Dyson said. "Zoom in."

The systems officer tapped a key and the long-range lens focused on one of the machines.

Dyson studied the big rig. It was a different type of MRV. It carried no markings. It looked vaguely like some of the MRVs they'd once purchased out of a South American unit.

"What do you make of it, sir?"

"Not ours. That's for sure."

As the strange looking MRV disappeared behind a building, another one came into view.

"That's one of the rigs from the 26th," the pilot said. "They're supposed to be on the south range guarding the atmosphere generators."

"So what the hell are they doing in the middle of the city?" Dyson muttered.

"Maybe we should call them and ask?" the pilot suggested.

"No," Dyson said. "Let's hang tight. This is too strange. Pass the word silently. Everyone on alert, but let's not make it look like we're on alert."

The pilot nodded.

"Message coming in, Lieutenant," the systems officer said. "Damn…"

"What is it?"

The systems officer looked up, his face ashen. "War's broken out on Earth. President Collins has been injured in an assassination attempt. The prime minister is dead. Forty senators are dead. Half the president's staff are missing and presumed dead. It's believed Black Death insurgents are responsible and that their next move will come here, on Mars."

"Maybe that explains why we were sent here in the first place," the pilot said.

Dyson gave the driver a sharp look. "Is there an order attached to that news?"

"We're to report to some guy named Cassini in Olympia. He's being installed as an executive governor, with full emergency powers."

Dyson didn't like it one bit. He moved the comm officer aside and took a look at the screen himself. He read the entire order, with all its directives about guarding infrastructure and the arrest of suspected individuals. It was signed by President Collins, and it certainly sounded like a reaction to the situation on Earth, but Dyson had never heard of military units being ordered around by a private contractor.

"Anyone know who this Cassini fellow is?"

The crew shook their heads.

"What do we do?" the gunner asked.

Dyson hesitated. He studied the order one more time, looking for something he didn't see.

"Lieutenant?"

Dyson sighed. "Orders are orders," he said grimly. "And we're going to follow them."

Chapter 12

New York City

James stood in fetid darkness. It smelled like a mix of burning oil and trash and waste. A miserable stench, even for this world.

Unable to claw his way through the rubble and back to the surface, he'd been forced to go deeper into the sub-levels looking for an exit. Using the micro-light on the lower rail of his pistol to guide him, he'd followed the hand carved tunnel until it gave way to an ancient, abandoned subway line. There he'd dropped onto a track bed devoid of rails or lighting or anything else that could be removed and sold.

Amid the overlapping graffiti, he noticed strange designs carved into the walls. The marks were unfamiliar to him, as if the underground had its own language and symbols. He guessed they were territorial marks, signs or flags to warn other groups away, as the sub-levels were known to house many factions and gangs who often fought one another for control and access to the surface.

An hour of hiking brought him past several dead bodies and a group of jerry-rigged supports wedged in place to keep the roof from collapsing in one section. At several points in the hike he'd heard strange noises emanating from various vents and grates in the floor, and the sound of water dripping was constant, but no one had challenged him.

Finally he'd reached an area that had once been a station, but after climbing up on the crumbling platform he'd found the exits sealed with huge piles of concrete and twisted metal. He couldn't tell if it was the work of the gangs, who wanted to keep people in and charge for access to the surface, or the surface dwellers who feared these underground tunnels and those who lived within them.

As James considered his next move, a series of muffled reverberations rumbled through the cavern. The double thud of distant explosions was unmistakable. Big enough to shake the city.

Whatever the hell was going on up top, the big guns were involved now. He wondered if Inyo's civil war had broken out, or if the coup against his father was being consolidated. There was even a slight possibility that the military had figured it out and were now moving against Lucien and the Cartel, but if the regulars were on the march it was more likely they were lashing out in revenge, blindly pounding any suspected enemies in the city.

Either way, he needed to do something about it. Exactly what he wasn't sure, but he couldn't do a damned thing if without getting back to the surface.

He dropped back onto the track bed and aimed his pistol down the tunnel. The tiny light cast a narrow beam that cut through the darkness and clouds of dust. Nothing but tunnel ahead. He picked up the pace, double-timing it now, racing for the next station.

A quarter mile on he began descending and rounding a curve, dropping another seventy feet before the slope flattened out. He was now on the second level. A third and fourth level of tunnels were known to exist below but James wasn't interested in going any lower. Not if he could help it.

Far up ahead he noticed firelight. He doused his own beam and continued towards it.

As he grew closer, something scurried across the tunnel from one side to the other. He only saw its silhouette, but by the way it moved, James thought it was an animal of some kind. Seconds later, other shapes fluttered after it.

James stopped his approach as a kind of whooping sound came out of the dark. Human voices, shouting and calling something out, distorted into an unnatural sound by the odd acoustics of the tunnel.

He edged closer to the side of the tunnel and gripped the pistol tighter. He could see shapes creeping towards him in the dark, hugging the walls. Suddenly one of them began running. The others followed. All of them charging for James.

With the light behind them they were nothing but shadows, dark shapes that seemed to be flying his way.

James raised his weapon and lit up the closest one with the blinding white beam. He saw a man with dreadlocks and a dark rat's nest of a beard. Crazed eyes seemed filled not with madness but fear. Startled by the light, the man tried to stop.

Instead of killing him, James clotheslined him around the neck with his free hand and slammed him to the ground.

He raised the gun, but the others continued the charge. He fired point blank, blasting two of the charging shapes. Three more rushed forward, one firing a lethal looking dart from a cross bow. Another raised a machete-like blade.

James dove out of the way, releasing the man he'd body-slammed and blasting the machete-wielding attacker.

The man with the ratty beard got up and ran. Only now did it dawn on James that he was clutching a satchel of some kind and that the others were chasing him. They raced past James and pounced on the runner like a pack of dogs. Two more appeared from the darkness and launched themselves at James. James flung one of them off, felt a knife slice his arm and then blasted the both of them in rapid succession.

He turned around just in time to see the satchel ripped from the dreadlocked man's grasp. A booted foot knocked the man down as another of the thugs raised a club to crush his skull.

James pulled the trigger once again. The crack of the gunshot and the flash of the muzzle lit up the tunnel. The bullet hit the pipe wielding lunatic in the head and sent him flying backward, half his skull blown off. The pipe clanged to the ground as the surviving muggers took off with their prize, racing into the darkness.

James lit them up with the micro-light but held his fire.

"Stop them!" the dreadlocked man shouted.

The shadows racing were easy targets, but James only had a nine shells left in the pistol. He wasn't about to waste them on purse snatchers running into the distance.

"Please!"

James doused the light. "I don't think so."

The dreadlocked man got up and began to chase them, but James caught him before he could get too far.

"God-damn you," the man said. "Do you know what you've done? There was medicine in that bag. Two hundred doses of Interferon."

Interferon was an expensive drug. In its newest form it cured the plagues, the same ones that had killed James's mother. It kept its potency for a very long time and was sometimes used as a barter currency.

"And what's a guy like you doing with Interferon?" James asked. "Paying someone off?"

The man looked up at him, squinting in the light. James noticed his dark pupils constricting. He guessed that living in the tunnels one got more used to the darkness than the light. He kept the beam aimed directly at the man.

Using his free hand, James searched the man for weapons. He didn't find any, and guessed if the man had anything to fight with he would have used it already.

"Trying to help people," the man said. "I'm a doctor."

Though the man spoke with conviction, James figured he was a dealer or courier or something similar. But it didn't matter. "If you say so, Doctor. Now how about showing me how to get out of this rat hole?"

"I can't show you anything if you make me blind," the man said.

James held the beam in place for a second longer and then moved it off line. The man seemed to relax with the beam out of his eyes.

James stood and stepped back, allowing the dreadlocked man to sit up. "Don't do anything stupid."

The man eyed him strangely. "Help me to get the medicine back, then I'll help you to leave. I know where they're going to take it. We can catch up to them."

"I don't have time for that."

"There are people who need that medicine," the man insisted.

"I'm sure there are," James said. "But I have bigger problems."

He cocked his head to listen. The pounding had resumed on the surface. "You hear that thunder? There's a war breaking out. Now you're going to show me how to get back up top, or you're going to rapidly outlive your usefulness."

The man listened intently to the sound of the distant explosions as if trying to fathom just what they were or to gauge how far away. "Fine," he said. "There's an exit tunnel a mile east of here. I'll show you."

"Leading up to the plaza?" James said.

The man nodded.

James shook his head. "Hate to tell you, but it's caved in."

"Are you sure?"

"Positive. That's how I got trapped down here in the first place."

The man looked glum. "The next exit on this line is three miles beyond that," he said. "But it's controlled by a group known as the *Long Knives*. They will want cash to let you back up to the surface. A transit fee."

"I don't have any cash on me," James replied.

"They might be willing to take your gun."

"And then kill us both with it," James said, roiling his eyes. "No thanks. What else you got?"

The man sighed and then looked to the left, down the tunnel toward the fires, back to where the thieves had ambushed him. "The only other exit within two hours of here is to the south of us. Further down the line."

James followed the man's gaze. The flickering light from small fires danced along the walls. Smoke obscured the ceiling as it drifted and vanished up pipes that led to the surface. He briefly wondered if the shafts were climbable, then discarded the idea. If they were, people would be using them.

"You don't seem too enthusiastic about heading south. Why is that?"

"Because the main tunnel is blocked. Has been for years. That means we'll have to go deeper before we can climb up again. It takes us into the *Badlands*."

"More gangs?" James asked.

"Worse," the man said. "Flesh eaters."

James wondered if the man was trying to trick him. He looked down the tunnel toward the fires and then back at the old man. There was only one way to find out.

"Better grab that pipe, old man," he said, pointing to the weapon on the ground. "You might need it."

Reluctantly, the man crouched down and picked up the pipe.

James nodded toward the fires and the man who was now his guide took the lead. James fell in behind him.

"My name's Bethel," the man said, glancing back.

James nodded. "Nice to know you. A word of warning, Bethel. If you lead me into a trap, I'll kill you before anyone gets to me."

"If we end up trapped," Bethel said, gravely, "I hope you do just that."

Chapter 13

James and Bethel moved deeper in the tunnels. They moved past the fires that marked the boundary of the *Badlands* and into the darkness once again. In certain places there was a tiny bit of light from an incandescent moss that grew in the walls. It was not enough for James to see by and he constantly bumped and stumbled over things, but it was better than nothing as using the micro-light would be a dead giveaway to anyone watching.

Bethel on the other hand seemed to feel his way through. Perhaps those large eyes of his had gotten so used to the darkness that this small amount of glowing moss provided enough light to see by. After a long time spent walking in silence, James finally asked about it.

"How is it you can see where you're going?" he whispered.

"Retina-max," Bethel replied.

Retina-max was a drug that enhanced night vision by five hundred percent. The military used it on night patrols. It gave the average soldier the night vision of a cat without the need for night vision goggles.

"How is it you have access to Retina-max and Interferon?" James asked, growing more suspicious by the moment.

"I told you I'm a doctor," Bethel said. "I worked for the government for many years. I know all the suppliers. I had a very successful practice. I lived in the *Cashmir* building. My clients were very important people."

Cashmir was one of the huge mega-buildings on the island. A smaller version of the Fortress, filled with extremely wealthy individuals.

"What the hell are you doing down here?"

"Does it matter?"

"Probably not, but I'm tired of walking in silence," James said.

"One day a woman came to me," Bethel said. "How she got through security I don't know. She was pretty, but not from our world. She had a four month old baby with her. He was dying from the plague. Against my better judgment, I gave her and her son doses of Interferon. I decided I'd figure out how to account for them later. If I could have patted myself on the back for my good deed, I would have. But as she was leaving she told me there were hundreds of children dying down here, maybe thousands."

Bethel's voice was deep and soft. It came through the dark like a wave rolling onto a distant beach.

"So you came down here to help them?" James guessed.

"To this day I'm not sure why," he said. "I had to see it for myself, I guess. I brought two cases of medicine. The gangs at the entrance took one of them and let me pass. But when I arrived it was worse than I expected. Worse than what you've seen so far. Children living off rats and refuse brought down from the trash dumps up above. So many were sick. And of course there were no doctors, not even false ones. I ended up coming back again and again. At some point I stopped going back. I sold off my things to buy more prescriptions on the black market. Now... now, I only leave to get medicine and supplies."

For some reason James believed the story. Maybe because it was spoken without a hint of pride. More like sadness, as if the man realized what a fool he sounded like.

"And I'm guessing you risk your life in the corridors of the cannibals to avoid giving half of your cargo to the gangs."

"I have very little left," he said. "I have to make it last."

James considered the man. He sounded both noble and crazy. Maybe those traits intersected more often than one thought. He started to laugh softly.

"What's so funny?" Bethel asked.

"Nothing really," James said, but then added, "It's just... someone I knew would have approved of your choice," James whispered sadly.

"*Noblesse oblige*?" Bethel asked.

"Something like that."

A sound in the distance ended the conversation and James stopped in his tracks. He put a hand on Bethel's shoulder.

For a moment they held still, listening for other noises. Soon enough, James detected the sound of footfalls soft to be sure but loose, uneven ground crunched slightly with each step. After a few steps the noises stopped.

In the silence and darkness James peered around. But he spotted no sign of attackers.

"You see anything with those cat's eyes of yours," he whispered.

Bethel peered into the darkness, holding very still. He slowly turned his head. "Behind us."

So they were being followed. Tracked. James wondered where they'd come from but he guessed cannibals would have well developed places to hide.

"How many?"

"Four. About thirty yards away," Bethel whispered back. "Their noses are twitching. They smell us. Or should I say they smell you."

James understood what Bethel was saying. He hadn't been down there long enough to take on the disgusting scent of the underground. He guessed that meant he smelled different, maybe even especially edible. He thought of the nine shells in the clip.

"How far to the exit?"

"We're almost there. About a hundred yards, maybe a little more." Bethel said. "I can see the marker."

Once again James wished he could see through the night. "Get ready to run."

Some kind of strange grunting noise came from the dark. James wondered if it was language or hunger pangs, then decided he didn't really care. He gripped the pistol, took a calming breath and exhaled.

"Go!"

Bringing the pistol up and thumbing the light switch, he lit up the cave behind them. In the bright glare he saw four men half clothed. Long stringy hair and facial growth made them look like animals. They reared back in the light and then charged forward trying to shield their eyes as they ran. They didn't get far.

James dropped three of them almost instantly only missed the fourth as he dove behind a pile of rubble. Only then did James see another group racing forward from further down the tunnel.

He fired into the pack, then cut the light and raced off in the other direction. He ran, stumbled and fell, then got up quickly. From behind him a whooping and yelling told him the flesh eaters had figured it out and were giving chase. Not interested in running blind, he turned on the light and sprinted through the rubble-strewn tunnel. Up ahead, he spied Bethel scrambling along the edge of the tunnel until he reached a pair of rusted pipes that stuck out from the wall like two fingers. He waved James toward him and then disappeared into a hole.

When James reached the hole, he stopped and turned, aiming the gun and its blazing light back down the cavern and firing once more. The shot forced the cannibals to scatter and take cover once again. As they did, James ducked through the breach and into a much narrower tunnel, more like a hand carved mineshaft.

It went up at a thirty-degree angle, as steep as a playground slide. It was climbable, but with a crumbling soil floor it was hard to get good footing.

James scrambled upward, using his feet and his free hand. He caught sight of Bethel up ahead and soon heard the weird grunting sounds of the flesh eaters coming in behind him. The further James climbed, the steeper the tunnel became. At one point he kicked loose a bunch of rocks, sending them back down the shaft and hoping to slow the pursuers.

Seconds later he caught up to Bethel. By now the sloping tunnel narrowed until it was just wide enough for a man's shoulders. The jagged walls of the tunnel and Bethel's feet were all James could see. Only now did he realize Bethel had no shoes on.

"Keep moving."

"I'm trying!"

Bethel was slipping and struggling on the slope of the steep tunnel. James braced himself and shoved the old doctor upward. With the boost Bethel got back on track, but before James could get moving a hand wrapped around his foot.

He shook loose but two more hands grabbed his ankle. They pulled downward. James tried to grab the wall to arrest the slide, but it was no use. He began to kick, pulling one leg free and swinging his leg violently. His boot smashed into the face of his captor. The sound of bones cracking and a sharp cry of pain told him he'd hit the mark.

Suddenly free, James began to scramble upward again. When the tunnel became vertical he found a rope of some kind dangling toward them. He used it to pull himself up and soon crashed into Bethel once again, who'd reached some kind of obstruction and was pounding on a metal plate.

"Open the hatch!" Bethel was shouting. "Hurry!"

The pounding continued, but nothing happened. The plating didn't move.

James squirmed around to look beneath him.

The crazed face of the closest pursuer came into view. Smashed nose and bloody teeth made the starved creature look even more deranged. James fired a shot, hitting the flesh eater between the eyes. Its head snapped back and it dropped away, taking two others with it. But the others were crazed like animals in a feeding frenzy. They pulled the dead man down and crawled past him, squeezing and squirming around the roadblock like ants in a nest.

Suddenly, James felt a rush of air. He looked up. The hatch had been opened and a pair of hands was pulling Bethel up through the gap.

James climbed higher and was pulled through by another helper seconds later. He fell out onto the floor and rolled, just in time to see another man slamming the solid metal hatch shut. A heavy bar was dropped across it and wedged beneath two bars, locking the hatch into place.

To force the cannibals away from the opening, boiling liquid of some kind was poured into a funnel that led to a hole in the metal plate. Screams were soon heard. Screams that faded as the cannibals fell and backed down the tunnel until they were gone.

James lay on his back, exhausted and thankful. It appeared he'd made it to another abandoned station. Torches burned around the open space. Further away the track bed was divided off into water filled sections like rice paddies. On closer inspection it appeared that some kind of algae or fungus was growing there. James had seen algae farms in various parts of the world, as algae became a staple of most diets. Though how algae could grow without light he didn't know. He guessed it was something else.

He turned his attention to the people surrounding him and Bethel. They all had grimy faces and dirty clothes, but they seemed somehow more squared away than the men who'd attacked earlier. They seemed angry at the intrusion but at least they weren't licking their lips.

"Thank you," James said.

"Who are you?!" one of them demanded.

"It's okay," Bethel said. "He's with me."

Chapter 14

On a wide city street in lower Manhattan, a group of two hundred armed men stood in loose formation. In the distance military jets screamed through the dark as huge explosions rocked a section of land that had once been New Jersey.

Here in the city things had finally gone quiet. Several riots had been put down. Suspected insurgent areas had been attacked without mercy. Collateral damage was high, but no one really cared anymore.

Despite that, the men on the street exuded a kind of nervousness and desire to get moving, as if they were missing out on the action. Beside them rested a long line of four-wheel drive vehicles and armored personnel carriers. The APCs were mostly empty now. Drivers and gunners only. Hitched to the back end of each one were empty flatbeds with fencing around the edges. They looked like cattle cars.

A burly man with a patchy beard climbed up onto one of the 4x4 trucks. He was known as Porter. He struggled with a limp and grunted as he reached the roof. A long row of tattoos down his right arm showed his allegiance to a mercenary band run by Lucien's family and the battles he'd fought in. He was considered the equivalent of a platoon leader.

Looking out on the motley group assembled before him, he raised the rifle in his hand and fired a shot into the air.

The sharp crack brought the men to attention. They ceased their conversations and turned his way.

"Listen up," he shouted. "You all know why we're here. We gave 'em less than a thousand for the last shipment. But we got the green light now. You boys fill up these trucks and there'll be bonuses for everyone."

A roar went up from the mercenaries.

"What if we run into trouble?" someone shouted.

At that moment a huge explosion went off down the block, blowing a hole in the concrete wall that sealed the old subway tunnel.

"Waste anyone who's stupid enough to challenge you," Porter shouted. "But once we deal with the primary resistance, we want everyone else alive."

The men turned and readied their weapons. A mix of rifles, pistols and shotguns.

"Not exactly crack troops, Porter."

The comment came from the APC's driver. A friend of Porter's. Part of his outfit for years. The way the mercenaries worked, there were core groups who stuck together and freelancers who were gathered up for jobs here and there and let go when the tasks were done. The men in the ragged formation, marching toward the gaping hole that led to the underground, were all freelancers.

"Doesn't matter," Porter said. He pulled a tarp off a large weapon mounted to the top of the APC. It resembled a small satellite dish with a long barrel protruding from the center. Heavy cabling suggested it was a directed energy weapon. "With this, we can put everyone in our path on the ground. By the time they wake up, we'll have 'em trussed up and ready for transport."

The driver smiled, turned the ignition and the big engine rumbled to life.

▲

Deep in the tunnels, James sat beside a fire as a group of women roasted rats on a spit, basting them with some kind of juice. Beside him several kids waited eagerly for their supper. The smell alone turned his stomach but he tried not to be obvious.

On the other side of the platform across a narrow bridge, Bethel was discussing things with some of the men. By the tone of their discussions and their sharp glances that came his way, he figured his presence here was part of the conversation.

With the cooked rats being peeled off the spit and the kids eating, James had had enough. He got up, crossed the bridge and made his way to the small group.

"I can't wait any longer," he said. "You need to take me out of here."

"No good," one of the men told him. "Fighting up top."

"That's half the reason I need to get back there."

"So you can lead them back to us?" the man snapped.

"Trust me," James said. "This is the last place I ever want to see again."

"You don't understand," Bethel added. "People have been vanishing. Entire clans. All their things left behind."

James was tired of this, but before he could say something a strange noise echoed down the tunnel toward them. As the sound rumbled through the station, James could feel it in his bones, like a deep, electronic buzz.

"What the hell is that?"

An instant later, a short burst of gunfire sounded off far up the tunnel, and several people came racing down it charging headlong into the station. Two women, three men, a couple of kids.

"Run!" one of them shouted.

The strange electronic distortion sounded again and a wave of blue light traveled down the tunnel, illuminating the walls in an odd pattern like the reflections from a lighted pool at night.

When the distortion reached the station it spread out and surged though the station like an explosion, but there was no fire or heat.

James managed to turn away, but the wave hit him and he felt all his muscles seize up simultaneously. A ringing in his ears went straight to his brain. He took a half step and stumbled, landing face first in the algae pond.

Some part of his mind recognized the weapon and its effects on his central nervous system. But it was too little too late and he began to sink.

As he floated downward through the muck, a hand grabbed him and pulled him back, hoisting him up and out of the water. It was Bethel, who'd been shielded from the blast by the other men. He pulled James up onto the platform.

"Can you stand?"

James managed to stand, took a few steps, and then tumbled to the ground again. Splayed out on the platform, he looked for his gun.

"Come on!" Bethel shouted, trying to haul James to his feet again. James stretched toward the algae pond, realizing the pistol had fallen from his grip and dropped into the muck at the bottom.

Before he could touch the water, Bethel dragged him back and pulled him to his feet again. They began to stumble forward together.

At the same moment, the deep rumbling sound began to emanate from the tunnel once again, like the shriek of some wild beast. As this call rang out, the blue wave of light surged forward, emerged from the tunnel, and mercilessly ran them down.

Chapter 15

Olympia Settlement, Mars

In a large control center in the half finished city of Olympia, newly appointed Governor Cassini was reviewing a message from Earth. It came from Lucien Rex himself. Because of the distance between Earth and Mars, it took nine full minutes for the message to reach him. That meant communications were less of a two way street and more of a question and answer session.

The first part of the message detailed the situation on Earth which seemed to be coming under Lucien's control. The second part indicated that a large batch of new laborers would soon be arriving.

"Four transports are lifting off tonight. You'll have ten thousand new workers on hand in thirty days. Put them to the task immediately. The first wave of the Cartel families will be following sixty days hence. They expect the city to be finished, and more importantly the other Core Units, shield generators and the additional atmosphere processors to be up and running. While some allowances are to be made, progress must be increased exponentially."

As Cassini listened, he stole a glance through the floor to ceiling window and gazed at the oval structure a few blocks away. The concrete housing contained the Core Unit: the main fusion reactor, the magnetic field generator that protected Olympia and the green fields around it from the deadly solar radiation.

Unlike Earth, Mars had no natural magnetic field, no north and south magnetic poles and as a result the radiation hitting the planet was enough to kill and sterilize anything known to man. The Core Unit changed that, it created what they called the Green Zone, an area of a hundred square miles where the incoming ultraviolet solar radiation was deflected and prevented from hitting the surface.

Within the Green Zone, people could walk in the daylight unprotected and not be burned, crops could be grown and livestock could graze. But while the Green Zone around Olympia was starting to resemble an earthly paradise in some ways, the rest of the planet was still barren. If Mars was to become what President Collins had wanted—or what Lucien Rex wanted now—additional Core Units had to be built. The ultimate goal was a planet-wide intersecting network that would allow all of Mars to look like Eden.

For now that was the most difficult task. Out where the new Core Units and shield generators were being constructed it was like the harshest of high deserts. Incredibly hot in the direct sun, bitterly cold in the dark.

Out there work could only be accomplished after sunset, when the double dose of solar radiation gave way to the grey twilight of Solaris Array. But even that had its difficulties. After the mirrors of the array went below the horizon, frost gripped the planet's surface almost instantly and frigid temperatures rushed in.

Laboring in such harsh conditions took its toll and the workers didn't last very long.

"The new Core Units and the shield generators must be the priority," Cassini told the adjutant. "Considering how the workers drop like flies we'd better overpopulate those camps to account for the attrition."

The adjutant took notes and nodded. "Maybe we should send the healthiest of the new arrivals out there," he suggested.

"Excellent idea," Cassini said. "Round up the medical teams and have them screen and document the new laborers. We're going to need a way to clear them for health threats and more importantly to keep track of them. But they can also grade the strength and vitality of the new arrivals so we can ship them to the appropriate location."

⚔

The intercom buzzed on Hannah Ankaris's desk. She ignored it for a moment, stunned by what she was seeing on the news feed from Earth. It showed a vehicle burning beneath one of the highways. It claimed the wreckage belonged to James Collins. The news was confirming his death at the hands of the terrorists.

Her heart felt as if it had frozen for a moment, skipping a few beats before beginning once again.

A year or so before, she'd been in a relationship with James. A contrived relationship that slowly became for her part love, part duty.

For his part, she was never sure if James loved her back or if he just enjoyed the fact that she was an outspoken critic of his father, the president. What he'd never known was that Hannah worked from the president's own intelligence service. She was a deep cover agent with no official position.

In his effort to survive, President Collins had long ago set hundreds of agents in covers that made them appear to be voices of the opposition. Some staged rallies, others became members of parliament and even important figures in the opposition parties.

Hannah's position was more passive. A decorated surgeon, she spoke out from her position as an opponent of the wars. At one point she was directed to make contact with James.

The president claimed it was for his son's own safety, but Hannah could see the distrust between the two. She knew her real mission was to see if James could be counted on. Over the course of a year she determined that he was utterly loyal, despite the simmering animosity between the two men and the almost pathological need to argue. That confirmed, she'd been ordered to Mars.

She did as she was told, but left knowing her feelings for James had become more real than fabricated. Staring at the photo of the wreckage, those feelings came pouring back.

She couldn't tell what kind of vehicle it was, there wasn't enough left of it to decide, but the explosion had obviously been massive. Huge sections of the building behind it had been blasted away. Whatever had been used on that vehicle, someone had left no room for doubt.

She looked away. Her heart was breaking; her mind was reeling. So much had happened so rapidly, but this was the worst yet. She took a deep breath and suppressed her feelings. She had to hide them.

Looking back, she tapped the screen and watched the next segment of the broadcast. It followed President Collins as he toured what remained of the

Fortress. His hands and arms were bandaged from what the announcer said was third degree burns, one arm was in a sling, but he was alive. He walked with a limp and then turned to give a speech. He vowed revenge and punishment for the terrorists and murderers. He promised a return to order for the people of Earth.

She stared at his face, freezing the picture and zooming in on him. It looked like him, it sounded like him, but something was wrong. The words he spoke were angry but the expression on his face was blank. Either he was more injured than the government was letting on or…

She began to think about the list of suspected individuals she'd helped Cassini and his thugs locate and round up. Some of them seemed to be random names. A few had been selected because their access to or knowledge of explosives and weapons made them possible threats, but many of them, too many in her estimation, were loyal supporters of the president. He couldn't possibly suspect that many spies had infiltrated his most important project, could he?

The intercom buzzed again, insistently, and she finally answered. "This is Doctor Ankaris."

"Alvin Davis is here to see you, Doctor."

"Send him in."

As she waited for Davis, her eyes went back to the news feed and the injured president. Something was wrong, she thought. Something was very wrong.

Chapter 16

Ten days later, Hannah found herself moving through one of the maintenance hallways near the west side of the city's sprawling architecture. She passed the work bays and the fabrications shops and storehouses of parts and supplies. At the end of the hall she dropped down a ladder and came to another hallway. It was dimly lit and the sides were cluttered with unused equipment and spare parts.

She was alone and feeling sick to her stomach. She kept her hands at her sides to keep them from shaking. The last ten days had been a nightmare. No contact from Earth, no information except the news reports and a small bit of anecdotal talk that trickled down from Cassini.

The rest of the Terra-formers were now living in fear. It came first and foremost via the terrorist threat against them. If the Core Unit and electromagnetic shielding were destroyed, there was not enough food, oxygen or shelter for the remaining workers. Half of them would die before help could arrive.

But another fear, in some ways more sinister, had gripped them as well. In the name of security, Cassini's men were questioning everyone. Each day additional members of the Terra-forming crews were being rounded up. A few were released but most of those questioned were held under guard. No charges were made and no visits were allowed. People began to fear their neighbors might be informants. They began to fear any stray words they might have let slip before the crackdown began.

Paranoia was growing. It showed in the drawn faces and the tired eyes of the remaining workers. It was palpable in the thick silence that now gripped the cafeterias and meeting places. No one knew the rules anymore. No one knew what kind of slip up might single him or her out for arrest and isolation. Worst of all, no one knew when or where it would end.

Hannah eased through the hallway with a mix of speed and caution, eventually arriving near the secondary recycling plant. Spotting a mark on a bay door, she knocked.

It cracked open and then was pulled wider to let her in.

She entered to find a half dozen others already inside. One man hugged her. The others just nodded. In the corner she spotted her friend Davis, the man who'd gone with her to find the half buried bodies of Lucien's slaves.

They looked at her expectantly.

"I'm so glad you've all come," she said to the leader of the group, a councilman named Julian. There were several other members of the disbanded council present, along with representatives from the technical teams and the maintenance crews.

"Davis told us you had urgent information," Julian said. "Though I must say, we're all a little surprised at the location and manner of this meeting."

"The current situation forces us to meet like this," she said. "It's for our safety. I'm hoping all of you can be trusted with the truth."

"Truth about what?" a woman named Isha asked.

"The orders coming down from Earth, the sudden imposition of Martial Law. The heightened presence of the military."

"Are you suggesting they're not necessary," Isha asked.

"More than that," Hannah said. "I'm suggesting they didn't come from President Collins."

They stared at her, hesitating.

"What are you trying to tell us?" Julian asked finally.

Hannah had thought about this question long and hard. After the initial attack, she'd desperately wanted to contact President Collins on the private channel they'd established, but all communications were now restricted. And she wasn't about to blow her cover by asking Cassini for access. She had no choice but to wait. But days had turned into weeks and she'd heard nothing from the president. It seemed to confirm her worst suspicions.

"I think a move has been made against the president," she said. "A coup d'etat. We know the president was attacked. At the very least he was badly injured. The prime minister and forty-nine members of parliament were killed. The president's son was also killed."

"But Collins survived," Isha said.

For days Hannah had wanted to believe this but she doubted it with all her heart. She looked at Isha and asked a simple question. "How?"

Isha stared.

"We've all seen the damage," Hannah explained. "If Collins was anywhere but the basement he wouldn't have survived."

"But the burns…"

"Too much to be touring military bases and giving speeches, too little for that type of explosion."

Julian's eyebrows went up. "You realize what you're suggesting?"

"Of course I do."

"Maybe it's a good thing," Julian said. "We've been talking about the president's *thirst for power* for months. If a move was made against him, we might be better off."

"That might depend on who takes his place," Hannah suggested. "We've all been critics of the president," she replied. "I certainly have been. And so have you, Julian. And yet he still allowed both you and I to come to Mars, to be part of the council. And while all our ranting against him has produced little movement, he's never tried to silence either of us."

"A mere concession to the façade of democracy," Isha said with disgust. "All departments and decision making bodies have been stacked in his favor. Allowing for a little dissent here and there just makes the process seem fair, makes the decisions seem more palatable when he rams them down our throats."

Julian nodded. "President Collins had always allowed for opposite voices," he said. "He just makes certain that his words drown them all out. It's part of his genius."

Hannah knew this. She'd once heard the president say that allowing people to dissent was a safety valve. But she understood it on a different level. One day, he often insisted, when the looming disaster had been averted and put behind them, separate parties and powers would be allowed again. Until then, however, he could not trust such a system to get Earth through the crisis. He'd once told her in confidence that he was an emperor who did not want anyone following in his footsteps.

She returned to the point at hand. "And yet in his moment of rage and retribution, Collins has not seen fit to have either of us questioned, accused or detained, even as some of his strongest supporters have been taken into custody."

Julian nodded. "Yes," he admitted. "Curious."

"Who would risk such a thing?" Isha asked.

Hannah thought she knew. Speaking it out loud might bring a death sentence if the wrong person was in the crowd. She took a breath. "Only someone who had much to gain if Collins was out of the way and much to lose if he remained in power. The only ones who fit that bill are Lucien Rex and the Cartel."

The room went deathly silent. The members of the gathering exchanged glances with one another. Isha shook her head softly, but Hannah couldn't tell if it was disagreement with her conclusion or just a way of warding off the thought that they'd gone from Collins to something worse.

Julian paced the room. The others watched him. But still no one spoke.

"It can't have escaped you," Hannah added, "that martial law is being imposed not by the military, but by these mercenaries who now claim to be working for the president. But I ask you: When has Jackson Collins ever needed mercenaries? When has he ever used anything but the professional army?"

Julian and several others nodded.

Isha shook her head. "We might get a better voice in this new government," she said. "Whoever's running it."

"How can you say that?' Hannah replied. "We're already living in a police state. Have you forgotten all of history? When has any group of people found more freedom by giving it up in the first place?"

"If Collins's supporters are taking the brunt of this, I say we let them," one of the group said.

"The military has run roughshod over us for years," Isha added. "If their power is being weakened I say it's a good thing."

"We can bide our time, strengthen ourselves at their expense," a third representative said.

Hannah glanced around the room. She was losing them.

They couldn't see beyond the immediate. Couldn't see what was over the horizon. "If it's a coup, the first phase will be to eliminate all direct support for Collins. But once power has been solidified, what do you think will happen to us? We'll no longer be needed. In fact, our independent minds will be a threat to whoever takes over. Surely you can understand that?"

No one replied immediately and felt as if she'd staunched the bleeding, but the question still hung in the balance. The group looked around at one another for direction and then, almost simultaneously, they turned to Julian. The man had remained silent for quite some time, mostly staring off into the distance.

"What do you think?" Isha asked him.

He looked up as if disturbed from a trance. A brief, sad smile appeared on his face. Finally, he answered.

"*First they came for the Socialists,*" he said, speaking in an odd distant voice. "*And I did not speak out, because I was not a Socialist. Then they came for the Unionists, and I did not speak out, because I was not a Unionist. Then they came for the Jews, and I did not speak out, because I was not a Jew. Then they came for me--and there was no one left to speak out for me.*"

"What are you talking about?" Isha asked.

"It is a quote," Julian explained, "with apologies for any mistakes I may have made. It comes from a poem of sorts, written and recited by a man named Niemöller, a priest who opposed the Nazi's in the nation state of Germany two hundred years ago."

"What does it mean?"

"It means, we must act," he said. "If we wait and allow those we think to be less worthy than us suffer, we will eventually all suffer together."

"So we're next," Isha said.

Julian nodded. "Sooner or later. But I'd say Hannah's right, it's only a matter of time."

Julian looked around and one by one the others nodded. They understood. They turned back to Hannah. "What should we do?"

"First, we have to find out exactly what we're dealing with," she said. "I'll see what I can do about that. And then we need to find out who among us might be willing and ready to fight."

A few of them looked ill at the thought, but they didn't reject it.

"We'll have to do it quietly," Julian mentioned.

"Agreed," Hannah said. "Be careful. Word of mouth only. Don't use any form of electronic communication, and start with those you feel you can trust implicitly. If word gets out to the wrong people, none of us will live very long."

A few of them nodded. All seemed gripped by the depth of the moment.

Across from her Davis pointed to his watch. "I think we should go."

"Let's meet here again in five days," Hannah suggested. "If I have to get word to you, Davis will bring it. No one else."

Davis moved to the door and opened it. He glanced down the hall in both directions. Looking back inside, he nodded.

One at a time the group began to file out, leaving some time and space between their exits and heading in different directions. When the others were all gone, Davis looked back at Hannah, nodded and then left.

For another minute Hannah waited in the room all by herself. But for the first time in weeks she didn't feel utterly alone.

Chapter 17

James Collins woke up to a splitting headache. He was cold, chilled to the bone and laying awkwardly on a metal floor. He moved to straighten his legs and realized others were lying beside him. Hundreds of the them, sprawled out, unconscious.

He had a strange sense of déjà vu. And for good reason. He'd woken like this at least a dozen times, only to see men wearing oxygen masks and backpacks walking though the dimly lit room with what looked like small fire extinguishers in their hands.

They moved here and there, checking through the heap of bodies and discharging a white fog over the mass of sleeping men and women as if they were spraying for lice.

In his vague memories, the mist drifted through the huge room and overwhelmed anyone who'd begun to wake up, including himself. Though he saw others slump to the deck upon breathing the gas, James could never remember breathing the mist in, until he woke up to experience it yet again.

Moving only his eyes, James glanced across the carpet of men and women. No one walked among them at the moment. The mist was nowhere to be seen.

Feeling weak but in pain from lying on the cold metal floor, James began the process of stretching and eventually getting to his feet. By grabbing a support column that ran through the center of the open space, he was able to pull himself up.

Holding onto the column to keep him up, James studied the mass of humanity. There were hundreds of men, women and children around him. Most of them snored and lay still. A few were moving, waking groggily. Their clothes were mostly tattered rags, their faces grimy and dark. He guessed most of them had been rounded up from the sub-levels.

James brought a hand up to his own face. Half of it was caked with dried blood from a scabbed over gash above his eye. The rest was sticky with salt from his sweat and what felt like a week's worth of beard growth on his jawline.

As he waited, the feeling began returning to his legs but they still felt weak and shaky. It might have been the drugs or the fact that he was literally starving. His stomach was so flat it felt concave.

He began to walk, moving awkwardly through the crowd, studying the faces, looking for Bethel. For a brief moment he wondered if Bethel had been killed or somehow escaped, but he soon found him lying near the far wall.

He crouched and shook him gently. "Bethel... time to wake up... "

As James shook him again, Bethel's weary eyelids opened revealing a sliver of white.

"Are you okay?" James asked.

Bethel didn't respond for a second. He seemed confused. He glanced past James, made a swallowing motion and then finally nodded.

"Can you get up?" James asked.

"I can try."

With James's help, Bethel got to a sitting position. But an attempt to stand was too soon and as Bethel's knees buckled, James eased him back down against the wall.

"What happened to us?" Bethel asked. "Where are we?"

"Someone stunned us," James said, remembering the flash. He looked around. "Not just us either."

Bethel followed his gaze taking in the mass of humanity around them. "Who was it? Soldiers?"

James thought about the possibilities. He might have vainly hoped it was the military, but a half conscious memory of the men who'd wandered through the cargo hold gassing the prisoners to put them back to sleep, told him all he needed to know. Long, straggly hair, baggy uniforms, odd, geometric tattoos.

"Private soldiers," he said. "Mercenaries."

Bethel seemed to take this news with less surprise than James might have thought.

"There have been rumors floating around for months," Bethel said. "People have been disappearing. Entire groups. Whole sections of the sublevels left suddenly vacant and empty. No one knows where they go. Most of us assumed it was an eradication program of some kind. Extermination of the undesirables. At least we're still alive."

James nodded. "If they were going to kill us they would have done it already."

"So we're hostages of some kind."

It made little sense. The gangs and clans of the slums were known to kidnap their enemies in fits of rage or revenge, but those unfortunate souls didn't live long. The wealthy and well off were often abducted for ransom payments and, for that reason, traveled with bodyguards. But indigents from the tunnels? It made no sense.

"Seems like it," James said. "The question is why? Why kidnap people from the sublevels?"

"Because no one would miss them," Bethel said bluntly. "Or raise a finger to look for them."

James nodded slowly. His mind was clearing. His thoughts becoming more coherent.

He put his hand against the smooth metal wall. It was frigid, covered in a layer of frost that flaked away under his fingernails. He scraped some of it off and watched the flakes fall. They drifted down like snow, only slower like puffs of pollen. He could feel a near silent hum resonating through the wall. Though it didn't seem like it, they were moving. The question was, to where.

He looked around, studying the shape and dimensions of their prison, thinking about the growth of his beard, the borderline starvation he felt and the men who'd kept them asleep for God knows how long. A thought came to mind, a possibility too ghastly to discuss.

Bethel seemed to notice. "You know where we are," he said. "Don't you?"

"We're nowhere," James whispered.

"What do you mean?"

"This isn't a prison," he said. "It's a transport. We're moving. Heading somewhere."

"Where?"

Before James could offer his guess, the main doors swung open and a squad of twenty armed men entered. Several of them remained near the door, weapons ready to fire at anyone who moved, while the others walked through the chamber dragging a cart stacked high with bottles of some peach colored liquid.

"Bet you dogs are hungry," one of them said, handing the bottles out. "This is mito-cellular protein and vitamin mix. It will restore part of your strength. Drink it slowly or you'll be puking all over the place, and it stinks bad enough in here as it is."

"Where are we?" someone asked.

"What's going on?"

The first question was ignored, the second answered with a blow from a baton that dropped the man who'd asked it to the ground.

"No questions!" the leader ordered. "You'll get your answers soon enough."

The men continued on through, handing out the plastic bottles and placing others beside those who were too weak to stand or still under the influence of the sedatives. As they finished up their rounds a second group entered.

These men said nothing. They traveled methodically looking at those who still lay on the ground or who seemed uninterested in the liquid rations being offered to them.

James watched this group sharply. As they moved, the leader inspected the faces and eyes of those he came across. The two men with him hung back, only becoming active when one of the prisoners rolled over and tried to conceal his eyes. They grabbed him.

"Let the inspector see your face!" one of them growled.

The man didn't comply and the mercenaries grabbed him and forcibly twisted his face around. The inspector studied him, shining a black light into one and then the other.

After a second he switched the light off. "Let him go."

Clearly they were looking for something, and for a moment James feared that something might be him. He wondered if they could possibly know they'd caught him in their net.

For the next few minutes this group moved among the captives like sharks in a lagoon. All eyes were on them, fearful and trembling. Eventually they grew close to where James and Bethel stood.

James pressed himself back into the shadows as the inspector dropped down beside another man lying on the floor.

After administering his black light test, the inspector shook his head and turned to the thugs helping him. "This one's got it. We have to remove him."

The thugs glanced at one another and then began to look around. Whatever the poor bastard had, they didn't want to touch him.

"You two," one of the guards shouted, looking at James and Bethel. "Get over here."

Bethel climbed to his feet but James hesitated, not wanting to be any closer to the thugs than necessary.

"I ain't gonna ask you twice!"

Reluctantly, James pushed off the wall and stepped forward.

"Pick him up," they demanded.

James grabbed the man's feet, while Bethel grabbed the man by his arms. They lifted the man easily. He was emaciated and light as a feather.

"Follow us," another of the mercenaries ordered as he turned for the door.

With little choice, James and Bethel carried the unconscious man across the large compartment. James could see him sweating and suffering minor tremors. There was odd pallor to his face, jaundiced and yellow.

"Where are we taking him?" Bethel asked.

"Keep moving," one of the thugs grunted, "and keep your mouth shut."

They carried the man through the door and out into a hall.

"This way," the inspector said, heading down the dimly lit passage.

James and Bethel followed him to the far end. A journey of over a hundred yards. As they went, James noticed the markings on the walls and the bundles of power and data conduits. A door with faded stencil marks read Cargo Bay Delta. Another, slightly newer paint job outlined Cargo Bay Gamma and a warning about oxidizers inside.

James was now certain. They were on a huge transport. A ship this big could only be going one place.

At the far end, the inspector stopped and used a keypad to open a door.

"Inside," he ordered.

James and Bethel made the turn. The room was the size of an average garage. A conveyer belt sat on one side and a sealed door sat a few feet down. Warnings written in three languages and surrounded by attention grabbing diagonal hash marks read "Danger Air-Lock."

Bethel had gone in backwards. He hadn't seen it yet. James almost hoped he wouldn't, but Bethel turned and glanced over his shoulder. Through a small portal three feet in diameter, the blackness of empty space loomed.

"Put him on the belt," one of the guards demanded.

Bethel hesitated. "Wait," he said, seeming to grasp what was about to happen.

"This man's ill," the guard shouted.

"He has shuddering sickness," Bethel replied, "which can be cured."

"Not here it can't," the guard shouted. "He'll infect the whole lot of you. Now put him on the damned belt."

The man stepped toward Bethel and raised a metal baton.

"No," Bethel shouted, "Listen to me! It's a simple treat--"

Before Bethel could finish the guard slammed the baton into his arm. Bethel winced and went to his knees.

"Please!" he shouted again. "All he needs is-"

Another blow landed. This time on Bethel's back. He cried out in pain but still held on.

A kick from the guard hit him in the face. "Let go of him, you filthy rat!"

The guard raised his baton high as if he would cave Bethel's head in. But still Bethel tried to protect the sick man in his care.

James reared back and yanked the sick man from Bethel's grasp. As soon as he'd pulled the man free, James heaved him up and slammed him down on the conveyer.

"He's on it!" he shouted, hoping to prevent Bethel from being injured further. "He's on the belt!"

Covering up from a reign of blows, Bethel glanced up, just as a last punch came flying in and knocked him to the floor.

Satisfied with the beating, the mercenaries stepped back. One of them went to the controls and engaged the conveyor belt. The sick man was carried forward into a small compartment designed for compressed waste. A door slammed behind him and was quickly pressure sealed.

A yellow warning light flashed twice and then went green. Without a trace of emotion, the man at the controls pressed the eject button. With a rush of air the sick man was launched out into space. He vanished into the darkness, venting oxygen and a mist of blood, as his body decompressed almost instantly.

In the center of the room, Bethel remained on his knees. His shoulders sagged and his eyes seemed locked on the cold steel deck.

"Get up," one of the mercenaries grunted.

Bethel didn't respond; he seemed to have lost the will to stand.

"I said, get up!" the thug yelled, raising his baton again.

Before they could start another beating, James grabbed Bethel by the shoulders and hauled him to his feet.

"Get them out of here," the airlock operator shouted to the mercenaries. "And finish the assessment before Gault has a fit. We'll be on Mars in two days."

The inspector opened the door. James and Bethel were forced out into the hall and marched back to the cargo hold that was their prison.

Bethel stumbled as the door clanged shut behind them. He was in a daze. James grabbed him to keep him from falling. But as soon as he was up, Bethel pulled violently loose from James.

"Why did you help them?" he said sharply. "They just murdered that man and you helped them to do it!"

James steeled himself against the accusation. "I didn't really have much of a choice, did I?"

"There's always a choice."

"Not with people like these," James insisted.

"All he needed was basic treatment," Bethel insisted. "A few days of antibiotics and he'd be fine."

"Antibiotics?" James said. "Are you kidding me? Look around you. We're just cargo to these people. Not even worth the cost of a bullet. You're lucky they didn't throw your ass out that airlock for fighting with them."

"And would you have let them?"

James leaned in close. Either Bethel was living in some delusion or he was deliberately antagonizing James. "Get this straight," he whispered through gritted teeth. "I wouldn't have been able to stop them if I tried. And I'm not about to get myself killed for something as pointless as a losing battle."

Bethel continued to stare back at James. "Sometimes you have to act no matter what the consequences are."

"And sometimes you have stay alive first and worry about everything else later."

Bethel looked away. He seemed hurt by the words. His face portrayed a type of sadness and disappointment, reminding James of the look his father often wore.

When he turned back to James, the look was gone. Perhaps the reality of the situation had set in. "I don't understand," he said. "I don't understand any of this. Can we really be two days from Mars?"

James nodded. He ran a hand over his own scruffy face. "We've been on this ship for weeks."

"You think they've kept us asleep?"

James nodded. "Reduces the chances of a rebellion. Saves them money too. We eat less, drink less."

"But now they're giving us liquid protein," Bethel noted.

James thought about that. "They must want us to have some strength," he said. "They'll probably feed us for the next few days and then, when we set down on the planet, they'll put us to work."

"Doing what?"

"Building pyramids for the new Pharaoh."

Bethel nodded. He seemed to understand what James was saying.

James grabbed one of the protein mixtures, broke the seal and took a swig. It was horrid, but he choked it down.

He thought of the argument in the cemetery, his father's warnings about the Cartel and their designs on Mars. They'd fallen on deaf ears and now... now it seemed like the Cartel had won. They had everything they wanted: the dying Earth, the blossoming planet of Mars, and the only man who'd ever stood in their way was gone.

James looked around at the others. They were sick and weak. The disposable members of society, the very ones his father had insisted mattered. And James was now one of them. He felt small and worthless. Defeated like he'd never been before.

He wondered how many others had died in the coup, if all his father's allies had been wiped out, and if the military had been splintered or a new civil war had begun. These questions were too big for him, too big for a captive. He needed to focus on smaller things. For now all he could do was survive.

Determined that he would at least do that, James took another gulp of the awful liquid and prayed it would give him strength. As he drank it down, he felt sick to his stomach but it wasn't the liquid meal that got him. It was the irony of life.

Had he listened to his father, he could have come to Mars as a prince, as the chosen one, a military governor and de-facto ruler of Earth's only hope. Instead, he would arrive as a slave.

Chapter 18

Olympia City, Mars

Hannah sat in Cassini's office, a chamber that had once been Chief Councilman Aaron's before his arrest. In the month since then, Cassini had given the office a military flavor, like everything else in the city.

While she sat and waited, he paced, dictating an order to one of his aides. Only when that was finished did he address her. "A pleasure to see you again, Dr. Ankaris."

"The pleasure is mine," she said. "I'd hoped we could talk about the prisoners. Schedule an examination so that I can assure the rest of the colonists that they're being treated well and are in good health."

She sounded both earnest and excited. She was a good liar.

"No need for you to see them," Cassini replied, flippantly. "I can assure you they're being well taken care of."

She nodded. There was nothing to be gained by pushing at this point.

He came around to the front of the desk and took a seat on the edge a little too close for Hannah's liking. The way his eyes lingered on her, Hannah guessed it wasn't accidental.

"But there is something I need from you," he said.

"What might that be?"

"We're trying desperately to speed up the Terra-forming work," he said. "To do that, President Collins has issued an executive order. New laborers are on their way. Ten thousand of them. They will land in a few days."

"Laborers?"

"Convicted criminals," Cassini said. "Itinerants, vagrants, the homeless."

Slaves. She almost let it slip. Somehow she managed to keep her disgust bottled up inside her.

"Forced labor?" she asked.

"In a way," Cassini pontificated, "but you shouldn't think of it like that. More like a second chance for these people. They are the poorest of the poor. The very souls who will starve first if we do not rapidly begin shipping more grain to Earth. Back home they live like parasites, but here they can contribute."

"How?"

"They can work out beyond the shelter of the shielding array, do the grunt work that must be done before we can expand; building new shelters, grading new fields and digging trenches for the aqueducts and the foundations of the new cities we need to create. Tasks that would give them a purpose, a reason for living, unlike their miserable existence on Earth."

He made it sound so noble. "They won't survive long out there."

"They'll work at night," he explained. "They'll live underground during the day."

"The conditions are still too harsh," she pointed out. "The air is too thin. It takes weeks to get used to it. You know that. Not to mention the possibility of them bringing disease or other contaminants here. "

"Yes," he said as if annoyed by these trifles. "And that's where you and your staff come in. You will set up a checkpoint of sorts. We have no time for quarantine, just a screening process. Your staff will give them hemoglobin boosters that will help them deal with the thin air. You'll also scan them for infectious diseases. Because we'll need to be able to track them, you'll implant identification and tracking sensors and then you'll clear them through. My people will take it from there."

She looked away, not replying for the moment. She knew it wasn't a request. Cassini had imprisoned anyone who defied him.

He stepped forward and crouched before her putting a hand on her shoulder as if to comfort her. Her stomach turned at his touch, but she didn't show it.

"It's necessary," he said. "You understand that… right?"

"I understand the goal," she said. "But you must know most of them will die, no matter what I give them."

He shrugged. "Don't worry about that. The president will be sending more to replace them."

She forced a smile, but she knew for a fact that Collins would not approve of this. Not after he'd sent her here to chase down rumors that the Cartel was already using slave labor.

The order gave her a sense of clarity. It meant the president was dead or at least no longer in power. The Cartel had taken over. There was no longer any doubt.

She stared Cassini in the eye and forced a sad but understanding look. "A cost-benefit analysis would suggest that you're right. Billions will die on Earth if we don't hurry. I'll get my people ready."

He smiled, a wicked and lusty smile all at the same time. He was enjoying this. "Good," he said. "I knew I could trust you."

Chapter 19

Empress Transport, Mars Orbit

As the nine hundred foot transport approached the curved red surface of Mars, it began to slow and descend toward the planet with the firing of retro rockets. They remained on until the huge vessel entered the atmosphere and its hull began heating up.

Continued use of the thrusters became dangerous at this point. Instead, a dozen air-brakes were deployed. Huge, metallic wings that increased the drag on the ship and slowed it to a velocity at which the heat from re-entry would no longer be an issue.

Seen from the surface, it crossed the night sky trailing a wake of smoke and fire like a meteorite or an angel cast out from heaven. When it had finally slowed to a manageable speed, the retro-thrusters were reactivated and the ship slowed to a stop before descending the last hundred feet vertically and slamming down on a landing pad made of packed gravel.

The gravel compressed and was pushed sideways like water on the ocean, spreading the ship's weight out evenly. Huge landing struts extended at a thirty-degree angle from a dozen spots on the side of the transport. Reaching the gravel, they wedged themselves into the surface like outriggers on a canoe.

With the struts in place the ship was stable, rock solid on its keel.

Inside the vessel that stability was welcomed. The descent had been a nightmare for the men, women and children in the cargo bays. The shape of the bay amplified the shuddering of the huge vessel. There were no seats or straps or hand holds to grab, and the hundreds of people in each bay were tossed around like loose change. Several ended up with broken arms or legs. Many more received nasty bruises.

Then came the heat of re-entry. Unlike the crew compartments, the cargo bay was not well shielded from the heat. In thirty seconds, the frost on the walls had melted and run down the plates as if the bulkheads were bleeding.

Thirty seconds later the walls had become too hot to touch and the huge bays became steam rooms as the water evaporated. The temperature peaked at one hundred fifty degrees, just before the loud bang of the air-brakes deploying could be heard.

From there the ship shook and shuddered as what sounded like a hurricane raged outside. The noise was horrendous, and the screams and cries of those who thought they were dying or descending into hell only made it worse.

When the retro-thrusters came back on James knew they were almost down.

"Brace yourself," he said to Bethel.

Using the rag of his shirt to wrap his hands, Bethel tried to hold on to one of the support beams. It was too hot.

"Easier said than done," he said.

James nodded and sensed the ship stopping and sinking. The final touchdown was abrupt and painful and sent those who were still standing tumbling back to the floor.

There they waited, sweating in the stifling heat, listening to the clanking sounds of the struts extending and the ratcheting noise of the air-brakes being retracted. All around them the hull creaked and popped as it shed the heat of re-entry.

With a final bang that reverberated through the hull, silence returned.

"Now what?" Bethel said.

"I'm not sure we want to know."

It took a while, but eventually the interior doors were opened. Cool air swept in followed by several dozen mercenaries. They pointed to the nearest of the prisoners, grabbing a few and sending them through the door.

"Let's go!" one shouted to the crowd. "Come on, move."

With ruthless efficiency, they began pushing and shoving the captives through the doors like cattle being separated in the pen.

James could see a type of fear in Bethel's eyes. He grabbed Bethel by the shoulder as the mercenaries closed in. "Stay with me," he said.

Bethel nodded and soon they were in the line being pushed and shoved forward, as much by the human wave of the other captives as by the mercenaries.

A woman stumbled a few yards ahead and was half trampled by the time James and Bethel reached her. James tried to help her up, but she fell again, her leg was broken. Bethel tried to reach back but the surging line kept moving, pushing him along like the current of a strong river.

The crowd swept over her and she disappeared from view.

"Stay on your feet," James urged.

They were pushed through the hall to an exit ramp. They trudged down it and out of the ship, thankful for a little more space and the feeling of the cold night air.

From there they were marched along a causeway of red gravel and dust toward a warehouse a hundred yards away. High fences on either side of the causeway kept them in the narrow channel.

James glanced behind them. The transport was a huge cigar shaped vessel. He guessed it was close to a thousand feet long, and two hundred feet from its domed top to the square bottom now resting on the surface of Mars. Its blackened hull crackled and groaned as it gave off the heat.

James couldn't see a name or designation but he recognized the type. His father had commissioned their design. Called them the Empress Class. He'd said they would be the key to bringing the abundance of Mars to the starving Earth. He wondered what his father would think seeing endless lines of prisoners streaming from its various holds.

"How many?" Bethel asked, trying to stay close to James.

"I don't know," James said, assuming he meant the prisoners. "Thousands I'd guess."

In the distance, lit up by a group of floodlights he saw another hulking transport lying silent in the dark. He wondered how many men and women had been brought here against their will.

A shove in the back got him moving again, and soon he and Bethel were herded into a huge warehouse where the captives were being separated into a dozen different lines. Men with cattle prods stood everywhere, their weapons snapping with electricity. On raised catwalks above the crowd dozens of others stood with rifles and shotguns.

The mercenaries were ready for resistance, but none came. Despite the overwhelming advantage in numbers, the captives were confused, exhausted and weak. It made them fearful. More than anything they just wanted to avoid any trouble.

At least most of them.

In one section a scuffle broke out. Screams echoed as the cattle prods were put to use. Several prisoners were quickly taken down and order restored as the offenders were dragged off.

Bethel stood on his toes trying to see over the crowd and assess what had happened. James knew better. A series of gunshots proved him right.

"My God," Bethel said. "This is madness."

"Don't do anything stupid," James whispered to him. "Keep your eyes down and do as they say."

Bethel went silent. A few minutes later they were at the front of the line. Two hulking men grabbed James and yanked him forward. They slammed him down into a metal seat and held him there. A sad eyed woman with grey hair sat across from him. From her uniform, James could tell she was a nurse.

"Hold his arm," she said in a monotone voice.

One of the thugs grabbed James's right arm and pinned it onto an armrest, twisting it so it rested palm up. The woman jabbed him with a needle, drew some blood and placed it in a scanner. Five seconds later a screen lit up with a green light.

"No pathogens detected," the scanner announced. "Blood type O negative."

"Congratulations," the nurse said, falsely. "You're healthy enough to work."

She jabbed him with another needle, one that reminded James of the inoculations he'd received periodically in the military.

As James stared at the red liquid being forced into his veins, the nurse went back to her computer.

"Name?" she asked.

James was silent for a moment.

"Your name?"

This was something he hadn't considered. He sure as hell wasn't giving them his real name. "Ares," he said finally, speaking in a soft voice and lying as convincingly as he could.

She tapped away on the keys and then spoke again. "Last name?"

This time he was ready. He shook his head. "Don't got one," he muttered, trying to speak as if he'd never been educated.

"No last name," she said, tapping the screen a few more times. It wasn't uncommon.

"Any technical skills?" she asked.

James hesitated. "No," he said finally and then added, "I did some welding once."

"No tech skills," she said to the computer. "Qualification: laborer."

With that done, she turned and grabbed something else from the worktable. It looked like a cross between a pistol and a medical probe. She brought it towards him.

"What's that?"

She placed it on his forearm and James pulled his arm away.

"Hold still," the guard grunted.

"Please," the nurse said. "It's just identification."

Despite his warning to Bethel, James couldn't help but struggle. It didn't last long. One guard slapped his head sideways while the other slammed his arm back onto the armrest, looped a strap over it and yanked it tight.

The nurse placed the weapon against his skin and held it there. With a tap of the trigger the weapon fired, shoving a tiny identification tag under the skin. It hurt like hell.

The nurse pulled the weapon back. James saw a tiny line of blood on the underside of his forearm. Beneath the skin he saw a thin, rectangular strip about an inch long. Before he could consider anything more, the strap was released and he was lifted up and shoved forward.

A moment later he was back out in the night air with hundreds of the others. There a line of huge trucks waited. The men, women and children from the transport were being herded towards them. In the darkness it was hard to tell anyone apart.

"Bethel!" he shouted.

"Keep moving!" a vicious looking man with bad teeth growled.

James continued forward but dragged his feet. "Bethel!"

Plenty of others were looking around too, searching for lost family members and friends. The mercenaries seemed content to allow it, as long it didn't get out of hand. Maybe they knew preventing it would cause a riot.

Finally, James spotted someone who looked familiar. He pushed through the crowd to find Bethel helping a child to search for his mother and father.

A shotgun blast rang out above them. "Come on people. Get on the trucks," a voice shouted. "We need to get your sorry asses into the shelters before sunrise or you'll all burn to death."

The captives began climbing onto the trucks with renewed haste.

The child spotted his mother who was screaming hysterically, and the two were quickly reunited.

"Get in the truck," the closest thug ordered.

James helped the child and his mother into the truck. The father arrived moments later, thanking them. Bethel climbed up and James followed, taking a seat near the back edge of the covered flatbed.

With snaps from the cattle prods, a few stragglers were forced on board and then a group of the mercenaries climbed in, standing at the back keeping watch.

A moment later the truck lurched forward. It bounced along, traveling quickly over the unpaved road. Red dust flew out behind it, obscuring the lights of the landing zone as the truck rumbled on toward the dark horizon.

▲

Back inside the warehouse, things were winding down. With the last of the new arrivals processed and shipped out, the mercenaries were mounting up on their own vehicles and heading back to Olympia, leaving the medical teams to tidy up and put away their equipment.

Hannah remained behind, helping with the work and studying the despondent faces of her staff. They were miserable, resigned to their fate, but hating every minute of it. Some of them openly resented her and her new 'friendship' with Cassini.

Still she went from station to station trying to reassure them. But little was said. After a month of martial law, everyone had learned to speak in code or simply keep their mouths shut.

"You did your job," she told them. "That's the best we can do for now."

Most nodded glumly or simply continued with their work. She arrived at a station to find one of the nurses struggling with the latch on a heavy case. She noticed that the woman's hands were shaking.

Gently, Hannah reached over and helped her. "Are you okay?"

"They're going to die out there," the nurse said, brushing strands of grey hair away from her face.

"We gave them the best chance we could," Hannah said, without much conviction. "The inoculations and the hemoglobin booster will help them deal with the thin air."

"They don't even care," the nurse replied.

"They're mercenaries," Hannah said. "They do what they're paid to do."

"No," the nurse said. "The *laborers*. They just go where they're told to. Like cattle. We even tag them like livestock."

We all do what we're told now, Hannah thought, though she didn't say it. "I heard you arguing with at least one of them," Hannah noted. "Near the end."

The nurse nodded, putting the tagging gun away in its case. "He said his name was Ares."

Hannah stooped and straightened up. "Ares?" she repeated. It was an odd name to hear. These people were the dregs of society. They had simple names. Ares was the name of a god.

"Yeah," the nurse replied. "The computer assigned him the designation, 4917 Gamma. Doesn't exactly have the same ring to it. But then the poor guy didn't have a last name to begin with."

On her handheld computer, Hannah typed in the designation 4917 Gamma. The basic information of the individual came up. No infectious diseases, no distinguishing marks. No obvious defects.

She tapped the screen and a photo came up. It was blurry, taken while the man was struggling by the look of it. Like all the new arrivals this one was filthy, his hair a rat's nest, his face bearded.

Still, he looked strangely familiar.

She zoomed in on the photo. For a second she felt dizzy and confused. The man looked familiar… Almost like…

She looked away, trying to clear her mind, but then she thought about the name he'd given and her heart began to pound with a surge of adrenaline.

"*I am Ares,*" she whispered to herself. "*God of War. I bring pain, destruction and death. And yet they still worship me…*"

The words rolled off her tongue as if she were speaking a poem in a trance of some kind.

"Doctor Ankaris?" the nurse said. "Are you okay?"

"Um…yes," Hannah stumbled. "It's just the name. It's a little ironic."

"How so?"

"Ares is a name from Greek Mythology. He's the counterpart of the Roman god, Mars," she said. "The god of war."

Chapter 20

An hour on the gigantic flatbed had brought the new arrivals out into the wasteland, well over the horizon from the landing site and the lights of Olympia. About the only thing of consequence they passed was a staging depot with several warehouse-like buildings around it.

It disappeared behind them as well, but eventually something new appeared up ahead. A looming structure of impressive size, lit up by floodlights and surrounded by tiny figures that streamed over it here and there, like ants building a nest.

The trucks pulled to a halt a half-mile from the looming monstrosity and the *laborers* were rousted out and assembled near a warren of holes in the ground.

A new squad of mercenaries arranged the captives into four groups like platoons in boot camp. They were made to stand facing the structure.

As they stood at attention, a hulking man with a shaved head and a tattooed face, climbed onto a platform in front of them.

"So you think you're in hell!" the muscle bound giant bellowed. "And maybe you are. But considering where most of you come from this might be an improvement."

The man laughed at his own joke, jumped down from the platform and began walking through the ranks like a general inspecting his soldiers.

"You're slaves now," he continued, his deep voice carrying across the crowd. "And I am your master. The first thing you need to know are the rules."

He raised the extra-large cattle prod above his head and sent a violent surge of energy from its tip. It snapped like lightning.

"To disobey is death," he growled. "To strike a guard is death. To kill a guard... is death to you, your family and all your friends. If there is any hint of a conspiracy or a coordinated act of disobedience, we will line you up and kill every third one of you at random."

The fear that swept over the slaves could be felt like a cold wind. Some of them glanced around. The slave-master let the fear linger and soak deep.

"I get the feeling he's done this before," James whispered.

Bethel said nothing. He was shaking in the cold.

"But if you work hard," the slave-master added, "and if you last a year, just one, solitary year, you'll have earned your freedom and become citizens in the realm that you're helping to build."

The slave-master walked past James and Bethel.

James resisted the urge to turn, but studied the man from the corner of his eye.

Bethel whispered. "What's with all the tattoos?"

"Mercenary kill records," James said. "Must have run out of room on his body so he marked up his face."

A baton hit James in the back of the knees, dropping him.

The slave-master stood over him. "I hope you dig as well as you talk."

James stared up at the man. "Doubtful," he began to say.

Before James had even finished the word, the slave-master jabbed him with the cattle prod.

James's whole body convulsed and shook. The pain was excruciating. When the ten seconds of agony were up, the slave-master released the trigger and pulled the weapon back.

James was panting, grunting in pain. He could hardly move.

The slave-master leaned down toward him. "You want some more?"

Unable to speak, James shook his head.

"Too bad," the slave-master said. "You've earned it."

He jabbed the cattle prod into James once again, and this time James howled in agony as the electric shock coursed through him.

When it was over, James was left on the dusty red ground in a heap of pain. He watched the slave-master's boots as the man turned his back and walked off.

Bethel looked down at him, about to reach over and help. James shook his head.

"The rest of you, understand this!" the slave-master shouted. "Work hard, you live. Slack off, argue or fight... and you'll die at my hand."

Chapter 21

Hannah sat in her office staring at a print out of the man who'd offered the name Ares to her nurse. As a precaution she'd printed a hundred other files, but this was the only one she cared about.

She stared at the photo long and hard, but she wasn't sure.

Could it really be James?

The face looked similar, but thin and drawn, and yet not as thin as most of the new arrivals. The man in the photo was filthy; he had bruises and gashes here and there. Scars that she didn't recognize, but it had been over a year since she'd seen James Collins. He'd been deployed in combat most of that time. Scars had a way of attaching to a man that lived in a perpetual state of war.

She'd almost convinced herself that she was wrong, that she was grasping at straws, when the memory came round once again. In it, she and James were lying naked on a couch with just a sheet wrapped around them.

"I think I love you," she'd said for the first time.

His reaction was unexpected. He set his jaw and looked away.

"What's wrong?"

"I don't want you to love me," he said. "I'm not worth your love."

"I'll be the one to decide that," she said smartly.

He looked at her coldly. A look that gave her a chill. "Then make the right choice. Don't tarnish yourself."

"What the hell are you talking about?" she asked pulling back and wrapping the sheet around her.

"I'm not like you," he said. "You heal people while I destroy them. You argue for democracy. I serve my father and his thirst for control."

She'd stared at him sadly, unable to explain that she'd been assigned by President Collins to connect with him, to observe him and see if he was trustworthy. She'd chosen to use lust as her way in and James, always eager to push his father's buttons, had been more than willing to fall into bed with the outspoken critic of the Collins regime.

Only it turned out that James was loyal to a fault. To the point that it was killing him inside. And among the three of them, the only ones spinning deception were her and the president.

But by then she'd fallen in love with him, at least that was the truth. And yet it was the only thing he didn't want from her.

"You don't get to tell me what I care about," she'd snapped. "I believe in your goodness."

"Really?" he said. "For every person you've saved, I've killed a dozen, maybe a hundred. For every surgery you've performed, I've destroyed a home or a village."

"For good reason," she said. "That's what happens in war."

They'd stared at each other for a long moment.

"I am Ares," he said finally. "The god of war. I bring pain, destruction and death... and yet they still worship me. I won't have you loving me. It would only make me despise you."

She'd said nothing more. As he showered, she'd left his apartment with her heart breaking. She'd never seen him again.

She looked at the picture once more, trying to see into the eyes of the man.

The door opened behind her. Hannah did not react. Methodically, without any haste, she slid the photo back into the stack. Only then did she turn.

It was Davis.

"I have the supplies you requisitioned," he said, sounding very official. "Do you need anything else?"

She understood. They all suspected the offices were bugged. He placed a box of medical supplies down on her desk and handed her an electronic clipboard to sign. A handwritten note was attached to it.

The others report little success in recruiting. The people are afraid. They want to know who's going to lead them and how they're supposed to fight against the mercenaries and their guns.

Hannah understood. She couldn't blame them. They needed a leader, a warrior to believe in.

She thought back to the photo. She had to find the truth. If the man in the picture was James, he would have more reason to fight than anyone. And many of those on the planet would be willing to follow him. She was grasping at straws, but what else did they have?

She nodded, took the slip of paper and handed the clipboard back to Davis.

Chapter 22

Secondary Core Unit Work Site

In the darkness, illuminated by the harsh glare of the mercury lights, a thousand slaves worked on and around the Core Unit. Those with more advanced skills were up in the structure, accompanied by a few techs from Olympia, welding pipes and installing the power conduits. The rest toiled near the base of the structure, excavating trenches and hauling steel plating and other material by hand.

James and Bethel were part of the second group and were currently lugging a seven foot steel beam designed as a cross brace. On Earth, the beam would have weighed nearly four hundred pounds, but on Mars it was half that and James and Bethel could carry it up the slope, with one man lifting each end.

They could lift it, but that didn't mean it was easy.

Both of them were struggling, feet slipping in the dust, arms and legs aching. Bethel was feeling the worst of it.

"You look like you're dying," James said.

"I feel like it," Bethel grunted. "The air is too thin. I can hardly breathe."

"I thought they gave us something for that," James asked.

Bethel nodded. "They did. But if they used what I think they did. It'll take a few days to build up the red blood cells in your system."

Talking made it harder to breath, and the short conversation was too much. After a few more steps Bethel stopped and dropped his end of the beam. He leaned over, hands on his knees, his chest heaving and falling. For a moment it looked like he might throw up.

As others passed by them, a guard aimed a flashlight their way. "Back in line," the man grunted. "Keep it moving!"

James dug in and got a better grip on the beam, preparing to shoulder more of the load. Bethel reached down and grasped his end, wearily hoisting it up.

They soon began moving again, with James holding most of the weight.

"Be careful," Bethel said wheezing. "You're helping someone other than yourself."

"Shut up," James said, with a smirk.

They finally reached the staging area and dropped off the beam. A second group of slaves placed it on a cart and wheeled it and two others toward an elevator. High above, acetylene torches flashed as the monstrous structure was slowly stitched together.

Bethel tried to take another rest, but James got him moving. "Come on," he said. "It's a lot easier going down."

They got in line with the other slaves and trudged down the hill, breathing hard and scuffing their tired feet. As they neared the bottom a high-pitched alarm began to wail. It sounded like the air raid sirens that had been so prevalent during the War of Unification.

As work ground to a halt all around them, James noticed one of the mercenaries check his watch.

"Back to the camps!" a voice shouted. "Sunrise in eight minutes."

The slaves who were still carrying things put down their burdens and turned around. The welding in the tower dwindled to a few sparks and then ceased. James turned his eyes to the east. He noticed a different shade on the horizon, a lighter grey.

One of the guards gave him a shove. "Get moving!" he shouted. "Unless you want to fry."

The wave of humanity began to sweep down the hill toward a shantytown made of metal siding, reflective tarps and holes in the ground.

James and Bethel followed, exhausted and moving slowly. By the time they reached the shelter, the tunnels and their nooks and crannies were all filled and spoken for. The only space left for the newcomers in the overcrowded camp were the spots beneath layered metallic tarps. Casting around for some space, they found an unclaimed spot near the entrance and all but collapsed to the floor.

"I don't think I'll last very long here," Bethel said.

"It will get easier as we adjust," James said, staring out at the changing color of the horizon.

"No," Bethel said, "this kind of work is hard on the body and mine's old."

As Bethel spoke, a wizened little man came by shouting something at all the newcomers. He had a thick accent and a high-pitched voice that made it hard to understand.

"This camp is not in a green zone," he said. "Move back. Stay inside. The sun will kill you. The sun will kill."

He moved on, warning others and James had to smile. "That guy seems to be doing alright and he's a lot older than you."

Bethel shook his head and then lay down, muttering something about there being no point to survival, but James wasn't really listening anymore. He was staring out at the horizon as it turned pink with the coming sun.

As he watched in fascination, a sliver crescent of light began to burn in a wide arc along the horizon. It looked as if the world was catching fire as it painted the sand a deep blood red. Despite all misery and pain, James stared in fascination, waiting for the sunrise. Waiting to feel its heat and light, like he never had on Earth.

Before the sun broke the horizon, the tarp was pulled down in front of him with a snap, blotting out the view.

James turned to see a pair of burly men who'd been acting like foremen of some kind, directing the other workers on the job site. They seemed better fed than most, a better class of slave apparently. They glared at him as if he'd violated some rule.

The little wizard of a man came up beside them. He waggled his finger at James. "It will kill you," he said. "Remember that."

Several hours later, the vast majority of the slaves were sprawled out on the ground, trying to sleep on makeshift beds of dirty rags or simply laying on the rust colored ground using their folded hands for pillows. Others were further back, down in the catacombs or beneath the shantytown's makeshift tin roof, trying to choke down more of the protein mix that seemed to be the only source of food.

James found he couldn't sleep, and much as he knew he had to eat, he had only one desire at the moment. Eventually it got the best of him.

He stood, walked toward the tarp and untied one corner where it was staked down.

No one stirred. No one tried to stop him.

He lifted the flap to the side, opening a gap of several inches. The sun had traveled high above and was falling behind them now. Shadows from the tent made a space of several feet where the solar radiation was blocked, or so James hoped. Quietly, he stepped through the flap and stood in the shade.

He crouched in the shade, staring at the wonders of Mars. Rolling plains stretched out before him, pockmarked by craters and shallow gullies that seemed to crisscross the surface. In the distance cliffs marking the edge of a canyon loomed, and beyond that the awe-inspiring presence of Olympus Mons bathed in the sunlight. It rose to a height of twenty-five miles, five times as tall as Mount Everest on Earth. It was the largest mountain in the solar system. And from a hundred miles off it was majestic.

The flap moved behind him and James turned.

"Thought maybe you'd had enough and decided to fry yourself," Bethel said.

James grinned and looked off into the distance. "I've never seen light like this," he said. "Never seen the real sun bathe the landscape. Nothing but the pollution and the acid filled clouds."

He turned back to Bethel. "There's something so pure about it. It's almost worth being a slave to see."

Bethel slipped through and let the tarp fall back into place. He crouched beside James. "When I was a child, my mother would take me to a place up in the mountains. Far to the north. On the longest days of summer, you could still see the sun from there, but even then it was shrouded, distant and cold."

Suddenly, James thought of his father and their argument about whether the Earth could even be saved. It seemed pointless at the time. But seeing the open plains, unspoiled by filth or trash or the endless sprawling structures required by the massive population, he felt differently. Gazing at the beauty of the landscape painted with real sunlight—even deadly sunlight—he finally understood what his father dreamed of in a way he'd never grasped before.

The Earth didn't have to stay as it was. It might take centuries, but if humanity could ruin the planet maybe they could heal it. Maybe if he'd sided with his father when the old man had reached out to him, the world would have still had a chance. But now...

"What have I done?" he whispered.

"What was that?"

James hesitated. Bethel had become a friend, his only friend in the world, but James could not reveal the truth to him. It would put them both in danger. Every camp had its snitches. This one would be no different.

"I mean humanity," he said vaguely. "What have we done? If things continue as they are, no one on Earth will ever see the sunrise again."

"Isn't that what this place is supposed to be about?" Bethel asked. "Buying time for the Earth to begin healing itself?"

"I suppose that was the president's plan," James said. "But something's changed."

"Changed?"

James hesitated again. "Have you ever heard of the Cartel?"

"The thousand families?"

James nodded. "Shortly before I met you, I heard that they were revolting against the government. That they were determined to take this place for their own and leave the rest of humanity to die."

"The fighting we heard in the tunnels," Bethel said. "Are you saying there was a new war beginning?"

"Could have been," James said. "I really have no idea what's happened since I fell down the rabbit hole. But the people working us are not regulars. And that tells me something."

"We have to do something," Bethel said. "You wanted to reach the military back on Earth. Maybe you still can. Maybe we can escape. No one seems to be guarding us."

James looked out across the open plain once again. Escape sounded deceptively simple. But it was complicated.

A night escape would be almost impossible. Guards were everywhere, walking among the workers, watching from small towers that sprouted all around the work site, riding around the perimeter in hopped up armored personnel carriers. James had even spotted a couple of old MRVs out beyond the fence keeping watch over everything.

The day seemed to be a different story—all the king's men retreated with the sunrise, slinking away like nocturnal predators to a shelter somewhere —leaving the camp and the worksite essentially unguarded. It was an illusion; Olympia and the Green Zone lay far out of reach, beyond an un-crossable desert watched over by the blazing sun.

James offered a sad smile. "They don't need to guard us," James said. "The sun is doing it for them."

"We have to do something?"

James nodded. *Sure. But what could slaves do, other than their master's bidding?*

Chapter 23

Governor Cassini was in his office getting measured for a new uniform, one more fitting for a governor.

"We have a problem," a deep voice called out to him.

Cassini turned to see Magnus Gault standing in the open doorway. "You're interrupting me," Cassini said. "This better be important."

"More important than getting your clothes tailored, I assure you of that."

Cassini motioned to the courtiers. "Come back in an hour," he said and then he sat down behind his desk and grabbed the staff-like scepter he'd begun to carry. It had a golden shaft and a black dragon's head on the top. All leaders should have a symbol; he felt this one was appropriate for him.

"What's this all about?" Cassini asked. "What kind of problem have you discovered?"

"I've been looking over your reports to Lucien," Gault said, holding up a small device and reading off of it.

"*The military situation is stable,*" Gault said, reading Cassini's words. "*All possible subversives have been rounded up and are being held in custody.*"

"Yes," Cassini said. "The Colonial Infantry has been disbanded. Some of the men have been mixed into our units. The rest are being held, as are all the commanders who resisted our new orders. We are in fine shape."

"Are we?" Gault replied. "There are four squadrons of MRVs unaccounted for. A full brigade from the 41st Armored Division."

Cassini nodded knowingly. He hadn't quite explained this to Lucien. "Yes, they are a small problem. They refuse to come back to Olympia. They claim to be hunting terrorists."

"You and I know there are no terrorists here," Gault said. "So why are you allowing this?"

Cassini was perturbed. He didn't like having Gault around. "Because they're a danger."

"Dangers must be dealt with," Gault said.

Cassini didn't like being questioned, but the world he and Gault inhabited was less stratified than the military. Rank meant little in comparison to power and the will to use it. He sensed Gault challenging him. It brought his own ire to the forefront.

"I'm dealing with them my own way."

"By ignoring them?"

"By letting them grind their strength down in this useless charade. They've been out there for a month now. Even if they're rationing their supplies they must be running low by now. A few more weeks out in the wastes without maintenance and their machines will be useless."

Gault sat back and put his filthy boots up on Cassini's desk. He seemed to be thinking. "Weak," he said finally.

Cassini knew how it looked, but he considered it shrewd. He stared at Gault. "You're in charge of our armed units," he said. "Perhaps you'd prefer to challenge them. Meet them in the desert for a showdown? After all, there are only forty-eight of them. If you take everything we have, you'll bring a hundred and nineteen units into battle. Not all of them top of the line like the machines in the 41st, but a capable force none-the-less."

Gault paused and ran a hand across his chin. Mercenary units that tangled with the regular armed forces had fared badly in the past. The regulars of the United World Military had been at war too long, they were too well trained, too experienced, too disciplined.

"I...um... see your point," Gault said at last. "But they're still a danger."

"They won't be for long." Cassini said, grinning. "The summer is just beginning. The dust storms will follow and when the storms come, the men and women of the 41st will be forced to choose. If they return to Olympia and stand down in the shelters, we will deal with the commanders harshly and impound their MRVs. If they remain in the field, they will die out there, choking on the dust, and the sun will bleach their bones."

Gault raised an eyebrow, which Cassini took as grudging admiration for his plan. "And if they decide to fight, rather than wait for their own inevitable demise?"

"They'll have to come to us. You'll be ready for them. And you'll have all the advantages."

Chapter 24

Secondary Core Unit Work Site

As dusk approached, the wailing siren rang out again, followed by the sound of a small convoy pulling up to the edges of the camp. The weary slaves roused themselves from sleep or other meaningless activities and began to file out through the various exits.

The second day of work was more brutal than the first, and though James found himself with more energy, his body ached with a type of soreness he could not remember. Halfway through the shift, the Solaris Array settled below the horizon and the cold rushed in. Their sweat-soaked clothes quickly chilled them to the bone.

At some point a worker refused to get up and was summarily shot. Another slave was caught trying to steal a sharp piece of metal that could have been used for a weapon. Instead of a quick death, he was dragged off to some unknown fate.

Little was said, and the work continued.

When the shift finally ended, the procession back to the camp began in earnest and even James found himself longing just to lay down on the hard, dusty ground and fall asleep. But as they approached the tents, the slave master and his men began separating a small number of the new arrivals.

"Don't look at them," James whispered. "Just keep walking."

It seemed like a good plan until the slave-master grabbed James by the shoulder.

"Ares!" he said, studying a hand held display that told him who James was officially. "Get on the truck."

Bethel paused.

"Keep moving," The slave-master grunted.

Bethel passed him by and James turned toward a covered flatbed truck like the one that had brought them in. He climbed in the back with thirty others and tried not to think too hard about where they might be going.

As the truck moved off, he watched the work site slowly disappear behind him while the sands around it grew brighter in the coming day. Despite the uncomfortable surroundings and his fascination with the natural light, exhaustion overtook James and he soon fell asleep.

By the time he woke up, they were entering Olympia. Miles of green fields led to a city of white buildings beneath a pale pink sky, so neat and clean it looked unreal.

An hour later he was sitting in one of the medical bays on the outskirts of the city. For a moment he was alone. Ahead of him on a tray were several hypodermic needles and a scalpel. He stretched forward, palmed the scalpel and hid it in his sleeve.

A second later the door opened and a woman came in. To his utter surprise, James recognized her instantly.

"I'm Dr. Ankaris," she said.

He nodded, trying not to react in any obvious way.

The lab tech who'd been studying him finished a scan and passed the device to Hannah.

She looked at it and nodded. "Set the others up in the main room, we'll do this as quick as we can."

"Yes Doctor," the lab tech replied.

As the assistant left, Hannah shut the door. She came over to James and placed a pair of long hypodermic needles on a tray beside him.

"Ares," she said, taking one of the hypodermics and drawing fifty ccs of some amber liquid from a large vial. "Is that your name?"

James didn't know if she was trying to make small talk to take his mind off the needle or if she had recognized him.

"It is."

"Look at me, please."

The words were clinical. As if she needed to examine his eyes. But when James looked up he could see more on her pretty face. Expectation and confirmation. He looked nothing like the man he'd been when they were together. But no one could change his eyes.

"James," she whispered.

He kept up the charade. "Excuse me?"

"You don't have to pretend," she said. "I know it's you. You can talk to me. I've scanned these rooms. There are no bugs. No one's listening to us."

He kept silent. The situation was so odd he didn't know how to respond. Her face was so kind. Her eyes red as if she'd been crying or not sleeping. Her lips trembling as she waited for an answer. All he wanted to do was reach out and embrace her.

"What are you doing here?" he asked finally.

Her eyes welled up at this. She reached forward and grabbed his hand, gripping it tightly. "I might ask you the same thing," she said. "The whole world thinks you're dead. "

"I almost was," he said. "I ended up in the sublevels. Apparently that's the hunting ground for slaves these days."

She nodded.

"I don't remember you having an interest in Mars?" he said.

"Your father sent me," she admitted.

"My father?"

She nodded. "I don't know how to explain this," she said. "But I'm not who you think I am. I was never part of the opposition. I was never a critic of your father's. Not really. I'm with Section 7."

James stared through the grime and pain trying to understand. Section 7 was a deep cover intelligence group under his father's personal control. Some considered them the president's secret police. "You were spying on me?"

"I was doing my job," she explained. "He asked me to spend time with you, because he was concerned with your views. But over time my feelings for you became very real, if that even matters."

For a moment the petty anger of having his father distrust him flared, but James quickly tossed it aside. None of it mattered. Not now.

In a bizarre way, hearing that she was part of Section 7 spurred a pang of hope in him. It meant she was sworn to uphold the Constitution, to defend the government that had just been attacked. She might have access to weapons, communications. She might be able to help.

"How bad is it?" he asked.

"Pretty damned awful," she said. She explained what she knew of the situation on Earth with the military hunting the Black Death, and the orders his father was supposedly giving.

"It's a lie," he said. "My father's dead. Inyo betrayed him. Sold him out to the Cartel."

"I assumed as much."

"We have to get in touch with the high command," he said. "They have to know the truth. If I talk to them. If they see my face, hear my words. They can rally the troops and we stand a chance of bringing this whole thing back under control."

She shook her head. "I have no access to off world communications. Everything is locked down and heavily guarded. Even if I could break in, the Cartel is in control of the relay satellites. Our message would never get through."

James looked up at the ceiling in frustration. "There has to be a way," he said.

"We can't reach Earth," she replied. "But maybe we can do something here. There are people who want to fight."

"Who?" James asked. "How many?"

"Most of the governing council," she said.

"Politicians won't do you much good," he said. "You're going to need an army. What about the workers?"

"They're afraid," she said. "They know the situation is bad but they won't act if they don't have any hope. They need a leader, someone to believe in. If they knew you were alive, they might be willing to—"

"No."

"But James—"

"I said no! The Cartel will kill me the second they find out I'm alive. They'll kill you just for knowing me."

"But if we kept it quiet..."

"It won't stay that way," he said. "Besides we can't beat these guys with small arms and Molotov cocktails. We need heavy weapons. Armor."

"We don't have access to any of that," she said. "The Cartel has confiscated everything."

"What about the military units my father sent here?"

"The men from the 26th and the 132nd were rounded up and..."

James could guess at the rest. They were probably all dead by now. "What about the 41st?"

"They were sent out into the desert when everything went down. They never came back. No one's seen or heard from them since," she said. "Rumor has it they were given poisoned rations."

James felt as if he'd been stabbed in the heart. His men. His unit.

Before he could muster a reply, the door swung open. A tall man in an ornate uniform stood there along with another man in military-like duds and a pair of guards.

"Governor," Hannah said, standing.

James glanced at Cassini and the man who stood beside him. In that instant he recognized him. The same son of a bitch who'd fired the missile into his wrecked car.

He quickly turned his eyes to the floor, like a good slave was supposed to.

"I'd like to introduce the new head of military operations," Cassini said. "Commander Magnus Gault."

Hannah shook hands with him and James seethed quietly.

"Gault will be taking over the military units while I will concentrate fully on running the city and speeding up the construction process," Cassini added. He stepped up and put a hand on her arm. "I hope you'll continue to help me."

Hannah smiled as if she was excited to see him. It made James sick but he understood. She was a soldier in a different kind of war. A dirtier war in some ways.

"Of course I will," she said.

"Good," Cassini said. "Now what's going on here? Some kind of epidemic?"

"No," Hannah said. "We had to rescan a few of the new arrivals. They received faulty boosters. It was limiting their ability to work."

"Is this one ready to go?"

"Yes," Hannah said. "He's all set."

"Good," Cassini replied. "He looks like a strong worker. He'll easily make it a year."

With that, Cassini turned to Gault. "Take him outside. He can wait there until the others have been inoculated, then deliver them back to the worksite."

Gault nodded at Cassini and then motioned toward the door. "Let's go."

James stepped through the door. The last thing he saw was the full hypodermic sitting on the tray. The booster he'd supposedly been given. But Cassini didn't notice; he was busy caressing the soft skin of Hannah's arm.

Chapter 25

By the time James and the other prisoners were dumped back at the work site, the next shift had begun. Despite their lack of rest, they were loaded down with machine parts and sent into the fray.

James took what he was given and hiked up the sprawling anthill that had been built around the base of the Core Unit. He was directed inside, where he climbed a dozen flights of stairs and made his way out onto a platform where the control room was being constructed.

He couldn't help but marvel at the immense size of the structure. It was like standing in the middle of an empty coliseum. The fusion grid down below was almost complete. The walls of titanium were nearly finished, plate after plate being welded into place. He couldn't vouch for the construction standards but if they were up to the job, the unit would be active in a month or so.

Then what, he wondered. Would the slaves be moved to a new task? Would they be needed at all? Surely they'd be worked to death, or simply shot when they weren't needed anymore.

"Put the parts down over here," a technician said. "Be careful."

James recognized the man's orange uniform as belonging to one of the original Terra-formers. The man looked worn out. James wondered what would happen to these men and women when their work was done. The Cartel would need some of them for maintenance, but not all of them.

James placed the parts next to a stack of modular electronic equipment.

"Thanks," the man said.

James nodded and turned around, heading back toward the stairway. Going down was far easier than climbing up and he soon reached the exit point. From there, he hiked back down the hill toward the staging area.

As he went, Bethel caught up to him. "What happened?"

James kept walking. He wasn't ready to discuss it. The meeting with Hannah had released a torrent of feelings. Some of which were reverberating like an echo. Tens of thousands would die here when the Cartel was finished with them. Billions on the Earth, lives James had scorned and now felt for. The guilt crashed over him in waves.

Hannah wanted him to do something about it. Bethel did too. But what the hell could he do? He was a slave. He was powerless and he knew it.

"What happened?" Bethel asked again.

"Nothing," James said. "Nothing happened."

"What did they want with you?"

James turned to Bethel, anger flashed across his face. "They gave me another inoculation," he said.

"That's it?" Bethel said. "They could have done that here."

James realized that. He wondered how long it would take the thugs who ran the place to realize that. He began walking again.

"We need to talk," Bethel said, catching up to him again.

"Leave me alone."

Bethel grabbed James by the shoulder. James stopped in his track, whirled around and glared at Bethel.

Before he could say anything, a scuffle broke out nearby. Over by the line at the water table. A young boy, maybe twelve or thirteen, was trying to push his way into the line. The guards were pushing him back.

"Get out of here boy," one of them said. "You've had your water."

"I get a drink," the kid said. "I did what I was told."

He stepped forward but was shoved to the ground by another guard standing near the water dispenser.

"Three more runs," the guard said. "Then you get a drink. Understand?"

The kid showed no signs of backing down or crying. "I'm thirsty," he shouted.

The guards laughed. "Then you'd better get your ass moving."

The kid stood slowly and turned back toward the staging area, looking dejected. But when the guards turned their attention away for a second, he darted back to the table and grabbed a bottle of water.

One guard lunged for him, but the kid was small and quick. He ducked and ran. Two other thugs chased him. "You're gonna regret this, punk!"

The kid raced into the crowd, but they parted as the guards came after him. He kept running and changing direction. Looking over his shoulder as he ran, the kid slammed into the slave-master.

He might as well have run into a wall.

Knocked to the ground, the kid looked up just in time to see that damned cattle prod headed for his chest.

The kid screamed in agony as it hit him.

The crowd froze, watching in horror.

After ten seconds of wailing, the slave-master pulled his weapon back.

The kid rolled over, curling up in the fetal position.

"You think that was funny?" the slave-master said.

The kid shook his head.

"I'll give you something to laugh at."

With that, the slave-master jammed the cattle prod into the kid again, just as he'd done to James, but this time he held it on until the child passed out from the pain.

The silence was deafening.

"Take him to north point," the slave-master grunted to a pair of his thugs. "Chain him to the dead machines."

Hours later, after the shift ended, arguments began breaking out in the shantytown of the slaves. James found it hard to tell what was going on, but it sounded like the kid's mother and father were arguing with each other, and a few big shots from the camp had joined in.

James had seen them before; they had pulled the tarp down in front of his face. One of them, the leader, seemed to go by the name Kek. With only a few days in the camp, James wasn't certain of much, but he was fairly sure Kek and his friend were collaborators of some kind. Probably trading information and promises for a little extra consideration; more food, better assignments, a shorter sentence in this hellhole.

As the argument went on, the shouting grew and the tiny old man began to make his rounds, pulling the tarps down tight, warning everyone about the sun. It was madness.

"Where did they take him?" the woman begged.

"Out into the desert," replied the father.

"To north point and the dead machines," Kek added.

"Why?" the woman screamed. "He's only a boy."

"You're lucky they only punished him," Kek growled. "And not the rest of us."

Others looked on, watching impassively. Their faces were blank. This wasn't the first heart-wrenching scene they'd witnessed, and it wouldn't be the last.

The boy's mother was inconsolable now, tears streaming down her face, shaking her head in disbelief. Her husband put his hand on her to comfort her but she slapped it away.

James couldn't take it anymore. He stood suddenly.

His movement startled everyone. They watched as he jammed the scalpel he'd palmed into the edge of the tarp and cut a large section out of it.

"What are you doing?" Bethel asked.

"What I can," James said.

He finished his cut, gathered up the fallen material and stuffed three bottles of water into the pockets of his pants and made his way for the exit. Before he could get there, Kek blocked his path.

"Where the hell do you think you're going?"

"I'm going to get the kid," James said.

"Like hell you are."

James took a step around Kek only to have the man grab him.

With a quick move, James knocked Kek's arm loose and shoved him out of the way. As Kek stumbled backward, James ducked through the hole he'd cut and walked out onto the barren plain. No one followed or tried any further to stop him.

"It's five miles to north point," Kek shouted from beneath the safety of the tarp. "You'll never make it."

James ignored him, turned north and wrapped the tarp around him like a shroud. He pulled it over his face just as the blazing orange sun set fire to the horizon.

Bethel watched him with pride. "Go, my friend," he whispered. "Go."

Chapter 26

With the sun rising fast, James used the tarp to cover his head, neck and back. He continued north, sticking to the higher ground, doing his best to avoid the soft red sand, but still the journey took its toll. The thin Martian atmosphere made breathing difficult and, despite the hemoglobin booster, it soon felt as if his lungs were failing. He ignored the pain and pushed forward, eyes burning and sweat pouring down his face.

As he pressed on James could hardly believe the difference between the frigid nights and blazing heat of the day.

Two hours into the hike he crested a small ridge and caught sight of a reflection, the sunlight glinting off something metallic in the distance. He pressed on, moving faster. Getting closer.

Through shimmering waves of heat, details began to appear. He saw the machines now, several dozen of them scattered in a random pattern.

North Point was apparently something of a boneyard. Cranes, earthmovers, backhoes and bulldozers sat scattered about. There were even a few armored transports and a pair of older model MRVs.

Feeling as if his skin was burning through the tarp and thinking of the young boy exposed in the blazing sun, James began to run, jogging at first and then sprinting down the hill.

It was a stumbling, awkward run made worse by the soft sand beneath his feet and the awkwardness of holding the tarp around him. He fell once, got up and then fell again. Finally he reached the flat ground and raced into the area.

He passed a few trucks buried up to their axles in the sand and then felt as if he'd stepped into a maze.

"Hey!" he shouted, his voice hoarse from the dry air. "Where are you, kid?"

He held still, but the only sound he heard was the pounding of his heart and the blood rushing thorough his veins. It was quiet on Mars; the open plains were more silent than any place he'd ever been in his life.

"I came to help you!" he shouted. "But I need to know where you are!"

Hearing no response, James began to search, checking one vehicle after another. He looked under and around them. He looked inside those with open cabs or hatches. It dawned on him that the mercenaries might not have bothered to bring the kid here, that the story of North Point might be nothing more than a cruel lie. Maybe they'd simply dragged the kid out into the desert and shot him, which meant James might have just thrown away his life for no reason at all.

"Come on kid? Don't tell me I just ran here for nothing."

Without any reply to help him, James continued the search. He skirted around the armored personnel carriers and past a crane that had toppled over onto its side. He came upon a dozen bodies, desiccated and drying in the air. They were adults, chained up and lying together. They looked like mummies.

The sight filled him with a mix of sadness and hope.

He stopped in his tracks and looked around. A dull, barely audible banging noise came from the other side of the crane.

Leaving the dead men, James rushed around the back of the fallen machine. All he found was a metal chain dangling from rigging and banging softly against the side of the crane in the slight gusts of the midday wind.

"Damn," he muttered.

He grasped the chain and then quickly let go. It was scalding hot to the touch.

He looked up. The sun was riding high, burning his hands and the exposed parts of his face. He'd have to take cover soon.

Feeling the pangs of despair settle over him, James shook his head angrily trying to chase them away.

"Not for nothing," he grunted. "Not for nothing." He moved on and continued the search, determined to find the kid even if it was too late.

Finally, after running himself in circles he spotted a shock of blond hair. He ran over and found the boy chained to the axel of an overturned transport. The kid had curled himself into the little bit of shade that the frame of the vehicle offered, but the mercenaries were no fools. They'd chained him in a way that left almost no shelter.

James quickly covered the child with the tarp and checked for and found a pulse.

"Thank God."

Without the tarp to protect him, James could feel the sun more painfully than ever. It stung his neck and scalp; it seemed to be burning through his clothes.

Grabbing a metal pole from the rubbish all around him, James tried to break one of the links. As he began to work, the boy stirred.

"Who are you?" the kid croaked. "What are you doing here?"

"I've come to take you home," James said.

"To Earth?"

James paused for a second and then went back to work, banging on what looked like a weak link in the chain. "No," he said. "Not that far."

The kid didn't reply. He looked pretty bad. His eyes were barely open and his skin was burned as red as the sand. James worked faster. After hammering at the damaged link uselessly, he stood up and looked around. He needed something stronger. He found a shovel beside one of the half buried machines and brought it back. He swung it with all his might. Slamming the edge into the link that connected the kid to the axel.

Still it held.

"Come on!" he shouted at the chain, his muscles straining and his arms burning in the sun. "Break damn you!"

With a few more blows, the link bent. And with one last savage impact the chain broke. It slithered off and rattled to the ground and coiling up like a snake. A dead snake, James thought. He dropped the shovel and scooped up the child.

"Stay with me," he said, carrying the boy to the front end of a tracked vehicle.

He placed the boy down in the shade, then went back for the shovel and began digging furiously. Soon he'd excavated a small den beneath the overhang of the rig, down between the two caterpillar tracks.

Gently he picked the child up and eased him down into the pit. With the kid settled, James dropped in beside him and then covered the entrance with the metallic tarp.

Chapter 27

In the shade of the big machine, a few feet down the soil was actually quite cool. It helped draw the sting of the burns they'd both suffered.

As the pain subsided James tried to get comfortable.

"We'll be safe in here," he said to the kid.

Safe from the solar radiation at least, he thought. No telling what might happen if the thugs came back, but from the look of the other victims James doubted they made a habit of it.

Across from him, the boy moved a little, but he didn't respond.

"You alright?" James asked.

The boy nodded. "I'm thirsty," he replied.

James had to smile. He pulled a bottle of water from his pocket, took a swig and then handed it to the boy.

"Don't take too much," James said. "You'll get sick."

The kid drank a few swigs and then handed the bottle back to James.

"You got a name?" James asked.

"Tor," the kid said.

"Tor," James said. "I like it…Good name."

"What's your name?"

"I'm Ares," James said.

The kid scrunched his face up as if he was considering the worth of James's false name. "I guess that's okay," he said.

"Good," James said, laughing a little. "I'm glad you approve."

The kid smiled a little. "Now what do we do?"

James leaned back. "We wait for it to get dark and then head back to the work site."

Silence followed. The kid seemed to be thinking. James was thinking too. A small part of him was calculating the odds, wondering what he'd do if the mercenaries found him, or if they'd notice the burns on his arms and face or if they came here to check and found that the kid was missing. None of the scenarios had a happy ending, but somehow that didn't change his mood. As he rested James felt a sensation he could barely remember. A feeling of...

Righteousness.

That was as close as he could come to putting a name on it. For the first time in as long as he could remember, there was no grey area in his mind. No conflict between what he was doing and what he thought was right. He considered the possibility that it might be the last thing he ever did, and that somehow it might also be the best thing he'd ever done, the purest thing, the only thing he could recall doing without anything to gain from it himself.

If they died out there, at least the kid wouldn't die alone. And if he was beaten and killed when he returned to the camp, then at least he'd died making a stand.

"Can I have some more water?" Tor asked.

James thought of how this had all started. The kid and his quest for a drink. He handed Tor the whole bottle. "You earned it."

As the boy took the water, James squirmed around until he could lean against the inside edge of the caterpillar track. As he got himself comfortable he noticed the metal strip they'd inserted in his arm. The identification strip. The tracking strip. He wondered if they might know where he was right now.

He guessed it was a short-range device. At such a small size it couldn't carry that much power. Still, as he stared at the dark strip he began to despise it and everything it stood for.

With deliberate thought, he pulled out the scalpel and began to cut into his own flesh. He didn't have to dig deep; the strip was just under the surface of his skin. His arm and fingers were soon covered in blood, but he continued the crude surgery, determined to remove the mark they'd put inside him.

"What are you doing?" the kid asked, looking at him as if he'd lost his mind.

'I'm trying to get this ID strip out," James replied.

"Why?"

He finally got his fingertips on the end of the metal strip, gripped it and began to pull. The strip slid one painful inch and then James yanked it free. The pain was excruciating and energizing all at the same time.

"Because, I'm done being what they want me to be."

Chapter 28

The sun had traversed the cloudless sky and was an hour from setting when it began to drop behind the broad shoulders of Olympus Mons.

The change in light was the first sign to those in the slave camp. If they wanted to eat or do anything before the taskmasters arrived and herded them to the staging areas, they'd better do it now.

From a spot against the wall, Bethel watched as the camp came to life. The arguments of the morning had faded into unspoken tension. The woman whose son had been taken lay forlornly on a shelf of rock. She had only a small rolled up wad of clothing for a pillow. Her eyes were streaked with darkness, as were those of her husband who sat beside her.

She looked despondent; he had a different appearance. After enduring hours of threats from the self-important group who seemed to think they spoke for the camp, the husband and father seemed almost to be hoping his son didn't return.

It would be easier that way. There would be guilt, but a different kind of guilt. Private guilt as opposed to facing the blame of the entire group for whatever repercussions followed. Such was the trial of those who lived in oppression and fear.

For his part, Bethel stayed beside the gap in the tarp, keeping his eyes on the desert. But the day had worn on and James had now been gone for ten hours. Even with the tarp to protect him and the bottles of water he'd taken, it was a long time to be out in that arid land.

As he clung to the tarp, Kek and his friend approached. "What are you looking for out there old man?"

Bethel kept his eyes on the desert. "The same thing I've been waiting for my whole life," he said. "A sign of hope."

The collaborators laughed. It was a mean, nasty laugh. "If you think your friend is coming back, you're crazy. He's dead by now."

Bethel might have believed him. Might have crumbled inside, but a sight had caught his eye. Out in the distance a trail of dust slowly drifting to one side. As he watched a figure came into view, the dust from his feet was blowing to one side. The man was wrapped in a shroud like a Bedouin in the deserts of old Earth. He moved solidly and relentlessly and he carried a child in his arms.

"Son of a bitch," Kek muttered and stormed back into the depths of the camp.

Bethel ignored him, his eyes on the approaching figure. "The Prodigal Son returns," he whispered to no one but himself.

⁂

As James grew closer, a murmur began to spread through the camp. Soon others were joining Bethel at the entrance. Pushing out into the shade from the big mountain, staring at the man approaching.

As he neared the entrance, they could see that he carried the child with him.

"He's dead," someone whispered. "The boy is dead."

"No," someone else said. "He wouldn't carry a lifeless body this far."

"Get him some water," another bystander whispered. "Get them both some water."

Soon there was a full crowd. They parted in silence as James arrived. He carried the child into the camp and laid him down at the foot of the bed where the mother was beginning to stir.

She looked dazed. At first she was afraid to speak.

"He needs water and food," James said. "But he's alive."

Those around the woman sprang into action, soaking rags in the precious water and laying them on the child's burned face.

"Thank you," the woman began to cry. "Thank you for my son."

James stepped back. Only now did Bethel see the burns on his friend's face and the bloody mess that was his forearm. Before he could say a word, Kek and his friend arrived.

"Who the hell do you think you are?" Kek shouted at James, stepping forward and slamming him into one of the corrugated metal walls. The sound reverberated through the covered space.

"When they find out he's not there, they'll come looking for him!" Kek shouted. "They'll kill all of us for this!"

James looked exhausted and spent. He remained against the wall as if the corrugated tin was all that held him up. "They'll kill you anyway," he said. "Eventually."

"That's a lie!"

Kek looked around at the crowd. "You all know what the deal is. How it works. We do our time. We get our freedom."

He stepped forward to grab James again, but this time James was ready. As Kek put a hand on him, James grabbed the man's wrist and twisted it outward. Kek winced in surprise, letting out an anguished grunt at the pain this caused in his elbow and shoulder. Even as he tried to escape the grasp, James swung forward and slammed his knee into the man's gut.

Kek buckled, but James held him up long enough to finish him off with a forearm smash to the face.

The burly man fell back, his nose shattered, his mind blurred by the concussive impact.

A woman in the crowd spoke up. "You shouldn't do this. You're causing trouble."

A man standing beside her added, "Maybe we should turn you in."

"We can save ourselves," the woman insisted.

"Save yourselves for what?" James replied.

The crowd hushed.

"To work until you drop?" he added.

"If we finish a year," someone spoke up. "We get to be citizens."

James cringed just hearing it. They repeated like a mantra, like an article of faith. A brilliant lie by the Cartel, just real enough to be possible.

"A year?" James said, almost laughing. "And how long have you been here?"

"Three months," the man said.

"Think you'll make it? Do you really think you have what it takes to last another nine months in this hell?"

The man didn't reply right away. "Maybe," he finally muttered.

"Maybe," James repeated, in a tone that said he doubted it. He turned to the crowd. "What about the rest of you? Anyone getting close? Anyone been here for six months? Five?"

No response. Only silence as they looked around at each other.

James stepped up his attack. "Have any of you seen even *one, single person* leave this hell hole on their feet?"

The crowd remained utterly silent. The wall of denial was breaking down.

James began walking around, looking at them closer as if he was examining them. He stopped in front of the man and woman who wanted to turn him in. They didn't look much better than the mummified bodies he'd found chained to the machines. "Look at you," he said to them. "You're half dead already."

Neither of them replied, and after a moment of bearing James's ruthless stare they averted their eyes.

"It's a lie," James said, turning back to the crowd. "No one leaves here, no one becomes part of the colony. The only land they'll ever give you is the grave they bury you in."

The woman pointed a bony finger at him. "I know what you want. You want to fight. You're crazy for even thinking these things."

James dismissed her with a wave and began to walk off, too disgusted to argue. Bethel stepped forward. He realized what James didn't, that this wasn't just an argument. It was a pivotal moment.

"He's not crazy."

Everyone turned toward him. A hundred pairs of eyes locked onto him, two hundred others listening.

"Some of you know me," Bethel said. "I was in the tunnels with you on Earth. I brought you medicines. I helped you when you were sick. People told me I was crazy as well, but sometimes things need to be done, no matter how hard they seem to be. "

A murmur went through the crowd. A few of them nodded. Some of them recognized him.

"So what do we do?" someone asked in a quiet voice.

Everyone in the room turned. The man who'd spoken was the largest person in the room. He had ink black hair, Polynesian features and a body like a grain silo.

"We can fight," James said.

"What do you know about fighting?"

"I used to be in the military," James said.

The big man shook his head. "Military man ain't no friend of mine."

"Well, I'm a traitor now," James added, grinning at the irony. "So hopefully that helps. But either way, I can tell you these bastards don't have nearly enough men here to guard a camp of this size. There are at least two thousand of us, no more than a hundred of them."

"But they have guns," the big fellow said.

"Which we'll have, after we take them."

"What about the armored personnel carriers?" someone else said. "They have heavy weapons, machine guns, and cannons like the *street sweepers*. They'll slaughter us."

"And what about the *thumpers*," the big man asked. "How are we supposed to deal with them?"

James thought about that. *Thumper* was slang for the MRVs, presumably because of the way their footsteps shook the ground as they stomped about.

Fact was while the APCs moved around, the MRVs just set up shop in the distance and sat down, like guards in a guard tower. No one knew better than James how absurdly expensive and complicated those were to operate. They went through parts like there was no tomorrow. And from what he understood, they wore out faster on Mars than in the toughest environments on Earth. It made little point having them stomp around the work site, stirring up the dust and putting more wear and tear on the transmissions and joints. They were just as effective sitting still. But that also made them vulnerable.

"Look," James said. "I'm not telling you it's going to be easy, or that a lot of us won't be killed in the effort, but you have a choice. You can die a slow lingering death, taking the abuse and waiting for them to drag your wasted shell of a corpse out of here on the day you can't answer the work bell anymore, or you can fight. If you want to live, if you want a chance at life, you're going to have to fight for it. And I'm telling you right now, if you people can take out the guards, I'll deal with the MRVs personally."

"And then what?" the big guy asked again. "If we take the camp they'll just come out from Olympia and slaughter us. What good is that?"

James was encouraged by the question. It meant this man had already thought about fighting, he'd taken the thought to its logical conclusion. *What would happen next?*

At the same time he noticed that the crowd had begun to follow the argument like spectators at a tennis match. No one else was chiming in anymore; the big guy was talking for them. James liked that too, it meant he only had to convince one person instead of the crowd. He turned toward the muscle bound fixture in their midst.

He understood the skepticism, the need for more. Every soldier needed hope.

"There are people in Olympia who will support us," he said, going out on a limb. "When I was taken away by the doctor, I was able to speak with them. They're ready to fight. They'll assist us if we can take the first steps."

A murmur of whispers moved through the crowd like a swell on the ocean. All of them knew he'd been dragged off the other day. Most of them were surprised when he'd come back.

They looked around at each other. They wanted to believe they could do something. But they were so downtrodden their sense of hope was almost gone. It was like putting a match to wet firewood and trying to make it burn.

They needed someone else to take the first step. James turned to his opponent in the debate. "What do you say big guy? You got any fight left in you?"

The big Polynesian man stewed for a moment, but his face soon hardened and his jaw clenched. Finally, he nodded. "Okay," he said. "I'll fight."

"You don't sound too sure," James prodded.

"I said, I'll fight," the big man replied forcefully. "You're right. I'd rather die today than do this for the rest of my life."

"What about the rest of you?" James asked.

A few nodded quietly.

"I'll fight," the father of the rescued child said, standing.

"Me too," said another.

Soon everyone was agreeing, getting riled up.

"Strike back!"

"Kill them for what they've done!" someone else said.

Others began to nod and pump their fists. A chant began. "Fight, fight, fight!" And soon they were all doing it. Hundreds of voices echoing off the walls of the cave. It was loud enough to hurt their ears.

Amid the clamor, the big fellow came up to James. "So we're going to fight," he said. "I should probably know your name."

"I've called myself Ares," James said. "But my real name is James."

He offered his hand and the big man shook it.

"My name is Kamahu," the big guy said. "You are a brave man. Fighting is worthwhile, but do you really think we can win?"

"We have a chance," James said. "First, we have to make sure our secret doesn't get out. That means we need to... *incapacitate* anyone who might rat us out. If you know what I mean."

James pointed toward Kek and his friend, who remained nearby but seemed shocked by what was going on around them. "You know they work for the guards right?"

Kamahu nodded. "None of us ever trusted them," he said.

"I'm sure they're not alone," James said.

Kamahu called over a few of his friends and they had a private conversation. The group quickly dispersed. "There are a few others we must worry about," he said. "But they will be taken care of."

"Good," James said, hoping that would be enough. "You'll need a few leaders. A group that won't hesitate. If they strike the first blows, the others will follow."

"I can name twenty or more who will be hard to hold back once they hear what we've planned," Kamahu said. "But how are you going to pull off what you've promised? How are you going to deal with those *thumpers*?"

James grinned. "Don't worry," he said. "I have a plan. But first, I'm going to need you to show me around."

Chapter 29

Word of the plan passed quickly through the camp. Some balked at the suggestion, but most quickly came on board. To gain their allegiance and boost their confidence, James made them promises about citizenship and equality, promises he intended to keep.

He also stretched the truth about the resistance in Olympia. Making it sound as if there were thousands waiting for a revolution. He felt a little guilty for this but he had no choice. If they wavered now, all would be lost.

With the camp buzzing in anticipation, James's biggest fear was that someone would get too eager and move too soon, or that the guards would notice the difference in the workers tonight.

"Remember, he said. "We have to take them out all at once. Go on the alarm that sounds for the mid-shift break. Do nothing before then or we'll all be killed."

"Why wait," one of Kamahu's handpicked lieutenants asked. "We'll be tired by mid-shift."

"So will they," James said. "They'll be drowsy and hungry and they won't be expecting anything. If you watch they're always on alert when they order us back to work. They expect resistance and arguments then, but they relax during the break and when the shift ends."

The men nodded.

"Besides," James added, "that alarm echoes all over the work site. It's the only way to coordinate the attack."

They stood and dispersed, and James turned to Kamahu. "Ready?"

Kamahu nodded.

With the plan locked in place and the suspected informants rounded up, James, Bethel, and Kamahu hustled through the tunnels that made up the subterranean part of the camp. They carried picks, shovels and a portable work light. They quickly wound their way around a dozen corners and down a long tunnel before running smack into a dead end.

"Can't go no further out," the big man said.

"This will have to do," James said.

James picked up the pry bar and looked toward the ceiling. He jammed it into the soft sandstone material and wrenched it sideways. A small bucket's worth of dirt, rock and sand tumbled down. After a few more stabs, the muffled sound of the air horn was heard. The slave-master and his friends were arriving for the start of the evening shift.

"You two better get out of here," James said. He handed Bethel the metal strip he'd pulled from his arm. "When you go through, punch me in."

Bethel took the identification strip, then he and the big man headed back down the tunnel. As they went James thrust the pry bar upward once again. He had twenty feet of soft sandstone to bore through and approximately four hours in which to do it.

Chapter 30

With the pale red sky fading to black and only the dim glow of the Solaris Array on the horizon, the mercenary crews began rolling up to the slave camp and rousting the laborers.

As usual the motivation was mostly negative—threats and curses. Bethel caught the end of it as he and Kamahu emerged from the tunnels.

"Come on you slackers," one of the guards shouted, firing a gun into the soil behind them.

Bethel and Kamahu dutifully hustled forward and caught up with the queue of workers streaming toward the worksite and the half-finished monolith.

As they neared the fenced in perimeter, they were corralled into a narrow chute that forced them to pass through the roll call gates. Armed guards waited on both sides. A computer kept track of the workers as they poured through. As each worker passed through, a tone sounded and the workers' names and numbers flashed up on a screen as they went past.

"Move your asses," one of the mercenaries urged. "The faster you get to work, the quicker you'll finish."

Bethel lined up in the queue, shuffling forward as the men and women in front of him went through. Finally he reached the gate. He stepped up to the scanner with his heart in his throat, wondering if the scanner would realize only one body had passed through as it read two identifications.

He moved forward. The scanner flashed his name and ID number and then Ares - Gamma 4179. It happened in a blink. Two separate tones sounded, almost one on top of another.

Someone watching closely might have noticed, but there were hundreds of workers passing through the gates side by side. The tones were constantly sounding with the screens flashing and changing rapidly. More importantly, the mercenaries were watching for slackers and escape attempts. No one was worried about people sneaking into the camp unannounced.

But just as Bethel had 'punched' James in, others were slipping though with the ID tags of Kek and the informants who'd been trussed up and sealed in the deepest section of the tunnels. It would keep the guards from knowing they were missing and going looking for them. Bethel just hoped none of the guards sought them out, located their ID tags and went looking to talk to them. They would be chasing a ghost if they did, but it wouldn't take them long to find out the tags were being carried by others.

Safely inside, Bethel headed to the staging area where the instructions were being given out. He found Kamahu again and managed to get assigned to the same work group. Today they would deliver power conduits that would be spliced together and buried to form a network. Based on the number of vehicles offloading the rolled up conduits, there would be miles of this stuff inside and around the Core Unit. Bethel couldn't imagine they'd get it all in place today. But two thousand workers digging trenches and splicing cable had a way of expediting the process.

With a grunt, Bethel lifted the heavy roll of shielded copper onto his shoulder and began to hike toward the delivery zone.

༺༻

As the workers began their assigned tasks, the slave-master grinned. Flashes from the welding torches high up in the structure showed the progress. At this rate the exterior would be finished in two weeks. From that point, work in the interior could proceed twenty-four seven. And most of that would be done by the techs from Olympia.

It meant the Core Unit would be completed on schedule. He'd receive his big bonus. And Cassini and Gault would know they could trust him with any project on the planet.

Considering the future to be bright, he walked from the entry gate to a waiting APC. One of his men stood beside it with a radio. Another sat in the turret on top of the vehicle. The armored truck's twin, rapid-fire plasma rifles were pointed toward the crowd.

"Ease up, Griggs," he said to the gunner. "The sheep are in the pen."

Griggs nodded, set the safety and tilted the weapons up into the forty-five degree position where they balanced and locked.

Down the hill, a squad of the slave-master's men were closing the gates. Raising the comm link to his mouth, the slave-master hailed them. "What's the count?"

Static came back for a second and then, "We're nine tags short."

That was less than usual. Under normal circumstances they lost a dozen per night. Occasionally someone was stupid enough to hide or attempt to escape, but most of the missing were found dead, or simply too weak to go on.

"Not bad," the slave-master replied. "Especially since we've been cutting their rations to make up for the added numbers."

"Did you round them up yet?"

"Yeah we found them," the voice replied. "Two of 'em are dead. The others are too far gone to do us any more good."

That was the way of things. "Clear them out, and put 'em down. Do it close. I want these slugs to hear the gunfire. It has a way of motivating them."

"Already on it."

With that bit of business taken care of, the slave-master climbed up on the APC and pulled out a flask of liquor. The long, boring watch was more easily stood with a little buzz going.

⦁

Deep within the tunnels of the camp, James continued to dig furiously. He was driving up through the sandstone at an angle. As he moved upward, he carved some ridges in the sides of the shaft and wedged himself into it.

Having carved his way through ten feet, he rested for a moment and looked himself over. He was filthy. Covered head to toe in red dust. His eyes were burning. His hands were wrapped in cloth, torn from his shirt, but they'd bled through that long ago. Another strip of fabric from his shirt covered his mouth and nose like a bandanna, an almost useless attempt to keep the dust out of his lungs.

He had no watch. No way to tell time. It felt like hours had passed but he had no real idea. All he knew was he'd better damn well not be late, or those he'd convinced to fight would be massacred.

"Come on James," he said to himself. "Break's over."

He stretched as best he could, coughed a few times and then climbed back up into the shaft. With a deep breath, he gripped the pry bar in his ravaged hands and attacked the stone above once again.

Chapter 31

Up above, the worksite was shrouded in a cloud of dust kicked up by human feet, and lit by the glare of the mercury-lights. The combination gave a red glare to the world as if it were on fire or perhaps some missing section of Hades.

The slaves moved as always, slow and steady, their efforts accompanied by the clank and banging of the metal work up above. They seemed immune to it. And even as several unannounced gunshots echoed across the plain, few of them reacted with more than a flinch.

They'd grown used to it by now. There were no sick days on this job.

As Bethel lugged the latest heavy load toward the drop zone he spoke with Kamahu. He'd found it was fairly easy to talk on the trail. The guards were congregated around the unit and the staging area.

"How are you doing?" Bethel asked.

Kamahu looked back at him. "Better than you by the looks of it," he said, then added. "Why are you following me?"

"You're a giant," Bethel said. "I figure you can fight."

Kamahu gave Bethel a quizzical look. "How about you? Can you fight?"

"I've been in a few," Bethel said.

"You win any of them?"

"Not really," Bethel said.

"Great," Kamahu said, shaking his head as if he was disgusted. "What good are you then?"

As it got closer to the zero hour the tension was growing. It was one thing to plan a rebellion, another thing altogether to carry it out.

"Well…I am a doctor," Bethel said. "If they fill you full of holes, I might be able to patch you up."

Kamahu stared blankly for a moment, and then he began to chuckle. The absurdity of the moment made both of them laugh. More than likely they would be dead in hours. Why the hell not laugh about it?

"Okay," Kamahu said. "You stick with me."

⸎

Deep within the tunnels, far from where James was digging, another man struggled against forces stronger than him.

Kek and his friends had been bound and gagged and dumped off in the most fetid, vile section of the tunnels, deep down where the waste collected.

To be honest, Kek was surprised to be alive. Had it been him, he'd have killed those who opposed him. But the man who seemed to be leading the slaves into a rebellion—the man who called himself both Ares and James—had insisted to his followers it was not necessary.

Intent on proving him wrong, Kek squirmed and twisted and strained against the knots. Finally, he'd managed to writhe his way up to the wall where he began rubbing the knot that tied his hands together against the stone behind him.

As he worked, Kek's mind burned with hatred toward the newcomers. The anger pushed him. As did thoughts of a reward he might receive from stopping the insurrection that was about to happen.

He worked relentlessly for hours, until he felt the strands of fabric giving way. When they finally snapped, he ripped the gag from his mouth and took a breath of the stinking air.

It almost made him vomit.

He reached over and ripped the gag off the man closest to him.

Both of them breathed heavily for a moment.

"Damn this air stinks," the other informant said.

"We won't have to breathe it long," Kek replied. "Those fools have done us a favor. When we turn these bastards in, our keepers will put us on the crew. We'll be out there with guns in our hands, not down here in this filth."

The other informant nodded. "Sounds good to me."

"Turn around."

The man turned and offered his wrists. Kek managed to untie them, but neither man could loosen the knots around their legs. The fabric had been wrenched too tightly.

"Grind through it like we did with our hands," Kek ordered. "And hurry."

⁂

In a higher section of the tunnels, James was also trying to hurry. He was slamming the pry bar upward desperately now. His mind playing tricks on him as to how many hours had passed. Several times he thought he heard the mid-shift horn only to pause and realize it was his imagination.

He jammed the bar upward and it stuck in the soft compacted mix of stone and soil. He pulled it back and almost dropped it. The space was claustrophobic.

It reminded him of the tunnel in the sublevels on Earth. He felt the same type of desperation; only this time it was for his friends not himself.

"Come on," he shouted to himself, as he slammed the bar upward again and again.

He could hardly feel his hands. He sensed his strength going.

"Don't give up," he shouted. With the next thrust the pry bar broke through the surface, moving easily.

Instead of pulling back hard, and yanking the rubble downward, James steadied it and himself. He switched off the dim work light so as not to give himself away and then cautiously wriggled the pry bar from side to side.

A trickle of rock came first and then, as he pulled the pry bar back, sand began to pour in through a roughly circular hole. It flowed like water and James hoped he hadn't just dug his way into a sand dune or drift of some kind.

When the stream of grit finally slowed and then ceased, James wedged himself upward once again.

Cold air was pouring in through the hole above him. Fresh, in comparison to the stale air in the cavern, it swept over him and drew most of the dust from the narrow shaft into the cavern below.

"That's more like it," James said, feeling like he could breathe again.

He widened the hole further and stared upward. The sky was epically black, dotted here and there with pinpricks of light from a few twinkling stars.

The Solaris Array had gone down. That meant the mid-shift break was right around the corner. "At least it's not dawn," he muttered to himself.

He inched upward and popped his head through the hole like a gopher. In the distance he saw the construction site and the looming tower of the Core Unit lit up by the harsh work lights. But where was the MRV?

He twisted around. To his dismay, the furthest tunnel in the slave camp hadn't brought him out quite far enough. He'd hoped to be behind the big rig, but he'd come out in front of it and off to the side. It was forty or maybe fifty yards away, sitting passively on its haunches with its angry face and lethal guns pointed towards the tower.

Crossing the ground toward the big rig would be dangerous. There was nothing to hide him. But he had a few things going for him. First, the MRV was set up to be seen. Instead of operating in a blacked out combat mode where every exterior light was extinguished, the MRV had both its position lights on and its main floodlights turned up to about fifty percent power.

There was a purpose to that. It made the big rig easily visible from the worksite and hard to forget about, but it would also ruin the night vision of the men who were manning it. As long as James avoided the lit up swaths of ground, he should be able to approach the rig unnoticed.

The second thing in his favor was universal: the tedium of guard duty. Personally James would rather fight than draw sentry's watch. And though it was a hanging offense in every army, plenty of soldiers had fallen asleep on a long, boring night like this.

"No time like the present," James whispered to himself.

He climbed out of the hole and began crawling slowly toward the rig. About half way there he was able to make out a hint of light coming through the armored windows from the control screens inside. He also noticed that the entry ladder on the right side was down and the top hatch propped open. It took a moment for him to see why.

Near one of the huge mechanical legs he spotted a tiny glow of incandescent red. For a second, it grew brighter like a firefly and then dimmed to an almost invisible ember. One of the crew had come down for a smoke. That, James thought to himself, was a problem he didn't need.

Chapter 32

The mercenary stood at the foot of his aging machine. Taking a draw on a cigarette and savoring the aroma. It wasn't much in terms of tobacco. In fact, most of the flavor came from composted muck. But it wasn't half bad.

He smoked about half the length of the cigarette and then tamped it out carefully before wrapping it in a piece of plastic to save the rest for later. Even these synthetic smokes were hard to come by on Mars. That made them too valuable to waste.

He glanced at his watch. The mid-shift horn should be sounding any minute. That meant it was time to move the MRV to a new spot, where the second half of the boring night would be spent. He slid the stub of a cigarette into his pocket, clambered onto the ladder and began to climb back up the side of the big MRV.

He'd made it to the third rung when a sharp pain he'd never felt before shot through him from the center of his back.

He might have screamed but at the same time a hand had clamped firmly over his mouth. It pulled him from the ladder and he was body slammed onto the ground sideways. Only now did he see the metal spike sticking out through his chest.

He grabbed for it feebly and then his hands fell away.

The last thing he saw was a filthy man—so covered in the red soil as to be nearly invisible up against it—holding him down and pulling the sidearm from his holster.

James made sure the thug was dead before he uncovered his mouth, then glanced around with the pistol at the ready looking for any sign of trouble. Nothing moved in the desolation around him and the only sounds came from the worksite in the distance. The other crewman had to be up in the MRV's cockpit. Someone had to remain at the controls even when nothing was going on.

Stuffing the pistol into his waistband, James climbed onto the ladder, scaled it to the top and eased his way toward the open hatch on the roof. Flat on his belly, he eased to the edge and looked down into the cab. He could see only the right arm of the MRV's driver. The man was sitting in the left seat, the command seat, unmoving until he reached up and tapped on one of the gauges.

James smiled. The unit was an old Mark V. They were good rigs, but they had hydraulic issues and bad sensors, always had, even new off the factory floor. That was half the reason the military dumped them. They were supposed to be destroyed like all military surplus hardware, but it seemed many of them had ended up in the hands of the Cartel.

James moved to a crouching position and then dropped through the hatch and into the cockpit, landing in the space between the two chairs. The driver turned with a start and, to James's surprise, was holding his own pistol. He swung it towards James and two gunshots detonated simultaneously in the small space of the cockpit.

Chapter 33

The sound of the twin gunshots echoed across the camp. The strange acoustics of the hill and the metallic wall of the Core Unit caught the vibrations and they echoed back, sounding like distant thunder from the cloudless sky.

Most workers kept going, another execution they assumed, but Bethel, stopped in his tracks. Kamahu was right behind him. Both of them glanced in the direction of the sound, back towards the lonely MRV in the distance.

"Do you think…" Kamahu asked.

"I don't know," Bethel said.

"Keep moving then," Kamahu said.

Bethel wrenched his gaze from the distant machine, hoping and praying that his friend hadn't been killed in the attempt. He noticed some of the guards pointing towards the camp. As he neared the drop off point he heard one of them on the radio asking what had happened. Unlike the earlier executions, none of them had been expecting this.

Bethel dropped off the parts he'd brought in and started wearily back down the hill. He found his legs shaking and his feet catching the ground. He nearly tripped at least twice. Up ahead, a group of mercenaries were converging by the gates and moving toward the camp.

Kamahu caught up to him. "They got him," he said. "They caught your friend."

"We can't be sure," Bethel whispered harshly, trying not to think about it. The first half of the shift was almost over. They were so close. Not now, Bethel thought. Not this close to the end.

"We have to tell the others," Kamahu said. "We have to call it off."

"No," Bethel said, sick to his stomach.

"Face it," Kamahu said, grabbing Bethel's shoulder and turning him. "He failed. He's dead. No reason we should die too."

Bethel tried to pull free but Kamahu's grip was like steel.

"We won't get another chance at this," Bethel repeated. "Who else will try what he tried? We have to hope. We have to believe. It's now or never."

Before Kamahu could reply, the sound of a commotion sprung up at the slave camp's entrance, just beyond the roll call gates. Spotlights came on and two men were seen running out from beneath the tarp. Even from this distance Bethel could see that the collaborators had broken free.

"We should have killed them," he muttered, fully aware that it was he who'd argued to keep them alive.

"It's over," Kamahu said dejectedly. "We're all dead now."

The collaborator and his partner ran up the hill toward guards, who seemed shocked and surprised at their appearance. The guards forced the men to their knees and blinded them with the spotlights, but it was only a matter if time.

Bethel could see them trying to explain, he could hear them shouting. And though he couldn't make out a word at this distance, he knew what they were saying.

The guards seemed wary, never lowering their weapons. And between the strange gunshots and this new commotion, work around them had ground to a halt.

Shoot them, Bethel thought. *Please, shoot them.*

But the guards didn't shoot and eventually the slave-master could be seen trudging towards them in the blinding glare of the spotlights. They spoke back and forth and Kek began to gesture wildly. He shook his head repeatedly, showing the wounds he'd sustained and the gash on his arm where the ID strip had been removed. Finally he pointed out into the work site, and Bethel felt as if the accusing finger were pointed straight at his heart.

In what seemed like slow motion, the slave-master turned toward the hill, his eyes squinting from the glare of the lights, his hands on a long barreled rifle. He motioned to one of the guards, and began to move up the hill raising the radio to his mouth as he went.

"We're dead," Kamahu said.

Almost without thinking, Bethel picked up a narrow strip of plating and shouted at the top of his lungs. "Attack!"

He flung the plating at the nearest guard and then lunged for him, tackling the man. Kamahu followed suit grabbing another of the mercenaries by the neck and clubbing him to the ground with his arm.

The guard Bethel had attacked flung him off and was pulling his handgun, ready to put Bethel out of his misery, when the clock ticked over and the shrill blast of the air horn sounded above the work site.

The blaring signal drowned out everything for several seconds, but as it faded a roar went up from around the camp and the slaves who knew of the planned rebellion acted in unison with those who didn't know. Three men swarmed the guard with the pistol and buried him in a pile, punching and kicking him into submission. One of them came away with the gun and began firing down the hill at the slave-master. While all around them hundreds of others were attacking any mercenary within range.

Within seconds, every man, woman and child on the hill had joined in; even those who knew nothing about the plan realized the moment to strike was at hand.

The viciousness of the attack took the guards by surprise, as the hatred for their taskmasters burst out from deep inside the prisoners.

▲

Down below the gates, the slave-master looked on in shock as the riot engulfed the worksite. For a moment he froze, so used to being in control, so used to dominating, he didn't know how to react. Few slaves had shown enough backbone to look him in the eye, let alone fight.

When he finally shook loose of his paralysis, he did so based on his primary method of responding to anything—utter violence. He began to fire into the crowd. "Kill them!" he shouted to the guards that remained outside the fence. "Kill them all!"

He mounted the APC beside them, shoved Griggs out of the gunner position and took over. As soon as the power came on, he swung the twin barreled weapon toward the hill, switched off the safeties and opened fire. Within seconds he'd stitched a line of blazing plasma across the closest section of the fence line, frying sixty people in the process.

Return fire soon came their way, courtesy of captured rifles and handguns. But while this volley forced the mercenaries on foot to take cover, the small arms fire was nothing against the armor of the APC.

Soon the other APCs and the guards outside the fence line joined their leader, and the angry slaves that had come surging towards them were driven back and scattered in retreat up the hill.

Certain that his quick thinking had turned the tide, the slave-master turned to the APC's driver. "Get the Vultures up and running"

"What should I tell them?"

A new surge of gunfire came at him, ricocheting off the gunner's shield. A chip hit him in the face drawing blood and ire. "Tell them to take aim inside the fence!" he shouted. "And to kill everything that moves!"

With that, the slave-master swiveled the turret, took aim and pressed the double triggers once again. The blazing plasma lit out across the field, leaving a swath of carnage and burning bodies.

⋏

The slaves' initial surge had quickly overcome any resistance from the mercenary guards, but in its wake the fencing around the worksite had become the front line of a battle the slaves were rapidly losing.

Bethel, Kamahu and a dozen others barely escaped being fried by the APC's plasma guns, and they were soon hiding behind a huge stack of pipes in the staging area.

As the gunfire grew in intensity, dozens more joined them, crowding into each other to keep out of the line of fire. At various spots around the hill, similar bands were cowering, trying desperately to survive the mercenary counterattack. About the only safe place was inside the tower of the Core Unit itself, which the mercenaries obviously didn't want to damage.

"Now what?" Kamahu asked.

"Why are you asking me?" Bethel shouted.

A series of explosions from unguided rockets blew out part of the protective wall, flinging a group of men and women into the distance like they were rag dolls.

"Give me that rifle," Bethel said. "I'll draw their fire. The rest of you run for the Core Unit. They won't shoot at you in there."

Instead of giving him the rifle, Kamahu stepped out and fired off a spread of shots. The group started running and Bethel grabbed Kamahu and pulled him back into the safety of the shelter just as the return fire set the desert alight once again.

"Let's go," Bethel yelled.

He and Kamahu took off running. They were halfway up the hill when even larger guns sounded, blowing apart the hiding spot they'd just left. A quick look behind them gave Bethel chills. Not only were the APCs firing at them but the closest of the MRVs—the mercenary's Vultures—had come stomping into the fray.

The hulking machine obliterated one hiding spot after another then crushed down the double fence with a giant armored foot. Its head turned to the side and unleashed a flight of missiles and cannon fire with devastating results.

As soon as this machine had cleared a section, the APCs came racing across the downed fence and mopped up any survivors.

Bethel looked away and kept running. With his heart pounding and his lungs feeling as if they might explode, he charged up the hill.

As they neared the outer edge of the Core Unit's foundation, the ground began to shake. From behind the bulk of the reactor another of the giant rigs appeared. The vast majority of the survivors were now trapped in between the two.

Bethel dove to the ground as the evil looking machine charged down towards them and unleashed a hail of rockets. But instead of laying waste to the ragged band of slaves the missiles screamed over their heads. Bethel turned just in time to see them hit the other MRV, which rocked backwards in a ball of smoke and flame.

The big machine looked as if it might recover when a final missile hit, penetrated the armor and blasted it apart from the inside.

"That's James," Bethel shouted. "It's got to be."

The machine pivoted on one huge leg and opened fire again, this time using the rotary cannon. The roar was tremendous. The air burned above them with tracers and the scream of forty millimeter shells racing past at a thousand miles an hour.

Covering his ears, Bethel watched as the armored personnel carriers took the brunt of it. Their plating was not up to the task, and the machines were riddled and burning in seconds by the combined effects of hundreds of small explosions.

Only one of the four avoided the onslaught, turning just in time and racing back towards the mangled fence with reckless abandon.

The cab of the MRV pivoted from side to side like a living dinosaur looking for any sign of challenge, and then with a roar from its engines began moving forward once again giving chase to the fleeing target.

▲

In the surviving APC, the slave-master was screaming at the driver. "Go! Go!"

The driver had the throttle floored and the tracked vehicle was racing out over the desert, rapidly picking up speed but to no avail. The renegade MRV was following and slowly gaining.

The slave-master spun the turret and pressed the triggers once again. The plasma fire lit up the hull of the MRV but the big rig shrugged it off and kept coming.

"Contact base!" the slave-master shouted. "Tell them we need help."

"I can't," the driver yelled back. "All frequencies are being jammed."

The slave-master could hardly believe what had happened. Never could he have dreamed of such a thing. He turned and depressed the triggers once again. Holding them down until the guns began to overheat. The hailstorm of plasma would have cooked almost anything it found, but the tungsten armor of the MRV was impervious to the onslaught. It shrugged off the attack and charged through the black cloud of smoke like an avenging angel coming from the depths of hell.

As the slave-master cycled the guns and tried to get them back up and running, he saw the missile pods deploying above the shoulders of the big rig.

"No!" he shouted.

The scream of a rocket launch followed. An armor piercing missile streaked towards him, the flare of its engine and the trail of smoke made it seem as if the missile was stretching out as it came. It hit like a clap of thunder, obliterating the fleeing vehicle in a single instant.

Chapter 34

In twenty minutes, the battle was over.

On the hill beside the Core Unit the slaves began gathering the wounded and the dead. At least three hundred had been killed. Another hundred or so were dying from burns or other wounds. The sight of it and the smell of burned flesh left many of the survivors retching, and very few had the strength to help Bethel tend to the wounded.

The young boy whose theft of a water bottle had started the chain of events was one of them. He came running up to Bethel with something in his hand. "I found this in the guard's shack," he said.

It was a first aid kit the size of a small toolbox. There wouldn't be much in it, but every little bit helped.

"Thanks," Bethel said.

He glanced over his shoulder. The heavy thudding of an MRV could be heard approaching, but shrouded in the darkness it was impossible to see the machine until the reflected glare of the work lights began to illuminate its angular, menacing shape.

As Bethel looked up from his work, Kamahu eased over to his side. "That's him right?"

"I hope so," Bethel said. "Otherwise we're in big trouble."

As it came towards them, Bethel studied it. It moved with a menacing grace, but because it walked instead of rolled, there was something different about it, something almost sentient. It seemed more like a mechanical form of life than a machine. The armored cab, now covered in black soot and burn marks, seemed to hold wisdom and intelligence. The sound of its ragged gears and overworked hydraulics suggested a weary soldier, like Bethel knew his friend to be.

It came to a rest nearby and settled onto its haunches, with the cab twisted off to the south as if it were watching for trouble.

Bethel returned to working on the wounded as Kamahu walked over to greet James.

"You were late," Kamahu said. "We almost got massacred."

James straightened up. He was covered in dust and soil, but the side of his shirt was soaked in blood.

"I ran into some problems," he said, and then dropped to the ground.

Bethel could see clearly. James was clutching his side.

"You're injured," Bethel said.

"The bastard got off a shot," James said. "It passed clean through my shoulder."

"You're losing blood."

"I'm okay," James insisted. "How are we doing here?"

James stopped in his tracks. He seemed stunned by the number of injured and dead. "What are you treating them with?"

"I have nothing," Bethel said. "The red soil helps the clotting and because of the solar radiation it's sterile, but there are no pain killers. Truth is, most of them won't last till sunrise."

James turned toward the distance. "Sunrise will be here in a couple of hours," he said. "We have to make our next move by then."

"How do you know we have that long?" Kamahu asked. "How do you know they're not coming now?"

James looked at him.

"I jammed the radios from the MRV," James said. "No one knows about this yet. But when these guys don't come back home in the morning…"

Kamahu nodded. "So what do we do?"

"We need to get to the warehouses down the road," James said. "The ones we saw on the way in. I'm pretty sure that's where the guards camp out during the day. They certainly don't come all the way from Olympia every night."

Bethel thought about that. It made sense. The landing site had been a three-hour ride in the big trucks, and Olympia was another ten miles beyond that.

"They'll probably have medical supplies there," he suggested.

"And more weapons," James said.

"What can I do?" Kamahu asked.

"Round up a group of men," James said, firmly. "Only those who really want to keep fighting. Meet me back here as soon as you can."

⋏

An hour later, James was lying flat on his stomach, peering over the crest of a ridge at the warehouse buildings they'd passed on the way out from Olympia. The road to the Core Unit ran by them on the right hand side, squeezed between the buildings and the sharp drop of a narrow canyon. It reminded him of the cuts and grooves carved by flash floods out in the American West, more proof that Mars had once flowed with water that remained nowhere to be found.

Ten yards back from the road, a high wall surrounded the buildings. The top curved outward and James guessed it was designed to catch and redirect the dust laden winds the way a breakwater redirected the waves, but it was also crowned with razor wire, spike strips and a few towers from which weapons could be fired. It reminded him of the compounds on Earth, and the walls the Cartel hid behind.

The central section of the wall was dominated by a wide metallic gate. Deep tracks in the ground leading up to it told him the MRVs and APCs used that gate. In fact, he could see three other MRVs in the yard beyond. They sat idle with plastic tarps covering their legs and other joints in a vain attempt to keep the fine dust out.

James wondered why they weren't inside the warehouses. But then he realized the doors to the huge buildings were not quite tall enough to let them enter. He wondered what sat inside those buildings aside from living quarters.

"Looks pretty quiet," he said, lowering the binoculars.

He felt a tug on his shoulder and turned to see Bethel packing some of the red soil into the bullet wound.

"You're leaking oil," Bethel said.

James had to smile. He handed the binoculars to Kamahu, who took a long look.

"How many men do you think they have?"

"Can't be more than a skeleton crew at this point. And most of them will be asleep. Everyone else would have been out at the worksite with us."

"Do you think we can take them?"

"I don't know," James said, sarcastically. "Maybe if we had a few more people..."

He glanced over his shoulder. A huge crowd stood behind them. Almost all of the former slaves who were still healthy had come along, waiting to charge into battle.

Kamahu shrugged. "You said only those who really wanted to fight. They all wanted to fight."

James smiled to himself. "I'll have to be more specific next time."

He eased back down the ridge and headed for the waiting MRV. "This time you guys wait for my signal."

Chapter 35

On the official maps the warehouse complex was supposed to be a simple staging area, but it was built under contract by one of the Cartel's companies and like the other outposts they'd turned this one into an armory. If the battle for Mars had ever come, they would have used this base and a dozen others from which to launch their attacks.

As it turned out Mars had been taken without a shot, and the mercenaries who'd expected to fight had settled down into easy duty, working the slaves, maintaining their bases.

The two men assigned to the tower beside the main gate at the warehouse complex were playing cards when they noticed a vehicle moving towards them in the darkness.

"Anyone due in?" the first guard asked.

The second guard checked his board. "Not for a couple hours."

As the MRV approached they could see it was one of the two assigned to the Core Unit's work detail. It moved slowly following the curved path that led up to the gate until it stepped into a gap between the high wall and the guard tower.

The armored cab of the MRV was now even with the observation deck, its menacing face all but filling the broad plate glass of the window.

"It's Vulture Two," the first guard noted, looking at the insignia.

"What the hell happened to it?" the second guard asked, studying the burn marks. "Looks like it caught fire."

As the second guard prepared to log it in, the first guard pressed the microphone switch. "Vulture Two, you're early. Is something wrong?"

A scratchy distorted transmission came back. "Turret actuator caught fire," the voice said. "Almost cooked us in here. When I find the mechanic that worked on this last I'm gonna beat him senseless."

"It's always something with these guys," the first guard said privately. "Better wake the mechanics."

As the second guard called down to the personnel bay, the first guard pressed the switch for the gate and a high-pitched tone rang out. Yellow lights around the huge gate started flashing and the gate began to draw back.

"Come on in, Vulture Two."

The MRV rose up a few inches, as they always did when getting ready to move, and then took a step forward. There it stopped, right in the path of the gate.

"Come on V2, keep it moving, " the guard said, his hand poised over the gate's close switch.

There was no response.

The guard pressed the talk switch again. "What's wrong now, V2?"

As the guard waited for an answer he saw movement in the distance, a group of men running towards the open gate. They were racing at all possible speed. Ahead of them dozens more rode on a flatbed.

They looked like…

"Damn," the guard said. He reached for the alarm.

"I wouldn't do that if I were you," a voice warned him over the intercom.

Both guards looked up. The top half of the MRV had turned towards them and was pointing both of its multi-barreled cannons into the guard shack. The barrels clicked around slowly, ready to fire at a moment's notice.

Without another thought the guard pulled his hand away from the alarm switch and—not knowing what else to do—slowly raised his hands.

Chapter 36

Sitting in Cassini's grandiose office, Gault took in the view of things. Through the curving line of windows, he could see from one side of Olympia to the other. Its buildings shimmered in a pink hue as their silver walls of tinted glass reflected the dim color of the morning sky.

In the center of the city, the Core Unit rose above them like a protective father—or a looming volcano. Gault knew better than most what would happen if one of those reactors went critical. He'd watched from the outskirts of Shanghai years before when the Black Death, using weapons supplied by the Cartel, had taken over a fusion plant, murdered the staff running it and then sent the huge reactor into super critical mode.

The plant went off like a hydrogen bomb. And from a distance of thirty miles, Gault's face had received second-degree burns before he could turn away.

Needless to say, only the poorest of the poor lived around Shanghai anymore.

The door opened, breaking Gault's reverie and he turned to see Cassini walking in.

"Are you in the habit of letting yourself into other people's offices?" Cassini snapped.

"You called me here," Gault said. "I don't wait in the hall like a schoolboy."

Gault had no real respect for Cassini. From what he'd seen, Cassini wasn't a fighter; he preferred to manipulate. Gault despised that kind of maneuvering. There was something cowardly in it.

"I did call you here," Cassini said, taking a seat behind the desk. "Because we have a problem."

Gault's eyebrows went up. "And what problem might that be?"

"We've lost contact with the work camp and the armory in sector five."

Gault had to think for a minute, he'd only just gotten done memorizing the maps and designations on Mars. "The second Core Unit?"

"Exactly," Cassini replied. "Lucien will have a conniption if something's gone wrong out there."

Gault fought to suppress a grin. "Yes," Gault agreed. "That wouldn't look good for you."

"For either of us," Cassini insisted. "Don't think I won't blame it on your lax efforts and weak enforcement of order."

Gault fumed. He should have expected as much.

"It's probably solar flares or something," he suggested. "Those workers are docile. They're half dead anyway. Where would they get the energy to fight?"

"We recently put another eight hundred out there," Cassini said. "They came on the freighter with you. That put the total workforce close to two thousand. The numbers may have made these slaves bold."

Gault knew what Cassini was getting at. Two thousand slaves. Less than a hundred guards. That was not a well-balanced mix. Little events could lead to sabotage, riots or worse. He'd seen that before, too.

"I'll have it checked out," Gault said, standing and wondering if he could turn this to his advantage.

He almost hoped it was sabotage or an insurrection of some kind. If he put it down with the requisite brutality, he could crow about it to Lucien and point out Cassini's weakness. He might even leap frog the manipulator and take over as governor. Spending his days in this fine office in the company of young women instead of out in the field had begun to interest him.

"I'll launch a pair of recon drones," he said, heading for the door. "We'll know in thirty minutes."

Cassini nodded, but also went further as if he knew something already. "Better get the heavy armor out of mothballs," he said. "I want those rigs prepared for battle if we need them."

Hannah was in her office when the call came in from Cassini.

"Governor," she said in her most polite voice. "To what do I owe the pleasure?"

"I'm sorry," Cassini said, "this isn't a social call. You need to get the medical bays ready for possible trauma arrivals."

"Why? What's happened?"

"A worker's riot at the second Core Unit. They've killed the guards and burned half the equipment…"

Hannah's emotions rode a wave as Cassini spoke. An insurrection at the Core Unit had to be James's doing. It meant he had come around to seeing things her way. It meant a slightest bit of hope in her mind. She could tell the others about him now. With a leader they could rally behind, a true resistance could begin. But Cassini's next statement crushed her spirit even as it began to rise.

"… I'm sending people in to deal with it. If any of these rebels survive, I want them brought back to health so they can be publicly executed."

She fought for balance. Trying to think of some tactic to dissuade Cassini from ordering the massacre, but she couldn't come up with anything that wasn't blatantly obvious. Her response made her sick. "Yes… I understand Governor. Anything else?"

He hesitated, then added, "Yes actually there is. You can come celebrate with me when the traitors are dead. It'll be just the two of us."

The comm clicked off before she could answer. Cassini wasn't waiting for an answer, because it wasn't a request, more like the whim of a dictator he fancied himself to be.

Hannah shook off the sleazy feeling that swept over her and got up. She had to find Davis and get word to the others. If they didn't act now, they would never get another chance.

Chapter 37

With the sun blazing down outside, injured slaves were brought into the sprawling, hangar-like buildings of the armory. With real therapeutic supplies and some help from two medics assigned to the station, Bethel treated as many as he could and made those who would soon die as comfortable as possible.

While Bethel ran himself near to exhaustion treating the wounded, James and Kamahu, chained the rest of the armory's skeleton crew to the water pipes in the barracks, leaving them under the watchful eyes of several angry former slaves.

After warning not to take revenge or allow themselves to be tricked, James stepped away and motioned for Kamahu to follow. Together they moved deeper into the complex.

Staring out into the yard, James counted a dozen earthmovers and huge bulldozers but saw only four MRVs. With the one he'd brought in, that made five. "If we're going to defend ourselves we'll need men or women who can man those rigs. I don't suppose there are any more ex-military personnel among our group."

Kamahu shrugged. "Doubt it," he said. "Can you teach us?"

"The basics," James said. "That's probably all we'll have time for. Send word around. I want to talk with anyone who has experience operating cranes, bulldozers or heavy equipment. That kind of knowledge will help."

Kamahu nodded. "So a counter attack is coming."

"Sooner or later," James said. "I jammed their transmissions during the battle, but it won't take long for someone to realize what's happened. Daily reports. Simple check-ins. None of those things are going to happen and the radio silence is going to be deafening. Once they figure it out, we won't have much time."

"But you have a plan, right?"

There was a hopeful look in Kamahu's eyes, one that said he was trusting James to see them through.

"I'm working on one," James said. With that, he pried open a locker to reveal twenty pulse rifles in a rack.

"First, we need to find anything we can use to fight with," he said, prying open another locker to reveal more rifles.

Kamahu joined him in the effort and soon they'd gone through every locker and storage room in the first warehouse. They'd found portable comm units, mining equipment and tools, more weapons and racks of body armor that had never come out of the packaging. As they went, James tried to make split decisions as to what might be useful and what might be burdensome. Kamahu wrote numbers and locations on a small pad, and called in some of his friends to distribute what had been found.

In the second warehouse, they found a fleet of small utility vehicles, all terrain scouts, some with four and others with six wheel drive setups. They wouldn't last long in battle but they had their uses. Finally, he and Kamahu forced their way into a storeroom secured with a heavy set of locks. As James flicked on the light, he saw the reason for such heavy security.

Stacked like lumber in small pyramids were a series of long tubes. Some of them were missiles for the MRVs out in the yard. But most lacked either a nose cone or fins for guidance. James eased up to them.

"Bombs?" Kamahu asked.

"Next best thing," James said. "Mining explosives. C-14."

"This is good?" Kamahu asked.

"Good for us," James said grinning. "Bad for them."

Chapter 38

Hannah stood on a balcony overlooking Olympia's main plaza. She was on the south side of the government building, several stories up. The balcony had an unswept look, red dust covering the chairs and tables, piling up in small dunes in the corners.

Few people came over to this side anymore. Not since the council had been suspended.

From this vantage point she watched a long column of MRVs marching through the city, heading out into the desert to do battle. The parade of deadly armor was impressive. Forty of the hulking machines, fully outfitted for battle. As they departed another twenty or so took up positions all around the city.

It was a show of force, far more than necessary to crush the slaves and their little uprising. There could only be one reason for that. Cassini wanted everyone to see what he had at his disposal, what he was capable of unleashing. He wanted fear to creep in and make a septic home in every soul on the planet. And by the sound of things, his plan seemed to be working.

Hannah had called for the group to meet, but no one had come and she'd been left to watch the display on her own.

Finally the door behind her opened cautiously. She turned, half expecting Cassini's thugs. Instead it was Davis and of all people, Isha.

She offered a sad smile of greeting. "Any sign of the others?"

Davis shook his head. "No one else was willing to risk a meeting on such short notice."

"Julian fears he's being watched," Isha said. "He sends his regards."

"He probably is being watched," Hannah said. "Maybe we all are."

"We've heard about a riot out at the second Core Unit," Isha said. "Word travels fast."

"Not a riot," Hannah said. "An uprising."

"Is there any difference?"

"Of course there is. A riot is simple reaction, born out of anger. An uprising requires an endgame." She nodded into the distance. "Someone out there believes they can win."

Isha ran a finger across the table. It left a trail in the thin layer of dust. "I think you put more faith in whatever this is than the rest of us."

"I have my reasons," she said.

"Which are?"

Hannah hesitated. She wanted to tell them about James, but she didn't quite trust Isha. She switched the subject. "You seem as if you'd rather it be a simple worker's mutiny."

Isha nodded. "People are afraid, Hannah. They're not likely to join in a suicide attack. Nor are they thrilled to hear that the riot has taken place at the site of the new Core Unit. Everyone knows what's going to happen when the next freighters land and the Cartel's friends and families begin arriving in droves. If that unit isn't finished there will be no place for us to live. We'll be the ones living in holes and hastily constructed shelters."

"All the more reason to act now."

"With what? Small arms and other weapons," Isha said. "What good are they against tanks and MRVs?"

"They're not much good at all," Hannah admitted. "Which is why we need to act now. While Cassini's army is busy with this uprising."

Isha looked out into the distance, staring at the departing column of MRVs. Her hands were visibly shaking.

"This is our chance," Hannah said. "We act now, or we act never and let them do with us what they will."

Davis came to her aid as always. "My people are ready," he said. "About a hundred in all. We have access to trucks and rifles. The techs have identified spots in the power grid we could attack that will bring down their communications and tracking networks. We can blind them. The construction battalion has already smuggled out a few caseloads of demolition charges. Some of the systems people have planned a computer virus to shut down their operating systems."

Hannah nodded. That was more than she'd expected.

Isha listened but continued to stare outward; she placed her hands on the rail to steady them. "I just thought…" she began. "I just thought we'd have more time. But you're right. We won't get another chance like this. I will urge those who trust me to join."

"Thank you," Hannah said. "Get word to the others. Let's meet back here tonight. Cassini and his thugs will be too busy with whatever this is to worry about us until then."

In the main room of the armory, James, Bethel and Kamahu were leaning over a display table. A satellite view of the armory buildings and the surrounding area was illuminated on the flat screen.

"We're right here," James said, pointing to the cluster of buildings, running beside a dark gash of the ravine. "They can't come at us from this direction because of the canyon that runs along the road."

He continued to study the screen.

"What about from the north?" Kamahu asked.

"Too rocky. They'd have to pick their way through and over these sharp ridges. Making them easy targets."

"Lucky for us," Bethel said.

"No luck involved," James said. "They built this place thinking they were going be the ones needing a defensible position in the fight for Mars. They chose this spot intentionally."

Bethel nodded. "Like I said, lucky for us."

James smiled. Using his finger, he traced a line from the armory along the road and toward Olympia City. "The only real option is to attack us from the east. That means they come over this ridge and right down the main road."

"Do you really think they'll come right at us?" Kamahu asked.

James turned toward the big man, "What would you do if some weakling threw a rock at you? Would you sneak around behind him and try to get him from the back?"

"No," Kamahu said. "I'd walk up and punch him in the face."

"Exactly," James said. "In this case we're the weaklings. They know what weapons were left here. They'll come in with ten times the firepower and demolish us head on."

"I hope that's not supposed to be your inspirational speech," Bethel said.

"Just the facts," James replied. "You have to know your enemy. Then you can plan accordingly."

As James spoke, the main power went out and the emergency lights came on.

"Looks like they've figured out where we are," Bethel said.

James nodded and looked at Kamahu. "It's time, gather the men."

Ten minutes later they were in the main hall of the armory. Several hundred men and women were gathered. They carried weapons now and many of them wore some semblance of body armor, though it would be of little use against the forces that were probably rolling their way.

James walked to the front of the room and climbed up on the loading dock as if it were a stage. Bethel and Kamahu followed him as the rag tag army in front of them, milled around, not exactly at attention, but ready to listen to him.

With the power out and the air processing units off, it was already getting a little stuffy in the room.

"It seems our enemies are trying to sweat us out," James began. "All I can say is…do they not remember where we just came from?"

A roar of laughter rose up from the men and they were put at ease. *If their leader could laugh and joke, how bad could it be?*

"They are coming for us," James said more seriously. "We knew they would, but if anyone doubted it, here's the proof."

The army grew more somber at this statement but they accepted it as soldiers should.

"And that's okay," James said. "In fact it's better for us. But I have to warn you, it's not going to be a fair fight. They know what we've got. They know the weapons we've picked up here. They know how many MRVs were in the yard. They may have doubts as to whether we can use them, but they're not going to be foolish enough to guess wrong."

A murmur ran through the crowd. The moment of doubt that James had to crush.

"But this isn't the time to fear," he said boldly. "This is the time to stand and to punish them for all they've done to you."

The murmur died and the room went silent.

"Listen to me and listen good," James continued, walking the stage and making eye contact with as many of them as possible. "Nothing has ever been given to you... Nothing. You've been shadows and ghosts your whole lives... To the rest of humanity you don't matter. You don't even exist... But if you stand up today... If you fight today...Today they will see you! Today they will hear you! Today they will know that *you... are... real!!!*"

A roar went up from the crowd. It shook the rafters of the metal building and must have echoed across the barren plains of Mars. A second shout followed and then a third, as if the workers wanted the whole world to hear them. To finally hear their voices.

James heard them, and he felt himself begin to choke up. These were the very people he'd barely given a damn about two months earlier. The very people his father had begged him to understand and to fight for. And now here they were, ready to fight alongside him, ready to die with him for a concept as abstract as freedom. The forgotten, the downtrodden, the rejected souls of the poorest of the poor. And yet, humanity's very last hope all at the same time.

"Never give up!" James shouted, raising his own rifle over his head. "Never give in!"

The army. His army. Repeated the words with bravado. They began to chant it over and over.

Never give up! Never give in!

Chapter 39

Clad in fatigues with a towel draped over his head instead of a helmet, James stood on the ridgeline peering through binoculars. He studied the shapes coming toward them.

"Smarter than I thought," he admitted as he studied the formation.

Whoever was leading the opposing forces had made a wise decision to spread his units out. The wide line would allow him to concentrate fire from all directions onto the defender's position, while the slaves would have to pick and choose their targets, firing here and there, diluting their fire instead of concentrating it. It would make an already unfair fight even more one sided.

And then, once the bombardment had softened them up, the phalanx would close in on the rebels, the ends would curl inward and the defenders would be caught in crossfire from three directions. At that point it would all end rather quickly.

"I don't see any infantry," James said. "Just armor. That's in our favor."

"Anything else in our favor?" Kamahu asked.

"Nope," James said, handing him the binoculars. "Not a damn thing."

Kamahu shook his head. "Have to say, I think I liked your other speech better."

James laughed and slapped Kamahu on the arm. He was the only one who'd be fighting in the open without body armor, because he was too big for even the XL size to fit. Instead he wore a cloak of white and grey, like some kind of Bedouin nomad.

"The men will look to you for guidance," James said, motioning to the hundreds of former slaves now digging in on the ridgeline. "Dressed like this they can spot you easily. Like it or not, you're their leader now. The job is simple. You get them to fire like crazy and then pull back once the heavy stuff starts coming in."

James pointed to the narrow road that ran down the ridge behind them, cutting between the armory and the canyon.

"Take the men all the way back past the armory," he reminded Kamahu. "Don't stop short."

Kamahu nodded.

"I've been meaning to ask you about your name," he said. "Sounds old. Does it mean something?"

"It comes from my grandfather's tribe," Kamahu said. "From our island in the Pacific, before it sank beneath the waves. It means *the quiet warrior*."

James nodded. "Well, I'll give you the warrior part," James said. "That's for damn sure."

James offered a hand and the big man took it. They shook and then parted ways.

A minute later James was climbing into his MRV. Bethel was already inside manning the radioman's seat, listening to the comm chatter over a set of headphones. A radar scanner of some sort showed the enemy approaching.

"Sounds like they've spotted us," Bethel said.

"I know," James replied. He sat down, strapped himself in and began to throw a few switches. The sound of the MRV's engine powering up was felt throughout the machine.

"Once they get a little closer, I'll throw on the ECM."

"ECM?" Bethel asked.

"Countermeasures," James said. "It'll jam up their radar. They won't be able to lock onto us from long range."

Bethel raised an eyebrow. "Won't that just bring them closer?"

James nodded. "That's the idea."

Silence descended over them as they watched the approaching mercenaries on the long-range screen.

Bethel grew quiet and very still. He seemed to be thinking deeply.

"You okay?" James asked.

"This is a first for me," Bethel said. "I've never seen the front end of war, only the causalities, the wounded and the dead."

"I'm not sure which is worse," James said. "Feels like I've been fighting since I could hold a gun. Twenty years," he added, his voice trailing off. "Twenty years with nothing but killing and death."

Bethel studied him for a moment and then spoke, the serious tone even deeper in his voice. "The fate of your family has always been to fight for those who could not fight for themselves."

James turned from the scanner and studied Bethel through hard, flinty eyes. "You know who I am?"

Bethel nodded. "I've known all along. I've just been waiting for you to remember."

"Why didn't you say anything?"

"No man can tell another who he is or should be. Each of us must find that answer in himself."

Chapter 40

Ten miles from the confiscated armory, Gault rode in the lead MRV. He would act as the gunner in this rig, but he was really there as a chariot rider, a captain on site to direct the battle. The mercenaries in the other MRVs were not as well trained, at least not in these machines, though he guessed they'd prove more than a match for the slaves.

As the big machine wallowed from side to side at its walking pace, Gault switched on the targeting radar. Waiting for it to lock on, he turned to the radioman.

"Order the others to bring up their scopes and clear their weapons," he said and then glanced over at the driver. "And bring us to three-quarters speed. I'm getting sick moving at this pace."

As the communications officer repeated Gault's order through the comm, the driver pushed the throttle forward and the big machine began to accelerate.

Riding in an MRV was much like traveling in a ship at sea. At low speeds they rocked from side to side as they loped along on the two massive legs. But at higher rates the ride was entirely different. It became smooth. The gyroscopic mounts held the cab steady and the hydraulic in the legs pumped ferociously with only fractions of a second of settling before the next leg extended. Like a speedboat planning across the water, it created a sense of skipping like a stone on the surface of a lake.

The biggest problem at high speed was the noise, which punished the ears. Between the relentless whine from the massive transmission and the throbbing of the huge engines that powered the machines, it was almost impossible to communicate verbally inside an MRV in battle. Because of this, the crews wore helmets with heavy ear protection. They communicated though intercoms and hand signals.

As the noise grew, Gault pulled his helmet on and cinched it tight. He turned back to the targeting display.

"Something's wrong," he muttered.

"What is it?" the driver asked.

Gault played with the controls trying to fine-tune the scope. "The range finding and directional lock are all screwed up."

Before he could say anything more, the radioman began to call out. "Units 3 and 4 report targeting issues… Units 5 and 9 are having the same problem. They're all reporting the same issue. It's just…"

Gault held up a hand, he didn't need any more confirmation. "They're jamming us."

Gault switched his targeting scope to infrared and noticed how bad the resolution was. On Earth, in the dingy light and the endless rain, infrared scopes were the preferred method for close quarters combat. But here on Mars under the twin assaults of the sun and the Solaris Array, the surface was superheated at high noon. It made the targets hard to pick out. They'd have to move in close. Very close.

The first twinge of doubt sprung up in Gault's mind. It came not out of fear but from the sense that something was not quite right. "How is it possible," he wondered aloud, "that these worthless, refugee slaves are able to operate our equipment?"

"They've picked a strong spot to defend from too," the driver noted.

Gault agreed silently. "So one of them knows a little military strategy. Fine. At least this will be somewhat of a challenge. Nothing bores me more than an easy win."

He opened the comm switch himself. "All units, accelerate to flank speed and switch to infrared," he ordered. "Close to one mile and show them no mercy."

⊥

From his own MRV James watched the phalanx of Gault's units spread out and begin their run. Through the shimmering heat of the desert they began to move faster and faster, kicking up clouds of dust behind them. From this range there was no sound. Just the sight of huge machines running through a mirage towards them. It felt like a dream.

James pressed his own comm switch. "Wait," he said, quietly, holding the line open and counting down the seconds in his mind. *Five, four, three...* And when he reached zero, "Fire at will."

He let go of the comm switch, locked his sights on the lead MRV and pulled the trigger.

The big plasma guns recoiled, unleashing their first shots. An instant later hundreds of other weapons opened up in unison. Most of the fire came from the rifles in the hands of the former slaves on the ridgeline, but larger more potent blasts came from the five MRVs.

It was impressive, if not particularly devastating to the oncoming stampede.

An explosion lit up the horizon as James's first shot found its mark. Seconds later other explosions and clouds of smoke showed additional impacts along the approaching line, but then the attackers returned fire and a hail storm of plasma blasts, tracers and missiles came blistering in at the rebel lines.

Not surprisingly the result was instant chaos.

The mercenaries had the numbers and the superior firepower, but the former slaves were dug in behind the ridge of stone. Even their MRVs stood far enough down the slope that only their weapons were exposed.

James was already moving. Moving and firing. His training and experience made him a more cold-blooded assassin for the moment. Move, set, fire. Repeat, repeat, repeat...

The salvos unleashed from his machine hit one mercenary vehicle after another with deadly accuracy. And soon there were a half dozen plumes of smoke drifting skyward from the victims of his onslaught.

Without automatic targeting the other MRVs were struggling. At best they'd hit one, maybe two of the attackers. The counterattack made it harder to see. Missiles hitting the ridgeline had blown fragments of stone and huge clouds of dust into the sky.

From the corner of his eye, James saw the MRV immediately to his right explode in a fireball. It had been standing still and firing from a fixed position as if it was a piece of artillery.

He tapped the comm switch. "Move and fire!" he shouted. "Move and fire. Just like I showed you."

The remaining two machines followed orders, moving awkwardly. But one of them was not firing.

"Tango Four, release your safeties," James called.

"Safeties?"

"The red switch on the right panel," James said. "Flip it over and press the button underneath it."

As James spoke, a pair of glancing blows hit them and both he and Bethel were jostled around. Reacting on instinct James redirected the machine to the right, spun the cab and fired again. A spread of missiles raced from the top of the rig, screaming towards the enemy and hiding them in a new cloud of smoke.

James used the distraction to move again, escaping just as several rockets hit the very spot they'd been standing in and showering the MRV with chunks of rock and shrapnel.

"They're getting closer," Bethel said.

"Not close enough," James replied.

Outside the freed slaves were firing at will, but their weapons were designed to be used against infantry rather than armor. With a great deal of luck they might cause light damage on a few of the attackers, but their most important role was distraction. With fire coming from all angles, the attackers had to spread their own fire out instead of concentrating solely on the MRVs.

In the distance, one of the attackers was weaving to the right in an uncontrolled motion. James let it go rather than waste time on a damaged machine. Instead, he lit up the vehicle that came in behind it.

By now, his wingmen were firing almost as rapidly as him. As if to make up for lost time, Tango Four unleashed all its missiles at once and followed that with a hailstorm of cannon fire that cut across the fields until the heat limiters cut in and shut down the system.

To James's surprise the tactic was quite effective, taking out two of the approaching MRVs and causing a third to change course and collide with a fourth. As he watched this the truth dawned on him.

"They're not trained all that much better than our people," he said.

"But there's a lot more of them," Bethel called back, grasping a handle as James maneuvered the vehicle.

James peered through the smoke of the battle. The incoming fire was picking up. The ridge they were hiding behind was getting obliterated piece by piece. During a brief moment of clarity, he spotted one of the enemy rigs hanging back. He guessed that was the commander directing the battle from the rear.

He wanted to take a shot at the bastard but the blowing smoke quickly obscured the machine once again. With enemy fire coming in from all directions now, they would have only moments before being overrun.

In quick succession Tango Four was hit with missiles from the left and the right. Like a stunned boxer it teetered for a second before a third missile blasted through the armor and sent it tumbling down the ridge.

A second later, cannon fire engulfed James and Bethel. The big plates of armor held together but the beating was intense.

Out on what was left of the ridgeline, huge explosions were blasting apart the defenders' lines, hurling bodies and soil skyward with impunity.

James tapped the comm. "Kamahu," he shouted. "Get your men out of there. Pull back. I repeat, pull back! I'll try to cover you."

⋏

Out on the surface, Kamahu heard the message and began running along the front line, shouting at the top of his lungs and waving for the men to retreat. They pulled out quickly and began scrambling down the hill, racing headlong toward the armory.

"Get back to the depot!" Kamahu shouted. "Go now!"

As the foot soldiers of the small army ran, James crossed in front of them firing at will. "Tango Three, get back to the barn if you can."

Tango Three tried to turn but it was unable to raise its left leg. Caught in one place it was a sitting duck.

"We can't move!"

"Get out!" James shouted.

It was too late. A river of cannon fire tore into the machine and its own remaining ordinance exploded.

"How many are left?" James asked.

"Only one besides us," Bethel replied. "They're running. And I think we should be too."

"Agreed."

With the abandoned and the defenders racing down the road past the armory, James yanked the controls to the side and the MRV turned and lumbered down the hill in huge pounding steps. Ahead of it, the slaves were running for their lives.

Chapter 41

From his vantage point behind the main force, Gault had been watching the battle with a mixture of surprise and horror. He'd seen a dozen of his machines destroyed and two others knocked out of commission. But they'd pressed on and destroyed the enemy's front line, taken out at least three, perhaps four of the defending MRVs and were in the process of turning the battle into a rout.

Still, there was something disheartening about his men's voices as they tried to coordinate their attack on the radio, a frantic, sometimes overwrought sense of each hit and miss. Then again, these weren't really his men, Gault reminded himself. They were just what he'd been given to work with.

"They're backing off the ridge."

"At least three of the MRVs are down."

"The others are running. They're trying to escape."

Gault smiled and nodded to the driver. "Go! This I don't want to miss."

Gault's driver increased their speed, took them past the burning wrecks of the other MRVs and toward the ridge.

"Bravo Units, stay up on the plateau," Gault ordered. "Everyone else converge on the armory and finish them off!"

⋏

On the far side of the ridge, the surviving slaves were running along the dirt track of a road that cut between the buildings of the armory and the steep canyon beyond.

James followed. Despite knowing he could pick off a few of their enemies as they crested the ridge, he didn't swing the cab around. It had to look like a collapse, like an army in disarray. The last thing he wanted was for their pursuers to slow down.

And they didn't.

The mercenary MRVs poured over the ridgeline as soon as they reached it. They came down seven abreast, blasting at everything in sight. Their missiles struck the warehouses of the armory. Their cannon fire scattered the fleeing slaves like a broom might sweep away a stream of ants.

James kept moving, racing past the far end of the armory and veering to the right, as if he might take the MRV deep into the desert beyond.

The attackers quickened their pursuit, charging forward with little sense of caution.

Using the rearward-facing camera, James tracked their progress. "Come on," he whispered to himself, "Just a little further."

As the others pressed forward, he noticed the command MRV stop at the top of the ridge to direct the battle. For it to come down would have been too much to ask for.

James pressed the comm switch. "Now!" he ordered.

⚔

In a bunker disguised as a garbage pit, two former slaves in body armor crouched beside a bank of controllers and plungers. At the sound of James's order, they leaned forward and began slamming their hands down on the plungers, one after another.

Out on the road, massive explosions blasted skyward, blowing apart two of the MRVs at the rear of Gault's armada, and carving a deep, un-crossable ditch from the side of the warehouse all the way to the edge of the canyon.

Another series of explosions took out the lead MRV and blasted a similar ditch at the front of the column. One of the MRVs tried to cross it only to find the width and depth too great. It tumbled forward and face-planted into the far side, effectively neutralized if not destroyed. The rest of the column ground to a halt.

"They're trapped," James called out, holding the comm open. "Finish them."

"Go," someone called back.

Almost immediately there was another rumble. But this time the explosion blew out part of the wall around the armory. From inside the warehouse, a phalanx of the huge bulldozers came rushing forward, shoulder to shoulder, monstrous blades raised and locked like shields.

The mercenaries reacted slowly and in a disorganized fashion. Some of them turned and fired, others tried to run back toward the ridge only to be blown apart by more hidden explosives.

As the mercenaries panicked, the bulldozers kept charging; side-by-side they formed an unstoppable wall of steel.

They slammed into the remaining MRVs like a tsunami, knocking them sideways, crushing some under their giant metal treads, forcing the rest of them backwards toward the canyon and then shoving them off the edge and into the abyss where the remaining stacks of explosives waited for them.

A wave of monstrous explosions flashed through the canyon, creating a fireball that mushroomed hundreds of feet into the air.

▲

From the inside of his MRV, Gault struggled to see through the smoke and dust.

"What happened?" he shouted. "What the hell happened?"

There was no response.

He toggled the radio and called again, but it was silent. Only static came over the comm.

"They're gone," his driver muttered, as the smoke began to clear. "They're all gone."

"They can't be."

"I'm telling you," the driver said. "They're not there anymore."

Gault could not muster a response. His mind was spinning, but despite his disbelief, he could soon see that the driver was right. His army had been annihilated, slaughtered by the outnumbered, worthless slaves. Aside from a few stragglers and the rigs he'd ordered to stay on the plateau, there was literally nothing left. Five machines out of forty.

He saw the slaves coming out from their hiding spots and opening fire. The two remaining MRVs were emerging from behind the armory. Both of them taking aim at him. The odds had turned.

"Get us out of here!" he shouted. "Get us out of here now!"

Chapter 42

James saw the carnage in the gorge from a higher vantage point than most. The majority of the mercenary machines had been destroyed on impact, crushed under their own weight in the fall. The explosives had simply been the exclamation point, designed to inspire fear and leave no doubt.

He glanced toward the ridge. The command MRV was turning and making its way up the switch back of the slope.

Impulsively, James gunned the throttle and the big rig began to accelerate along the road. He raced toward the ditch and used the wrecked mercenary MRV as a stepping stone, clambering across to the other side. At full speed he raced between the craters left by the mining explosives and set his sights on the ridgeline.

To the foot soldiers of his army the move came as a surprise and several groups had to run and dive out of the way to avoid being crushed by the pounding feet.

Trying to target the fleeing rig, James dialed up the plasma guns and unleashed several shots. They raced toward the fleeing target, hitting all around it but nothing direct enough to put it out of action.

"What are you doing?" Bethel asked.

"That's the leader," James told him. "I'm not letting him go."

A series of bursts came back at James and Bethel as Gault's rig neared the top.

James switched to missiles.

"Missile bay exhausted," the computer informed him.

"Damn it," James grunted. He switched to the cannons. They had only a hundred or so armor piercing rounds remaining in the massive ammunition drums but if he could get close enough they would do the trick.

Up ahead the mercenary MRV directed a last shot down into the valley, crested the ridge and disappeared.

James held the throttle of his own machine to the stops, causing it to leap as it reached the other trench and kept going. At sixty miles an hour the huge metal beast ran toward the ridge and leapt onto the slope of rubble, soil and stone. Unlike Gault, James avoided the switchback, using the speed and momentum he'd built up to race straight up the hill.

The huge claw-like feet dug and churned, pounding and straining as they propelled the rig upward. James tilted the shuddering cab forward to keep the momentum going.

"You don't have to do this," Bethel said. "We've won."

"You don't understand," James insisted. "This is our chance to finish it. We get this guy, they'll be in disarray. The war might be over."

"James, he's beaten already."

With James urging the MRV on like a stallion, they surged over the top of the ridge.

In the distance, Gault's MRV was fleeing, racing headlong back toward Olympia, dashing between three other MRVs that stood like sentinels with their guns waiting and trained on James and Bethel.

"Oh my God," Bethel shouted.

It was too late for James to even utter a curse. They'd lost so much speed on the climb that they'd reached the top like a man exhausted, barely moving. The MRV was a sitting target and he knew it.

Flashes from the mercenary rigs caught his eye and the whole cabin shook as the first impacts tore into the machine. The rig shuddered from the blow and almost toppled back down the hill. James steadied it and moved it forward returning fire for a second before a new wave of impacts staggered them.

Under relentless assault from three sides, the machine was rapidly bludgeoned to death. It staggered forward until a missile hit the hip joint on Bethel's side of the rig, caved in the armor and toppled the mortally wounded machine.

It fell sideways and crashed into the red soil like a dying animal collapsing in the sand.

Inside the mangled wreckage, James fought to breathe. The cabin was filling with smoke and flames were licking around the edges. Bleeding and battered, with his head ringing from the missile impact, James fought a weird sense of disorientation.

Broken panels fell about him, dangling on their wires. Only then did he realize that the rig was over on its side. Frantically, he grabbed for the seatbelt release. As it let him free, he slid out of the chair, grabbed a support rail and pulled himself up to where his friend lay unmoving.

"Bethel!" he shouted.

The doctor was a ragdoll hanging in the belts. James punched the release and pulled him free. They tumbled back and came to rest on what had been the starboard bulkhead.

James dragged Bethel along it, found the hatch and hit the emergency release. The top hatch was blown open by a series of explosive bolts, and James pulled Bethel through it.

Outside now, he crawled forward, still dragging Bethel along with him. He quickly located the ridgeline and began moving that way, trying to keep the smoke and the wreckage of the MRV between them and the mercenaries.

Bethel began to come around. "You had it won," he mumbled.

James grimaced in pain and slid forward. He could feel the soil vibrating as if a big bass drum were being struck. He looked up as the last of the slaves' MRVs crested the hill.

"No!" he shouted. "Go back!"

It was too late. Just like he had, this last MRV walked into firestorm.

It took a series of missiles to the cab and exploded. The concussion wave threw James backward and he landed in the sand only semi-conscious at this point.

As his senses returned, he realized all too keenly what he'd done. He'd taken certain victory and turned it into utter defeat. He wanted to throw up, wanted to fall face first into the sand and die, but he remembered Bethel and crawled back towards him.

As he reached his friend, one of the mercenary MRVs began shouldering its way through the smoke.

It made it past the wreckage of James and Bethel's machine and stopped. It sat on its haunches in perfect killing range. But instead of tilting the cab down to target the two men on the desert floor, it stared out beyond them, looking into the distance.

What are you waiting for? James thought. *Finish us.*

Then, without warning, the MRV turned around and took off running, sprinting back through the smoke and heading towards Olympia.

James stood awkwardly and as the smoke drifted he caught sight of all three machines racing away in a sudden retreat.

It made no sense. He should have been dead. The slaves in the valley behind him should have been getting obliterated by now, but instead the mercenaries were turning tail and running for the hills.

James watched them go, noticing that the smoke on the battlefield had begun to blow sideways. Sand began pelting the back of his legs and the plateau grew dark as a menacing shadow passed over them.

James turned to see a massive wall of red dust rising up behind the armory. Two miles high and as wide as the horizon, it obscured the sun and bore down on them like a nightmarish wave ready to crash.

As James watched, the leading edge of the storm whipped past the armory, and aced up the hill hitting him with the fury of a hurricane.

Chapter 43

The surviving rebels huddled in the undamaged sections of the armory as the violent winds shook and sandblasted them. The sound of the wind alone was fearful, it was made worse by the wrenching sound of items being torn loose from the outer structures or the sudden echoing bangs that shook the buildings as items, picked up and thrown by the wind, slammed headlong into the thin metal walls.

Because of the endless noise, it was several minutes before anyone recognized the sound of a fist banging on one of the steel doors.

Finally realizing what he was hearing, Kamahu, ran over to the door. He looked through the small viewport and saw a man with his face wrapped carrying another man over his shoulder. He unlatched the door allowing a blast of sand and wind to whip through, all but shoving James and Bethel inside.

For his part, James was barely breathing. He all but collapsed lowering Bethel to the floor. "Get one of the medics," he croaked, pulling the cloth away from his face. "Hurry."

As Kamahu ran off, James looked down at Bethel. "Hold on."

He tried to peel some of Bethel's clothing from his body, but it had been burned and melted to his skin.

"It's too late," Bethel said looking up at him.

Looking around, James spotted an oxygen tank with a mask. He grabbed it, set it down and turned the valve. As soon as the oxygen was flowing he placed the mask over Bethel's nose and mouth.

Bethel took a few shallow breaths and then pushed the mask away. "It's too late," he repeated, in a wheezing, gravelly voice. "My lungs are gone. Burned up. I can feel them… filling…with fluid."

James looked up. "Get someone over here!" he shouted.

Bethel shook his head. "There's nothing to be done." The words were a painful whisper.

"I shouldn't have taken you with me," James said. "You should have been here with the wounded."

"I needed to keep an eye on you."

James felt emotions roiling inside him—rage, pity, guilt—all of them surging uncontrollably. "I've destroyed everything," he said, his own voice cracking.

"No," Bethel said. "You've brought these people something."

James shook his head. "Pain and death."

"You're wrong," Bethel managed. "They have something they've never had. Hope."

James looked away. He could barely listen. He was sick of people talking about hope. All it brought was misery when it was dashed.

"Hope won't do them much good now," he said. "The only thing keeping us safe is the storm. When it breaks…"

He didn't have to finish.

"You can't give up," Bethel said. "You have to find a way."

"There is no way," he said.

"There must be. Find one."

Bethel began coughing up blood, even as Kamahu and the medic came running.

"A leader," Bethel said, before coughing again. "A leader…has to try, has to give everything in the effort…everything…he…has…"

As the last words came forth, Bethel seemed to relax. His eyes closed and his chest fell once more, never to rise again.

James moved the oxygen mask towards his face, but the medic stopped him.

James glanced up, but the medic just shook his head. "He's gone."

Bethel was gone. The armor and the heavy weapons were gone. As far as James could see, hope itself was gone.

He found he couldn't move, couldn't even lift his head. In the middle of the sprawling room, surrounded by hundreds of people, he had never felt more alone.

Chapter 44

Olympia City

Gault's last surviving MRVs raced back into Olympia with the storm right on their heels.

They raced down the central boulevard, the same road they'd so arrogantly marched out on, made their way to the hangars and stomped inside.

Gault was already out of his machine as the last of them parked and the gaping hangar doors were shut tight against the howling wind. He looked around. The room was already coated in a fine layer of dust and it was painfully empty. Only five of the forty MRVs had returned.

"Seal everything," he said to the maintenance crews as he marched for the corridor that would lead him to Cassini's office.

He needn't have bothered. Cassini met him in the hall with two adjutants at his side.

"What happened to the rest of your squadron?" Cassini demanded.

Gault didn't feel like explaining. He kept marching. His mind was churning. By a narrow margin he'd avoided death, but the magnitude of his defeat would mean a similar fate when Lucien Rex learned what had happened. Failure was not tolerated among the forces of the Cartel.

Cassini quickly caught up with him. "Answer me Gault!"

"They're gone," Gault shouted, whirling on his so-called governor.

"What?"

Cassini's mouth was agape and it made Gault wish he'd lied, but he couldn't count on the other crews keeping their mouths shut.

"How?" Cassini demanded.

Gault had to think quickly. "A trap," he said. "The whole thing was a trap. They were too well prepared, too well trained in their use of the machines. They must be more than just slaves."

Cassini was more used to building lies than Gault and he saw through the tactic instantly.

"You failed," he said, with surprising boldness. "If there was a trap, you walked yourself right into it and let the slaves catch you. We have to inform Lucien."

To everyone's surprise Gault lunged at Cassini, grabbing him by the throat and slammed him into the polished surface of the wall. The adjutants moved to assist Cassini but Gault pulled his sidearm and blasted them down without even looking their way.

As the men fell in pools of blood, Gault shoved the hot barrel of the pistol up underneath Cassini's chin. "You should have brought guards with you, not pencil pushers like yourself."

"If you kill me, Lucien will-"

Gault cut him off with a renewed shove of the pistol and Cassini's teeth closed on his tongue, spurting blood, which was soon dribbling from the corner of his mouth.

"Lucien is thirty days from here," Gault explained bluntly. "And getting further off every day. He can't help you. And quite frankly, he doesn't give a damn who kills who, as long as the job gets done."

Cassini seemed to accept this, and as Gault released him, he sensed that the governor had been effectively neutered and surpassed.

"Now, listen to me and listen clearly," Gault said. "I will finish these slaves off. And I will allow you to take some of the glory, but if you speak with Lucien beforehand, if you tell him what's occurred…Well, at that point I'll have nothing left to lose, will I? And I might be prone to doing something rash and even… violent. Do you get my meaning?"

"You're insane," Cassini mumbled.

"Who isn't these days?"

"Alright," Cassini said. "I'll cover for you. But what do you propose to do?"

"Spread the word that we put down a slave rebellion and the other machines are standing guard over the damaged camp."

"That should deal with the rumors," Cassini said. "Then what?"

"Bring the rest of the units back to the city. Even those guarding the other camps."

Cassini's eyes all but bulged out of his head. "But the camps need to be watched or we risk another insurrection."

"The storm will keep those slaves in place," Gault said, secure in his mind. "And if it doesn't, we'll deal with them later. But this threat must be taken seriously."

Cassini licked his lips, no doubt aware that he was now taking orders from his subordinate. "Fine," he said at long last. "And what do you propose we do after the outlying units return?"

"We use them without concern for collateral damage."

Cassini paused. Even if he didn't quite understand, he knew enough not to ask any more questions. "Alright," he said. "I'll give the order."

Gault nodded. He felt a wave of hope. *He would get a second chance. And if he could end this slave rebellion with enough brutality and blame a few others for the defeat, he might just save his own neck.*

Chapter 45

In a mechanics workshop connected to the main MRV hangar, a pair of journeymen technicians worked to repair the main hydraulic pump on one of the damaged MRVs. Other mechanics were crawling over the machines in the hangar working on the instruments of their own imprisonment.

With no one else in earshot the first mechanic spoke quietly. "Do you see the damage to those rigs?"

His assistant grunted an acknowledgement without looking up.

"What the hell do you think happened out there?"

"No idea. Not sure I want to know."

"Come on, look at the burn marks. These are heavy plasma burns."

The second mechanic kept his head down and kept working. He didn't want to talk. A guy could get killed for talking.

"Notice something else," the lead mechanic said. "This hangar bay is empty."

"The other rigs are guarding the prisoners."

"In this storm?" The lead mechanic shook his head. "Hell no. This was a battle. Those other rigs are gone and they're not coming back."

"Come on, can we just do our job?"

The lead mechanic kept up the chatter. "Something is going on here. I'm telling you. I hear things. And I've heard rumors that there might be a resistance forming up. We should-"

At that, the second mechanic grabbed him. "Look man, I have a family. I'm not doing this. I know what you're thinking and I'm not gonna be a part of it. You do whatever you want. I won't say a word, but don't drag me into this."

The first mechanic shook free. "Doing what?" he asked. "I was just pointing something out. Just talk."

They went back to work, toiling in silence for a few minutes before the second mechanic finally spoke. "Of course," he whispered. "If there was an uprising, it wouldn't hurt if this hydraulic pump failed again in the next battle."

The first mechanic grinned. "Or if Johnny misaligned the launch initiators in those missile pods."

The second mechanic allowed a smile. "Hell," he said. "The quality of Johnny's work, I'm surprised it hasn't happened already."

They laughed quietly. "Keep working," the lead mechanic said, "I'm gonna make my rounds."

Chapter 46

Out at the armory, the storm continued to gust in undiminished intensity even as dusk came on.

James listened to it from inside a semi-darkened supply room as the walls shook and rattled around him. With great effort, he cinched the straps on a suit of body armor until they were tight. With practiced hands, he connected a line from the camelback oxygen tank that fit the armor, to the helmet he would wear. A quick test of the flow told him it was working.

He was alone except for Kamahu.

"Are you sure you want to do this?" the big man asked.

"I have to," James said quietly. "I have to try."

"I was caught in a sand storm a month ago," Kamahu said. "It wasn't as bad as this one, and I only had to make it back to the caves from the far side of the work site. It almost killed me. What you're trying to do…it's suicide."

Kamahu was probably right, but it was their only hope.

"If I can make it to Olympia, I can sneak into the city during the storm. Their scanners will be down. They'll never see me. I can make contact with the people I told you about. Hopefully they're ready to fight. Hopefully they can help."

Kamahu looked around as the wind continued to rattle the structure. "I'll go with you," he said finally.

James smiled but shook his head. "No. You stay here. They need you. You're their leader now."

"What should I do with them?"

"Try to keep their spirits up. Keep them together. If I can find help we'll come to your aid."

"And if you don't?"

"Fight to the end," James said. "Don't let them take you alive."

Kamahu nodded and offered a hand. James shook it and felt his hand all but crushed in the big man's grip.

After the hand shake ended, both men remained silent and Kamahu escorted James to the door and opened it for him.

James stepped through and stopped in his tracks. In the main hall, formed up like platoons of soldiers, stood hundreds of the former slaves. Men, women and children. Even the injured that could stand were there.

"Ten hut!" Kamahu shouted.

His voice was like a gunshot and the sound of the men and women snapping to attention and saluting was like a thunderclap that echoed off the walls.

James didn't really understand it. In his mind, he'd done nothing but lead them on a foolish suicidal crusade. But they seemed to think differently. Perhaps a moment of freedom and a taste of pride were worth dying for.

James could only stare. He was proud of them. And he knew what he had to do. He would get them help or die trying.

He returned their salute and headed for the exit. Standing beside the door, he slid the helmet over his head and locked it into place. With the flick of a switch the oxygen began to flow.

He gave the thumbs up, and Kamahu pushed the door open against the blowing wind.

James nodded and stepped through, moving out into the swirling wind. Instantly he was buffeted by the gusts, which pushed him sideways and threatened to topple him over—the way his emotions had done for most of his life. But as he stood in the gale and considered what he now faced, James found his mind to be quiet. Despite the odds and the pain and exhaustion, there were no more questions.

He moved to one of the six wheel scouts and climbed on. The electrically powered vehicle had a theoretical chance of making it through the storm, since it's engine didn't need air to breathe. James tapped a button and turned the power on. A blue white headlight cast a well-defined beam out into the swirling dust. The power indicator registered 99%.

Ready to go, James glanced back toward the warehouse. Through his gold tinted visor, he saw the Kamahu standing there in the open doorway.

James cocked his head as if to say, *What are you doing?*

In response, Kamahu lifted the rifle he carried above his head. "Never give up!" he shouted. "Never give in!"

His voice boomed through the storm, louder than the banshee-like wind. The words had never carried more meaning.

James nodded once again, and then turned and drove out into the tempest.

Chapter 47

Gault paced the floorboards of Cassini's office relentlessly and Cassini found himself growing tired just watching.

An aide came in with several reports.

"The camps are reporting in," the aide told Cassini. "They indicate-"

"I don't care about the camps," Gault bellowed. "How long till this damned storm ends?"

Cassini wondered that too. It was the worst he'd seen since arriving. The satellite coverage showed a third of the planet obscured.

The aide scanned through the information he'd been given. "Not for at least twenty-four hours," he said.

Gault shot him a dirty look.

"Maybe less."

Gault ground his teeth. "It had better be less," he growled.

Cassini didn't like this news any better than Gault. "Twenty-four hours. Those slaves have had too much freedom already."

As the aide left them, an intercom tone caught their attention. "Yes," Cassini said.

"Governor," a harsh voice said. "I think we have another problem."

"As if we don't have enough already, " Cassini replied. "What's wrong?"

"The small arms lockers have been tampered with," the voice replied. "Their sensors indicate all weapons remain in racks, but a physical inspection revealed that the spare rifles and pistols have all been taken."

Cassini looked up at Gault, who shook his head. His men hadn't done it.

"You're right," Cassini said into the comm link. "That is a problem. Round up your men. It seems we have more than one insurrection to deal with."

▲

Out on the plains, James continued his journey, pushing on through the storm and the dead of night, piloting the small ATV through the storm.

He couldn't take the main route to Olympia for the simple fact that it was the most direct route and would likely be guarded. Instead he was angling across the plateau, out into the barren wasteland of the planet, trying to cut the corner a bit.

It was slow going. After two hours, the headlight on the ATV began to dim. James switched it off and slowed down, but the batteries were dying fast. Thirty minutes later, the ATV ground unceremoniously to a halt.

James sat on it for a moment longer. He'd covered about half the distance or so it seemed. He'd have to do the rest on foot.

Climbing off the ATV, he stretched his legs, got his bearings and flicked on a small light on the right shoulder of the body armor. It illuminated no more than ten feet in front of him, just enough to keep him from tripping or tumbling down a canyon.

He adjusted the flow of oxygen and began walking. He'd need more now that he was on foot. And he needed to move quickly if he hoped to get to the outskirts of Olympia before dawn.

He began hiking and was soon sweating in the cold and dark. A heads up display on the helmet kept him on line, but he noticed his vision getting worse as the hike wore on. At first he thought his eyes were failing with exhaustion, but then he realized the visor of his helmet was slowly getting sand blasted.

The navigation pack failed shortly thereafter. Whatever signal it worked off of was being blocked by the storm. And the directional icons and their little green lines came and went intermittently for a while before they vanished permanently, replaced by an annoying icon that read: *No Signal.*

He kept going, walking as straight as he could even as the wind and the sand pushed him around. Soon his legs grew heavy. He began to trip over small rocks. He noticed his feet seemed to have no feeling.

He turned the oxygen flow up to full, but almost immediately a yellow light on the tank lit up and a warning appeared on the heads up display inside his helmet.

O2 supply low.

Reaching for controls on his arm plate, James dialed down the flow to the lowest possible setting and pressed forward. The reduced oxygen supply only aggravated his weary state, and soon he was stumbling through the night like a drunk.

The uneven ground made the process more difficult. With increasing frequency, he tripped and fell, laid low by unseen rocks or simply blown over by the gusting wind.

Eventually, he put a boot down on some loose gravel and sprawled forward once again. His hands went out instinctively to break his fall, but there was nothing to grab. He tumbled forward down a steep slope, sliding and rolling, until he was tossed out at the bottom and rudely deposited onto the flat desert landscape again.

The warning indicator began to flash once again. *Oxygen level critical.*

James reached for the shut off valve to save the remaining supply but saw that the line from the tank to his helmet had been ripped out during the fall.

Oxygen depleted.

"Now you've done it, James," he grunted to himself.

He switched a lever on the side of the helmet that opened tiny vents in the mouth guard for him to breath the surrounding air. They were filtered to some extent but in two breaths he could already sense the odd metallic taste of the Martian sand.

With great effort, he rose to his feet and began to trudge forward once again. He had to keep going; somehow *he had to keep going.*

Each step became agony. A battle between his will and his own aching muscles that would eventually be lost. The lack of oxygen and water were causing his legs to cramp. He wanted to fall, to lay down in the soft sand and die. Some part of his mind told him it was okay. He'd done enough.

"Keep going, God damn you," he grunted. "Keep going!"

A false step put him down once again. This time, as he got to one knee he heard something. Something other than the sound of the wind and the sand.

Fifty yards off, a pair of sharply defined spotlights snapped on, blinding him. The high intensity beams cut through the storm like the eyes of some demon come to claim his body for perdition.

James knew all too well what those lights came from.

"No," he muttered to himself.

The lights began to move and the ground began to shake as the huge machine began stomping towards him.

It shook James from his lethargy. "No!"

He got to his feet and began to run. He could lose them in the storm; he knew he could. But thirty paces into his flight, another set of lights snapped on in front of him and James skidded to a halt. As he turned, another set lit up and then another.

With nowhere left to run, and no energy to run with, James fell to his knees defeated. The lights from one machine moved forward, until the big machine appeared through the swirling dust like a nightmare come to life.

James felt his shoulders sag and his spirit fail as he awaited the inevitable. From the chin of the MRV a wave of blue light spiraled forth, it cut through the storm, much like the stun beam that had been used on the tunnel dwellers.

As the wave of energy swept over him, James fell forward, unconscious in the dust. His last thought was simple: *this is the end.*

Chapter 48

James awoke in darkness. The wind and blowing sand were gone. He was sitting on a chair, his hands cuffed to a small table in front of him.

A tiny chemical light sat in the middle of the table, its whitish glow soft and steady.

"About dammed time you woke up," someone said.

Two more lights came on. Halogen beams but nothing fancy. They were work lights. The kind mechanics use to see what they were working on in tight engine bays. From what James could see they were mounted on a scaffolding of some kind. Hastily rigged up and aimed down toward him.

Where the hell was he?

A shadow moved forward in the lights. As it got closer, the light painted some of the features on the man's face. He had a snarling look, a full bushy beard and a scar on the right side of his jaw that left a gash in the beard like an access road cut through a dense forest.

"Who the hell are you?" the man growled, his voice echoing as if they were in a large room or a cave.

James remembered he had ripped the ID strip from his arm. Maybe they hadn't seen the gash. Or maybe with the bullet wound in his shoulder and the other injuries, these men had simply overlooked it.

James chose to remain silent. He might learn more if the interrogator asked a few more questions. But instead of more questions, the interrogator stepped back.

"Jog his memory," he said to someone else.

Another thug moved in, rolling up his sleeves. He stepped between James and the light and threw a right cross that caught James in the jaw, sending him tumbling off the chair. He hit the ground and lay there, his hands held up where they were still cuffed to the table.

The force of the blow seemed to wake James up. He spat out some blood and small chip that had probably broken off one tooth.

"Don't you dumbasses know anything about interrogation," he managed. "You want someone to talk, you don't break their mouth."

With that the brute kicked him in the stomach, a blow James had expected and steeled himself against. The impact was jarring and painful, but not half as bad as it must have seemed to the men administering it.

"Where did you come from?" the interrogator asked. "And how did you find us?"

That was a strange question, James thought.

The interrogator stepped forward and righted the metal chair. A quick look told James it had been ripped out of the front end of a truck or some other vehicle.

"Help him up," the interrogator muttered.

The thug taking orders hoisted James up, putting two beefy hands on his collar, yanking him off the floor and depositing him back onto the old seat.

James noticed a full beard on this one too, scruffy and unkempt. What he didn't see, despite looking for them, were the cryptic markings of the mercenaries.

"Where's all your ink?" James asked.

"You think we're mercenary scum, like you," the enforcer replied angrily.

James's mind began to spin. His thoughts leaped about in huge bounds. If they weren't mercenaries then they had to be…"You're regular army?"

"41st damned Armored Division, you son of a bitch!" the enforcer shouted. "And by God we're gonna know who you are before tonight's over."

James felt his mind whirling. He began to laugh hysterically. He couldn't help it. He glanced around, trying to peer through the darkness. Where the hell was he? A firebase. *The 41st had built themselves a firebase and hid out there.*

"What the hell are you laughing at you son of a bitch?"

James couldn't explain it fast enough. He couldn't find the words.

A club-like blow from the enforcer's arm to the back of his head shattered the moment of good humor.

When he looked up again his eyes were filed with righteous fury. His voice grew low and menacing. "You wanna know who I am?" he growled. "I'm your goddamned commanding officer. James R. Collins. Rank, Major. ID number, 410-33-797."

The interrogator and the enforcer seemed stunned for a second by this statement. They looked at one another in confusion. Then they got angry.

"You lying son of a bitch!" Another punch came his way, but James took it and stared back at the man who'd thrown it.

"This guy's out of his freaking mind," the interrogator said. "Get the shock machine."

James stood, fast and angry, the cuffs pulled tight against his wrists, yanking the table up into the air. Shocked by the sudden move, the interrogator stepped back a few inches.

James stared him in the eye. "You listen to me soldier! I am James Collins, and you will obey my orders. Now go find Lt. Dyson or another officer and bring them back here. Or I promise you'll spend the rest your life wishing you had."

"What?"

"Did he say what I think he said?"

You heard me!"

"He's got to be a damn spy," the enforcer said. "No one from those camps would know Lt. Dyson?"

"Get him in here!" James shouted.

"Shut your mouth!"

James lunged to the side, yanking the table with him. If this really was the 41st, Dyson or some other ranking officer would be watching.

"Dyson!" James shouted into the darkness. "I know you're out there. You get your ass in here and talk to me. You know who I am."

The interrogator and the enforcer had been thrown into a state of shock by all the shouting but were suddenly coming out of it.

"Hit that man!" the interrogator shouted to the enforcer. "Take him down!"

The enforcer came first, slamming the end of a baton into James's stomach and dropping him to the ground.

"Shut him up! Knock his ass out!"

"Dyson," James shouted. "Perrera would kick your ass for this if he was here."

The baton was raised in the enforcer's hand, ready to come smashing down when a voice from the dark prevented it.

"Wait!"

The interrogator and the enforcer stopped their attack and stood at attention.

James heard the sound of boots crossing the stone floor toward him. They echoed slightly like everything else had.

A new figure moved into the light. He was cleaner cut but still a little ragged for a military officer.

"You're relieved," he said to the interrogator.

"Sir, with all due respect, I don't think it's safe for you to-"

"I said, get out!" the officer shouted. "Now!"

"Yes sir."

The interrogator and the enforcer turned and moved off into the darkness as the officer crouched down and studied James where he lay on the ground.

"My God," the man whispered. "You look like hell."

James had no doubt who he was talking to. "You don't look much better, Lieutenant Dyson. But it's damn good to see you again."

Chapter 49

James spent much of the next hour receiving fluids and explaining what he'd been through, while Dyson filled him in on their tactical situation, explaining the odd stalemate that had developed, leaving the 41st wandering the desert like the lost tribes of Israel.

"So where are we anyway?" James asked. "What is this place?"

"The original survey site for Olympia," Dyson explained. "They dug enough living space out of the rock to house the first crews, but the ground was too unstable for heavy construction so they moved. Later surveys put the city in the valley, ninety miles from here."

"Ninety miles?" James said. "I thought I was a lot closer than that."

"At some point you must have wandered off course," Dyson said. "Assuming you were trying to cut the corner, you've come at least thirty miles in the wrong direction."

"Story of my life," James said. "What's our strength?"

"We've got thirty-seven working rigs. We've had to strip the others for parts. But even with that, most of our mechanics are back in Olympia. So we've really just been trying to hold on. We've done what we can to protect the MRVs but with this storm and the limited supplies, we're all but out of time."

"Food and water?"

"Water we can make," Dyson reminded him, "but even on half rations, we're down to the bottom of the barrel on food."

"I heard they might have tried to poison you," James said.

"They did try," Dyson admitted. "But we were kind of expecting something."

James grinned at Dyson's foresight. "So what was your plan here?"

"We've been trying to contact the high command, find someone who knows what the hell is really going on, but all the signals out are being jammed. Lately we've been considering raiding parties or even trying to re-take the city. But from the info I have they outnumber us three to one."

"Maybe not," James said. "We took out a whole battalion of their rigs out at the armory. And I have reason to believe a resistance movement has been growing among the Terra-formers. If we can get word to them as we march on the city, we might be able to turn this thing around. But we have to move soon. And by *soon*, I mean *right now, a*s soon as the men can mount up."

Dyson's eyebrows went up. "In the middle of the storm?"

"The storm will give us cover," James said. "If we can hit them while they're still hunkered down in the shelters, we'll have the advantage."

"And these rigs will be useless forty-eight hours later," Dyson noted.

"They'll be useless in a few weeks anyway," James said. "It's now or never, lieutenant. Now or never."

James managed to get an hour of sleep as the men of the 41st sprang into action, turning the dormant firebase into a hub of activity. With great energy, they began tearing the protective covers off of the MRVs and arming them to their full capacity. Missiles were loaded into the launch tubes. Racks of armor piercing rounds were carefully coiled and packed into the magazines of the Gatling guns.

They worked through the night, lit up floodlights in the orange swirl of the storm. It was difficult work under such conditions but not a single man or woman complained. As the job neared completion and morning approached, the storm's intensity began to lessen.

Having shaved his beard and donned a uniform, James walked out amid the final stage of preparations. He crouched beside one of the goliaths and scooped up a handful of sand from a windblown pile that had formed against the machine's armored foot.

It was the finest powder he'd ever held, almost like water in the way it moved. He tilted his hand and let the dust slide off. It caught the wind, vanishing before it reached the ground as if it had evaporated in the thin air. It dawned on him that these tiny particles were all that had stopped the mercenaries from killing everyone in the staging area and ending the rebellion before it began.

Strange, he thought, that something so small could have made such a large difference.

"We're almost ready," Dyson announced, walking up.

James stood. All around the makeshift yard the soldiers he'd known and led on Earth were preparing for the biggest fight of their lives. "The men look like they're raring to go."

"They ought to be," Dyson remarked. "We've been losing out here, without firing a shot. Wandering the desert, waiting for someone to take us into the Promised Land."

"You'd have gone eventually," James said.

Dyson shook his head. "I don't know."

There was guilt in Dyson's words. The kind James felt after witnessing his father's building explode. As if he'd stood by and done nothing, when he'd actually done all he could.

"You kept the unit together," he told Dyson. "That can't have been easy. Not under these conditions. If humanity gets a second act, you'll be the main reason for it."

Dyson took the compliment for what it was. But he knew the limits of his own style. There were caretakers, he thought, and then there were leaders. And now—in their hour of need—the leader of the 41st had returned to them as if he'd been brought back from the dead. The men took it as a sign, an omen of destiny, and if Dyson read them right, they were ready to storm the gates of hell if necessary to put an end to the Cartel's madness.

James followed Dyson up into the command vehicle and took the gunner's position, while Dyson settled into the driver's seat.

As the machine powered up, James grabbed the comm. There were no speeches this time. None were needed. He simply gave the order, broadcast to all the units simultaneously. "41st, this is Major Collins. Time to roll."

Chapter 50

In the same storeroom where the resistance had initially met, Hannah, Davis, Isha and Julian had now been joined by three dozen others. Plans were being made to strike and hold strategic buildings. Weapons were being divided up and placed in crates for distribution. A hundred rifles and fifty pistols soon to be handed out at clandestine meetings in three different locations.

"If the mechanics can take the hangar bays, we might be able to keep the Cartel's men out of their MRVs," Hannah suggested.

Davis and his crew nodded. "We can take them," he said. "Just not sure how long we can hold out."

"I'll try to get you some help," Hannah said.

"From where?"

"The detention facility," she said. "If my count is right, Cassini has almost five hundred people crammed into the holding cells. Half of them are former members of 26th. They'll be ready to fight."

"Assuming they're in any condition to do so," Isha said. "Are you sure you wouldn't be better attacking a different target?"

Having seen how they treated prisoners and slaves, Hannah had no doubt that many of them would be in bad shape. "I helped Cassini round up those people," she said. "I had my reasons but mostly I was just protecting myself. I'm not going to let them rot in there any longer."

Isha seemed to understand that, but she still looked concerned. "Fine," she said, "but why now? Why are we rushing? You said you wanted to wait until the mercenaries went back out to the Core Unit after the storm. But they're still cooped up here with us."

"I have my reasons," Hannah insisted.

"I think it's time you explained them."

Julian and some of the others nodded. Hannah had become the de-facto leader of the group but she was not unquestioned. "You have to trust me," she pleaded.

"Perhaps you need to trust us," Julian said.

There was no way around it. She nodded and closed the door, sealing them off from the others. When she was certain she had everyone's attention she spoke. "I've received a message," she said, "transmitted from the desert. The remnants of the 41st Armored Division are marching on the city as we speak. They'll be at the gates in less than an hour."

A hush fell over the group.

"Are you sure?" Julian asked. "Are you sure it's not a trick?"

"I'm positive," she said. "But they're badly outnumbered. And they'll be at a disadvantage once they enter the confines of Olympia's streets."

"So we distract and harass the enemy," Julian guessed.

Hannah nodded.

"If the 41st can get into the city we have a chance," Isha said. "A real chance."

There was excitement in her voice that told Hannah she'd figured the revolt was a lost cause prior to this. It made Hannah realize Isha was braver in some ways than she had been.

"As good a chance as we'll ever have," Hannah said. "But this information carries risks. It *cannot, under any circumstances,* fall into Cassini's hands. In other words, no one in this room can be captured alive."

⋏

With the stolen weapons in their possession, Hannah and her small militia rushed through the underground catacombs which hid the power conduits and the high pressure pipes that were used to heat and cool Olympia. Part of the original phase of construction, the corridors spread across the city like a web, with the Core Unit and the main government building at the center like a spider waiting for a meal.

Aside from the technicians who repaired and monitored the hidden systems of Olympia, few people used the tunnels any more. The streets above were wide and pleasant, the tunnels cramped and dark. But the tunnels were a more a direct route to anywhere one wanted to go.

At the front of the small force she'd gathered, Hannah came to a door protected by a coded lock. She turned to Davis. "Are we in the right place?"

Davis studied a readout on the handheld display. "This is the main intersection in sector four. The tunnel branches on the other side of the door. Access to the detention area will be found a hundred yards to the right. The left tunnel will lead to the government buildings, about five hundred yards onward."

With that confirmation, Hannah pulled a piece of electronic equipment from her pack and began to override the security protocols.

"Are you sure this is going to work?" Isha asked.

Hannah nodded, "Let's just say it's not the first place I've broken into."

The electronic lock pick finished its job and began flashing.

"Divide and conquer," Hannah said. "Here we go."

She pressed the green button and the pressure-sealed door released and slid open. Before it reached its maximum width the sound of plasma blasts rang out and several of those standing beside her were thrown to the ground, their clothes on fire, their skin melting and charred.

Hannah slammed herself against the wall, taking cover behind the doorjamb, and instinctively fired back.

A quick glance confirmed what she already knew. Mercenaries by the dozen were firing from covered positions in the long underground tube ahead.

Chapter 51

Out on the open plains, the storm was fading fast and the convoy of MRVs racing towards Olympia was rapidly becoming more visible.

As the dust tapered off, the green fields surrounding Olympia came into view. For the first time James saw them in the light.

"Beautiful isn't it?" Dyson said breaking his trance.

"Worth dying for," James said.

"You may get that chance," Dyson replied. "We're jamming all radar signals, but they're gonna see us before too long."

As if to prove his point, a warning light began to flash. A target appeared on screen.

"What it is?" James shouted.

The third member of the crew, a systems officer name Lasky shouted the answer. "Recon drone."

"Do they have us?"

Lasky locked in on the drone with the MRV's cameras. "It's turning back to Olympia. Trying to get home. I'll jam the frequencies, but if she gets through…"

Instinctively, James grabbed the firing controls and rotated the cab upward.

With great speed, he locked missiles on the high-flying bird and pulled the trigger. Two missiles ripped from the housing, trails of fire streaking toward the fleeing craft.

The recon drone crossed the barrier into the reddish-brown mass of dust. The missiles followed quickly, disappearing into the clouds.

The next seconds seemed like hours, and then an explosion lit up the clouds of dust from the inside, like the back lighting of a huge electrical storm in the dark of night.

"It's a kill," Lasky said.

"Did she get the message out?" James asked.

"I'm not sure, Sir. It was on its second cycle. But the data may not have passed through the storm."

Almost immediately gunfire lit out from the dust cloud, tearing into the MRV beside them. James whirled and spotted a lone machine, half hidden in the dust, standing guard on the approaches to the city.

Before he could fire, another unit lit up the sentry with a battery of cannon fire. The old mercenary rig was no match for the assault and was quickly reduced to a burning pile of junk.

It was bad news. Half of their strategy depended on getting into the city unnoticed, but there was almost no hope of that now.

Dyson looked at James. "Well?"

"Keep going," James said.

"If they meet us at the gates, we'll be decimated before we get inside," Dyson said. "You know that."

James did know that. It didn't matter. "There's no turning back now. Signal the other rigs. Things are about to get hot."

Chapter 52

In the tunnels beneath the government building, a firefight was raging.

Gault and Cassini were in the rear of a large squad of mercenaries as they tried to advance down the tunnel.

Cassini took cover as Gault launched a series of grenades down the tunnel. The explosions sent shockwaves flying in both directions and even Gault was knocked off his feet.

When the smoke cleared he saw the rebels had backed off, but not by much. He couldn't believe they were dealing with such stubborn resistance. Since the initial wave of gunfire, they'd moved forward by only fifty feet.

As the dust cleared, Cassini looked up furious. "Why don't you just blow us all up?" he shouted. "Then we'll have nothing left to worry about."

Gault ignored him and yelled into his communication device. "Bravo Team, where the hell are you?"

A voice came back. "We're doing our best to get in position. They've changed the codes on the doors. We're having to cut through everything we come to; it's slowing us down."

"How long will it take?"

"We'll be in position in five minutes. Just keep them pinned down and we'll have them trapped."

"Make it quick," Gault grunted.

He fired a random shot down the tunnel and then ducked. As the next wave of return fire ricocheted around them his comm squawked.

"Gault do you read? This is the command center. You'd better get back here. We have a problem."

"I'm a little busy right now," Gault grunted. "You'll have to deal with it yourself."

"I think you're going to want to deal with this," the voice said brazenly, "or we'll all be dead."

"What the hell are you talking about?"

"One of our drones spotted a column of heavy units moving toward the city. They've already taken out the sentries."

"Heavy units? What kind? From where?"

"The video is sketchy, but I'm pretty sure they're leftovers from the regular army."

"Damnation!" Gault cursed. "Scramble everyone. I want everything we got out on the streets, now!"

Gault stood to leave, but a panicked Cassini grabbed him. "Where are you going?"

Gault handed the comm to Cassini. "Our nightmare is now complete; the army you should have destroyed is marching on the city."

"What do we do?"

"We win," Gault said, "Or we die."

⋏

As the tunnel rocked with plasma blasts, Hannah and her people found cover wherever possible. After several minutes of fighting, the tunnel had filled with a smoke from burning debris and gunfire. Even then, Hannah realized the mercenaries at the far end of the hall were not pushing very hard.

"Julian, we need to break up into groups," she shouted. "They're probably surrounding us."

Julian was not a fighter. He put on a brave face but he looked to be falling into shock.

"Julian!"

"What?" he finally replied.

"Take half the group back to the last intersection," she shouted. "Do whatever you can to hold it while I figure out a way to get through."

"Do you have a plan?"

"Not yet," she admitted, "but our path is straight down this corridor and the mercenaries are in our way."

"That's suicide. There's got to be a better way?"

"There's no way around this junction," she shouted. "Now move before we get caught in a cross fire."

Julian nodded and waved a few of his people over. They spread the word and soon half the team was abandoning their positions and racing back down the hall.

As they went, Isha moved up beside Hannah, ducking behind a stack of equipment as a new wave of plasma fire came in. "So how are you going to get through that army?"

Hannah wasn't sure. In fact, considering the density of the smoke she couldn't even see the enemy. She looked up, scanning the array of piping and electrical conduits. An idea came to her. "Who works down here?"

Isha thought for a moment. "Santiago," she said. "He works primarily on the cooling units."

"Get him up here."

Chapter 53

As the last of the dust vanished, the outline of Olympia took shape ahead of James and his army. A silver city gleaming in the red light.

"Approaching the west gate," one of the units called out. *"Small arms fire coming at us from the towers."*

James tapped the transmit button on the comm. "Take out the gate and towers. Hit them hard. The heavy units will be waiting on the other side, so be ready and launch as many smoke grenades into the area as you can. If we don't break through the choke point we're dead. Once inside, scatter and make your way to the center of town; if we take the command building the rest of them will not fight that hard."

Confirmation came in from the various squad commanders and the convoy continued to charge.

Small arms fire increased as they reached the outskirts of the city and the big guns of the MRVs began to answer. Soon the mercenary defenses were silenced and the 41st began streaming into the city.

The radio chatter decreased but took on a strange tone.

"Alpha Two, do you see anyone?"

"Negative, no resistance on the north road, continuing on."

"This is Charlie Three, nothing but small arms fire on Main Street either."

James and Dyson weren't even dealing with that.

James and Dyson passed the west gate to find several structures reduced to burning rubble, but to everyone's surprise there were no MRVs there to greet them.

"Where's the welcome committee?" Dyson wondered.

"No idea," James said. "Not waiting around to find out either." He grabbed the comm. "Blue Team, you're with me. Everyone stay sharp. In case this is some kind of trick."

⁂

It was no trick. At that very moment, the mercenary army was trying—and failing—to get out onto the battlefield.

"Clear the hangar doors!" Gault shouted from atop his rig.

"We're trying," one of the mechanics said. "They've been welded shut. It's sabotage."

Gault could hardly believe what he was hearing. The army was bearing down on them and they were trapped in the parking garage.

"We're getting a cutting torch now," the mechanic shouted.

Gault wasn't waiting. He dropped into the gunner's seat, flipped off the safety and opened fire. The mechanics dove helplessly out of the way as the rotary cannon stitched a hundred holes in the huge doors and a missile released an instant later blew the central section of the door apart and out onto the street.

"Go!" Gault shouted.

The pilot shoved the MRV's throttle forward and Gault's machine rumbled to life, knocking down what remained of the doors and pushing out into the sunlight.

Within minutes the mercenary forces were flowing from three different hangars and massing for a counter attack.

⁂

James heard the sudden uptick in fighting clearly as the yellow and red groups ran headlong into the charging mercenary forces and explosions lit up Olympia's central boulevard.

Desperate radio calls went back and forth. Tracers and plasma fire filled the sky and the pall of black smoke from burning buildings and machines grew rapidly. It looked bad.

"We need to get in there," James said to Dyson.

Dyson nodded, and James hit the comm. "Units Three and Four, you're with us," he said. "The rest of you continue on to the main square."

The blue squad split up, with three units continuing to the center of the city and the others following James, Dyson and Corporal Lasky towards the main battle. As they neared the brawl, they came across six or seven MRVs burning and down.

"Ours or theirs?" Lasky asked.

James shook his head. The machines were too charred to identify as friend or foe.

Several blocks ahead, a trio of enemy vehicles crossed their site line at an intersection.

In the blink of an eye, James let four missiles fly, and seconds later, two of the three were obliterated. The first machine in the group survived, making it safely across the opening.

Before they could follow up, new enemies appeared, this time firing from the right. By the time Dyson had maneuvered the MRV into a firing position the enemy rigs had ducked behind one of Olympia's housing structures. James held his fire.

"We're at a disadvantage here," he mentioned to Dyson.

"How's that?"

"We actually care about the people in these buildings."

"They clearly don't share that worry," Dyson mentioned.

As another building took the brunt of someone's gunfire, James could not disagree. Looking around, it seemed like half the city was burning already.

Chapter 54

The catacombs beneath the city had begun to shudder from the battle going on up above. While most considered that a bad sign, Hannah knew better. It meant the 41st had finally arrived.

Hannah scanned the infrastructure with Santiago and Isha. "Which of these pipes carries the superheated water?"

"What are you planning?"

"This tunnel is downgrade toward the mercenaries," Hannah said. "If we blow one of the main lines we can flood them out of their position."

Santiago scanned the various conduits above them. "There," he said pointing to one of the large diameter pipes. "That's the one, high pressure water from the Core Unit, keeps the city toasty while cooling the reactor. I'm guessing you plan on breaking it?"

Hannah nodded.

"Don't get any of it on you," he said.

"Why? Is it radioactive?"

"No," Santiago replied. "But it's three hundred degrees. Half of it will turn to steam as soon as the pipe bursts."

"I'll be careful," Hannah said.

"You'll need to be more than careful," he warned. "You'll need to be at least fifty feet away or you'll be broiled alive."

Hannah took that to heart. There were a lot of ways to die, none of them good, but being steam broiled sounded worse than most. She began prepping two explosive charges.

"I'll go find a cut off," Santiago volunteered. "That way, once it's blown, we can divert the flow."

Hannah nodded and looked up at the conduit above them. She needed a way to get the explosives down range and yet keep them close to the conduit. Taking the strap from the rifle, she hooked the explosive charges to it and then handed the rifle to Isha.

"Make sure you cover me. It's wide open up there."

"I'm not a good shot," Isha said.

Hannah pointed down the hall. "Just keep firing that way. It doesn't matter if you hit anything. Just keep them pinned down."

Isha nodded, rested the rifle on the edge of a stack of equipment and waited.

"Now," Hannah said. As Isha and a few others began firing, Hannah climbed the maintenance ladder with all the speed she could. Despite the suppression fire, stray bullets and bursts of plasma fire still came her way, but she kept going and was soon hidden in the nest of conduits and perched next to the steam pipe.

She unhooked the rifle strap, looped it around the pipe and connected it back up again. That done, she set the timer for fifteen seconds, hit the start button and shoved it down range on the pipe. It slid about a hundred feet before stopping and exploding.

Hannah never saw it, she was back on the ladder, sliding down the rails and hitting the ground floor just as the explosions blew the pipe apart.

The foot wide conduit burst and a large section dropped toward the floor. A gusher of high-pressure water blasted out the end and the entire passage way instantly filled with steam. In seconds, a boiling torrent was surging down the tunnel toward the mercenaries.

From his position behind a stack of equipment, Cassini heard and felt the explosion. For a second he exalted, thinking Gault's pincer movement had finally worked, but the wave of steam and boiling water came blasting through the tunnel towards him. The steam blinded him, burning his face. Screaming, he turned away and tried to walk, only to stumble into the flood. Trying to get up he was trampled by his fleeing men.

The water seared him and he opened his mouth to scream again but instead swallowed some of it. Shaking and convulsing in a kind of pain he could not believe, his nerves shut down and he passed out, falling face first back into the scalding river, drowning and boiling simultaneously. As the flow built further, his body and those of his men were washed down the corridor to the low point where the water drained away.

As the hideous screams faded and the corridor grew unbearably hot, Hannah became certain that the mercenaries had fled their positions or been killed.

She called out through the swirling steam. "Santiago, shut off the water."

As Santiago diverted the water to another channel, the sound of the torrent began to fade. Meanwhile Hannah crawled forward to where Isha remained crouched in the fog.

"Ready?"

She got no answer and it took a second before Hannah why. Isha was dead. Her body propped up by the wall, a bullet wound through her neck.

She cursed silently, but there was no time for sadness. She took the rifle back and called to Davis. "Get the rest of the team up. We need to move now!"

Chapter 55

As the battle for the city raged, Gault directed his men from a fixed position in front of the main buildings of government square.

Watching a bank of monitors in his machine, he had seen the battle in the city go back and forth, but the strange geometry of Olympia's streets had begun to play into his hands. By using the buildings for cover his units could fire with impunity, and then back off and force the men and women of the 41st to move out into the open or risk destroying the very city and civilians they were trying to save.

It all seemed to be working perfectly. His people were bleeding the 41st dry in a war of attrition. Though the regulars were winning on a 2 to 1 ratio, that would not be enough especially with the last of the units from the outlying areas yet to arrive.

"Contact the reserves," he ordered. "Have them flank our enemies and end this madness."

The communications officer to his right gave the order and the last of the MRVs moved out into the streets, leaving Gault alone in the city's central square.

It wasn't long before he could sense the effects of this latest move. The intercepted radio calls from the 41st told the story.

"*This is Bravo Two. We're getting pinned down on grid one, five, zulu. Enemy units on both corners. Need assistance.*"

"*We're trying to get to you Bravo Two, see if you can—*"

"*Say again Alpha. We did not copy.*"

"Alpha?"

"Alpha's gone. Pull back Bravo, pull back!"

Gault could sense a type of panic setting in amongst the regulars as their numbers dwindled. It brought a smile to his scarred face.

"Finish them," he whispered to himself. "Finish them."

⁂

A half-mile from Gault's position, James was even more aware just how badly the battle was going. Rockets and missiles streamed in from every direction. They were ducking and weaving like a fighter in the ring just to avoid obliteration. There was little chance of getting off a well-aimed shot.

"This isn't good," Dyson said.

As the words left his mouth, the MRV beside them took a direct hit and exploded like a roman candle going off.

Three more rockets streamed in barely missing them, but a fourth hit their right leg, glancing off before exploding. The big machine began to limp.

"Losing hydraulic pressure," Dyson shouted. "Switching to back up."

James could see clearly that they were being surrounded. He made the fateful call. "All units," he called out. "One final charge. Break this noose or we're going to be destroyed."

There was no response. Their antenna had been sheared off in the last hit.

"Go," he shouted to Dyson.

"Alone?"

"The others will follow! Now move!"

Dyson did as ordered and soon they were turning back into the teeth of the enemy's fire. James began to fire without aiming. But even then, they didn't make it far before the hits began to add up.

Cannon fire dented the right side. Explosions in front of them blinded their view forward. Then a direct hit, rocked the cab. Warning lights lit up on every panel. And James flashed back to the defeat at the ridge that had taken Bethel's life.

"No!" he shouted.

"There's just too many of them," Dyson called. "They're all around us."

Chapter 56

From his spot in the main square, Gault could see it all unfolding on the tracking screen like a chess master hovering over the top of the board. The snare was closing. It would soon be over.

But just when it seemed to be all over but the shouting, things he could not explain began to occur. One by one his own units flashed yellow or red as their telemetry feeds indicated heavy or fatal damage. Some of them blinked off the screen completely as if they'd been removed from the game.

The radio chatter sounded confused, as if the armies of the 41st had somehow flanked them.

"Watch your six, Vultures. Pull back."

"We're taking hits. Indirect fire. It's coming from…."

"From where?"

"Everywhere… They're everywhere"

Finally Gault could stand it no longer. He pressed the comm switch. "What the hell is happening out there?"

"Gault," one of the commanders replied. "We have to retreat."

"No!" Gault shouted. "Do not retreat!"

"We have to. We're being overrun."

"By who?"

As far as Gault could tell the 41st had less than ten units still in the battle.

"I don't know," the commander replied. "Trucks, ATVs, bulldozers. There are hundreds, maybe even thousands of men and women on foot. They have bombs and---"

The signal cut out and the commander's icon turned red and then vanished.

Gault failed to understand, but he could wait no longer. "All units, pull back," he ordered. "Retreat and regroup at Government Square."

⚔

Out in the center of the chaos, James could hardly believe what he was seeing. On the very cusp of defeat, assistance had come from out of nowhere.

"My God," he said, watching a four-wheel drive scout race by with a familiar figure at the controls. "It's Kamahu."

"Who?" Dyson asked.

"Old friend of mine."

Riding on the trucks, ATVs and bulldozers taken from the staging area, Kamahu and several hundred slaves had charged onto the field of battle. They attacked without fear. Some of them rammed bomb laden ATVs into the legs of the mercenary MRVs, tumbling off at the last minute in what looked like suicidal fashion. Others hurled explosives as they raced by, swirling around and confusing the enemy. Waves of gunfire issued from the back of the big flatbeds, like broadsides from an old sailing vessel.

The mercenaries reacted quickly, and their fire was murderous as it poured onto the freed slaves, but the attack continued long enough for James and his forces to recover.

"This is our chance," he called. "Make it count."

With everything they had left, the 41st tore into the confused mercenaries. In minutes the line was broken and the few surviving machines were turning tail.

James recalled his mistake from the staging area and chased more cautiously this time. But he was not alone, and soon the fleeing units were run down, hobbled, subdued or destroyed.

⚔

Gault saw it all in living color. Aside from a few latecomers that had yet to arrive, his forces were gone.

"Gault, this is Control. Do you read?"

Gault ignored the call.

"Gault! Come in!"

In a fury Gault answered, "My God man, what is it?"

"Cassini is dead. We've been pushed back to the command center. The rebels have picked up help from the prisoners and the other citizens. We can't hold out much longer."

A sick feeling hit Gault's stomach. The emptiness of utter defeat.

Damn these people, he thought to himself.

As the words rolled around in his mind he began to smile and then a laugh bubbled up from deep down, a sickly, deranged laugh. "Yes," he whispered aloud. "Damn them all to hell!"

"Sir?"

Not sure he could trust the command crew to fulfill his next orders, Gault pulled out his side arm and blasted them dead in their seats.

Pulling the dead pilot out of his chair, Gault took over, turned the MRV around and took dead aim at the towering Core Unit looming over the city.

If he was going to die, he might as well go out in style and take all of humanity with him.

Chapter 57

Hannah had managed to rescue a hundred soldiers of the 26th armored brigade from the detention center. They fought with revenge in their hearts for those who'd been killed or tortured by the mercenaries, and few of the mercenaries they encountered lived to surrender.

With their help and a sudden uprising from the citizens in general, the little rebellion had grown into a human wave. They swept from building to building and soon overran the control center.

Finally in control, Hannah looked out through the glass wall ahead of her. A thick cloud of smoke hung over the city while fires burned in many of the outer buildings and explosions continued to be heard. As she studied the visual evidence, one of the men from the 26th studied the mercenary's tactical board.

"What's it look like?"

The soldier looked up smiling. "Mercenary units all but obliterated. A few coming in from the north, but they won't make it far. It's over.

"We've won," someone shouted. "We've won!"

Just then a wave of cannon fire ripped through the glass wall in front of them. Hannah dove out of the way, but others weren't so lucky.

As the gunfire ceased, bigger detonations shook the building.

Hannah got to her feet and risked a glance. The last mercenary MRV was blasting away at something. Firing everything it had at the walls of the Core Unit.

"Oh my god," she whispered. "We have to stop that rig from destroying the Core Unit," she shouted, "or this whole city will go up in a mushroom cloud."

"No way we can stop that rig with these weapons," the soldier replied.

"Find a radio," Hannah ordered. "Get in touch with the 41st. Or all of this is going to be for nothing."

⋏

James and Dyson were tracking toward the government center when long range fire began pelting them from afar. The shots were inaccurate, but substantial.

"They're coming across the two mile bridge," Dyson said. "I count three of them."

Two Mile Bridge was not two miles long but was named for being situated two miles from the edge of Olympia on the northern route.

"Yellow Four," James called. "Take the rest of the units and deal with these guys. Do not let them into the city. We're continuing on to the government center."

"*Roger,*" Four replied. "*We'll take care of them.*"

As the last MRVs peeled off to finish the enemy, James tried to get their systems back on line. He managed to cycle the ammunition feed in the rotary cannon bay and clear the jammed link. He was working on repowering the targeting sensors when another desperate call came in.

"*41st Armored, this is Hannah Ankaris. Do you read?*"

James was thrilled to hear her voice. "Hannah, this is James. What's your status?"

"*We've taken the government center and the control building but we have a problem. There's one mercenary heavy left in the square out front and it's blasting the hell out of the Core Unit. I think it's Gault.*"

"The Core Unit?" Dyson said. "Why would anyone--"

He didn't have to finish.

"We're on our way."

Chapter 58

Gault had taken a shot at the government building out of shear spite but his real target was the fusion reactor at the heart of the Core Unit. He had every intention of blasting through the containment building, destroying the cooling system and setting the fusion reactor into an unstoppable meltdown that would result in a thermo-nuclear explosion.

He laughed as he fired away at the wall. To hell with the settlers, to hell with the army and the Cartel and Lucien Rex. To hell with all of humanity as far as he was concerned.

As he loosed the last salvo of missiles and waited to see the effect, he began to grow frustrated. The thick, concrete walls were gouged and cracked from his assault, but they were also five feet thick.

Undaunted, he resumed the attack this time opening fire with the plasma cannon. Each hit was devastating, superheating the concrete and blasting chunks of it free due to simple and sudden expansion from the heat.

He continued to fire, maneuvering closer, certain he'd almost completed his task.

A call interrupted his revelry.

"Gault, this is Major Collins of the 41st Armored Division. Cease your attack on the Core Unit and stand down or you'll be destroyed."

Gault had no intention of standing down. But the call stunned him just the same. *Collins... James Collins. It could not be. But of course it was. Who else would it be?*

Disgusted more than anything else, Gault ignored the call and continued to fire, this time augmenting the plasma fire with the bursts from the armor piercing rotary cannon. The heavy shells did more damage than he'd expected, and soon the whole square was filled with a cloud of concrete dust. As it cleared, Gault could see that he was almost through. He lined up to fire, ready to end it for one and all.

Dyson had the throttle on the MRV wide open but the big rig was struggling and wheezing, and James could tell the limping machine would not make it much further.

"We're losing hydraulic pressure to the right leg," Dyson warned.

"Compensate for it," James called back.

"I can't. The fluid reservoir is almost empty."

They were so close, only a single glass and steel building between them and Gault. A single obstacle to go around.

"Take us to the right," James ordered.

Dyson maneuvered for the turn but the MRV stumbled like a drunken man about to fall. Before it toppled, the right leg stiffened and the rig seized up.

"Dyson."

"I'm sorry. There's nothing left."

James looked around in desperation. He could actually hear the pounding being unleashed on the walls of the Core Unit on the other side of the building. In a distorted reflection of a third structure he could see Gault's MRV unleashing the hellacious onslaught, but he could not reach him.

He had only one choice. He turned the cab to the left, locking the turret's sights onto the building between them. "God help me," he said, and then he opened fire.

The rotary cannons spun and unleashed a wave of armor piercing shells that quickly carved a tunnel through the building between them and out the other side. With a sight line that ran straight to the back of Gault's rig, James flicked the selector to missiles and let the last of his birds fly.

They launched without hesitation and took flight through the wrecked building like fiery arrows through a darkened cave. They caught Gault's machine center back, just above the spot where the cab rested on the chassis, where the armor was weakest.

The impact buckled the plating and the explosions sent the machine tumbling forward. It crashed face first into the street and then blew itself apart from the inside.

Chapter 59

In the moments after Gault's rig exploded, James, Dyson and Lasky remained on full alert, waiting for a hit that never came. Soon the reports came in from all over the city. The mercenaries had been captured, killed or had run out into the desert where the slaves were pursuing them on the remaining vehicles. James didn't imagine many of those caught would live to become prisoners.

When the main computer in their MRV gave up, the ghost and the cooling system failed. James knew they had no choice.

"Abandon ship," he joked. "Time to meet up with the resistance."

The three of them grabbed rifles and climbed out of the wrecked vehicle.

As Dyson made contact with members of the 26th, James made his way to Gault's obliterated rig. It had mostly burned out, but the charred remnants continued to smolder and issue black smoke. Three blackened bodies told him all he needed to know about the occupants who'd been inside.

James looked around. The city was burning, the air so filled with smoke that it blotted the sun from the sky. The darkness and carnage brought to mind Earth and all the battles he'd fought under the clouds of carbon, but unlike the home planet, this one still had hope. As if to prove it, the smoke thinned and the disk of the sun appeared, red as blood, but still shining as the smoke drifted past on the wind.

Chapter 60

A week after the battle the mood was upbeat as the newly formed government of Mars began ratifying a constitution that guaranteed rights and protections for one and all. In the damaged but hastily repaired government building, James sat in the balcony listening to the final vote and smiling as the gavel went down.

The speaker of the new government read out the results in a booming voice that everyone could hear without a microphone. "One hundred and fourteen votes *for*, and zero votes *against*! The constitution is passed unanimously."

The hall erupted in a chorus of cheers as Hannah, now the leader of the newly formed government, smiled beside James.

"We don't really need a PA system as long as he's the speaker," she said.

James laughed. *Of that there was no doubt.*

Up on the podium, Kamahu was celebrating with the others, shaking hands and grinning broadly. There were no more slaves or laborers on Mars, only citizens. Everything would be shared and the work on the other sites would resume once Olympia had been repaired.

As a crowd of the new senators came to speak with Hannah and Julian, James was thankful to have turned down any part in the government.

"I'll leave you to this," he said.

"Where are you going?"

"To get some air."

As the celebration got under way, James left the great hall and made his way outside. A long walk took him out of the city and onto a dirt road that ran beside green fields on one side and golden brown on the other.

For now at least, the smoke and dust were nowhere to be found and the sun was high overhead. In truth, it was a day unlike any James had ever experienced.

He made his way past the fields and came to a place where the oldest trees on Mars stood, trees planted by the first settlers. They were maturing now, fed by the irrigation and the morning mist.

There, under a weeping willow tree next to a stream of clear water, a burial mound lay, silent and still. No headstone had been crafted yet, but one day James would carve one on his own.

He sat down beside the mound and smoothed some of the dirt with his hand. "I wish you could see this place, my friend. It's incredible. You can watch the sun rise and cross the sky. You can feel its warmth on your skin and watch it set beneath the arms of the trees. You can hear the water running and drink from the stream. It feels like heaven. And I'm going to name it after you."

With that, James reached into the backpack he had with him, pulled out two shot glasses and filled them with crystal clear water from the stream. "One for the living," he said, "and one for the dead."

As was the custom, James raised his shot glass to the setting sun and then to Bethel's grave. After drinking from his own glass, he placed it down beside the second one, leaving them both at rest on the rich, maroon soil.

Chapter 61

Three Weeks Later

James walked down a long marble corridor in the upper echelons of the government building. Beside him, a man read information off various documents as they walked at a military pace.

At the end of the corridor two heavily armed guards snapped to attention and opened the double door to a well-lit situation room. Hannah was there as were the senior senators and the ranking officers of the military.

By the time James arrived the meeting was already in full swing and little progress had been made.

"Madam President," one of the senators pleaded. "We must respond. We must tell those who control Earth that we have declared independence."

A message from Lucien Rex to Governor Cassini had been looping on the comm system for days, repeating every ten minutes for the past two weeks. It started off cordially, demanded information about the situation on Mars and ended with a threat to the late Governor.

Nothing else had come, and despite their efforts to reach surviving military units on Earth, nothing they'd coded and sent seemed to have gotten through either. Now on this third week, a new message had arrived. It seemed Lucien had guessed fairly well what had occurred on Mars.

"So much for biding our time," Dyson said.

The plan had been to remain quiet, to play for time while they rebuilt their limited defenses and to come up with a plan for dealing with Earth.

"Can you play it again," James asked. He hadn't seen it yet.

Hannah set the message in motion. Holographic images appeared in front of all attending. Lucien spoke, "To the illegal criminals in possession of the Mars colony: We demand immediate communication at this time, or you will force us to take drastic measures. You have no rights to Mars. It belongs to the people of Earth and its food supplies are critically needed. You have twenty-four hours in which to respond, or we will be forced to take drastic action."

The members of the cabinet and the military all conversed.

"How do they know?" someone asked.

"They might have spies here," a second senator said.

"We should start checking everyone," a third added. "We can bug those who are suspected."

"It's against the constitution," Hannah replied. "We will not resort to being as they are."

"Then we might not survive," someone else said.

The way James saw it there were probably spies in the mix somewhere but they were irrelevant. "Spies or not," he said. "Lucien and the Cartel are in a desperate situation. The Earth is still dying, three months closer to collapse than it was before all of this madness started. When word gets out that Mars has been taken, the people will panic. Most will assume that none of the promised food will be coming forth. The riots in the street will become unstoppable."

"Good," someone said.

"Is it?" James replied.

"Lucien and his kind sought to leave us to that fate. Let them be consumed by it."

James had to admit there was something poetic to the thought, but not when one considered the vast amount of human misery that would accompany it. In its death throes, the Cartel would do all they could to survive, even if it meant exterminating the rest of Earth's population.

The colonists would be safe on Mars for a while, but not forever. As James thought of the people he'd met in the sublevels and the settlers trying to scratch out a living on the barren plains and all the rest who had no voice, the words of his father returned to him. *Do you really think we can save just ourselves?*

He spoke his mind. "You misread the Cartel if you think they'll sit around and die with the masses. They're backed into a corner, sooner or later they'll come out fighting."

The cacophony of voices died as James spoke. They looked at each other. And then to him. "What do you suggest?" Hannah asked.

He was the leader by default. A title he'd never wanted, yet it was his to bear. His family's legacy, perhaps.

"We help them," James said. "All of them. Even the Cartel."

⋏

In a similar room, seventy five million miles away a very similar meeting was taking place, the only difference was the tone.

"I don't know how you're going to fix this situation Lucien, but you'd better come up with a solution and fast."

Lucien Rex stood his ground. "Are you threating me Jonathan?"

"No, I'm letting you know that soon it will every man or woman for themselves, even in this room. My experts tell me that we're losing major ground to the rebels, insurgents, and terrorists. Their recruitment is growing and they're reaching into the highest levels of the government and military now. We have nowhere to run anymore, and soon they will be unstoppable. Do you understand? Our wealth cannot protect us forever."

"You've doomed us all with your arrogance, Lucien." The accusation came from a woman named Whitestone. It was yelled across the table.

"We could have rigged the lottery," she added. "We could have slowly added to our numbers, pried more favors from Collins. But no, the Great Lucien Rex had to be king. Well, congratulations. You're king now. King of a dying world."

Lucien turned angrily. He'd been taking this brow beating for the past forty-eight hours, ever since the news arrived that Mars had not just gone dark but that his forces had been overthrown and utterly defeated by rebels and elements of the military. While a few spies remained hidden there, they could do nothing about it. The planet was firmly in the hands of the enemy, and it had the great barrier of space as its protector.

"You fools," Lucien shouted, "Collins was never going to let us near his paradise. Not before the lifeline of this planet ran out."

The room went quiet as Lucien looked over their faces. "None of you wanted that. We took a vote, or are your memories so short? Now, we're all in this sad and unfortunate position together. But if we fracture, we're doomed."

"We're doomed anyway," a man named Abbas growled. "Isn't that what you told us? The Earth is dying."

"The window is not yet closed," Lucien insisted.

"It will be soon," Abbas said. "We must counter attack. Take Mars back at all costs."

"I'm afraid that's more difficult than it sounds," another of the Cartel said. "The orbits of Earth and Mars were at their closest point four months ago. They're separating now. Mars is almost out of range already."

The room became like a morgue. The true weight of their situation held them all in check. Because Earth orbited the sun much closer and faster than Mars it was rapidly pulling away. To launch transport for the red planet now, was like swimming against the current. It meant more fuel had to be carried and burned, more food and supplies used on the journey itself. As a result, less in the way of weapons and arms could be carried. The fact that several of the largest transports were already sitting on Mars made things worse.

Nor was a quick effort possible. To assault the planet, plans would have to be made, long detailed plans. The military would have to be consulted or the Cartel's grip upon them solidified. That also was easier suggested then done. Despite promises and bribes the High Command had already grown wary of Lucien. While the common enemies of chaos, anarchy and the Black Death kept them linked together a day would come when the military would assert itself again; a nightmarish scenario that none of them could have conceived when they voted to take over the government would come to fruition.

"So what do we do?" Abbas said.

"Yes," Whitestone added. "What do we do?"

One by one the others turned to Lucien and posed the same question. They would not fracture perhaps, but only because none of them wanted to lead at this moment.

Lucien didn't have any answers, only questions of his own. He tried to figure out where it had all gone wrong, how Mars had slipped from his grasp. Finally he got ahold of himself. It didn't matter what had happened, it only mattered what was about to happen. And then, at that very moment, something did.

"Lucien," an aide reported over the comm system. "We're receiving a transmission from Mars."

All eyes widened. "Patch it through," Lucien said. "Immediately."

The comm system lagged for a second and then a screen at the front of the room lit up. As always with such distant communications it was a one-way message, but even before it began Lucien understood that his plight had become even more desperate.

He rose from his chair, silent but with his mouth agape in surprise. "Collins," he whispered.

On the screen, James Collins stood proudly in his full military uniform. For Lucien, it was like seeing a ghost. Not only because he'd been assured months ago that James Collins was dead, but because the young man was the spitting image of his father, looking almost exactly like the late president had thirty years prior when Lucien had first met him.

Finally, the image began to speak. "To the members of the Cartel, I address you as Military Commander for the Olympian Republic and the free people of Mars. This message is for you and in particular for Lucien Rex. I call to discuss your surrender."

"In return for your imprisonment and trial as war criminals, ten billion metric tons of dehydrated grain will be delivered to Earth and the rest of your families will be pardoned and exempt from prosecution. These terms are non-negotiable. I expect your answer in twenty-four hours. If I don't receive it, or if you reject these terms, I'll be coming for you. Make no mistake: the next war will be fought on Earth in your homes, not in ours."

Chapter 62

James stood on a balcony, high atop one of the few untouched skyscrapers in the city of Olympia. His gaze wandered the cityscape. In some parts the settlement was in utter ruin, in others, it was as if war had never come to it. Not a scratch. Cranes moved silently in the dusky skyline and down on the street workmen moved about the broken and shattered buildings, removing debris by the truckload.

As the sun set behind the great mountain Olympus Mons, stars began to form in the sky like a magic trick, blinking suddenly and quickly out of the darkness and into existence.

As James pondered the future, Hannah walked onto the balcony and put her arms around him.

He smiled and then asked the question they both knew the answer to. "Any word from the Cartel?"

"No response yet," she said. "But they still have a few hours. Do you really think they'll accept our terms?"

James hesitated. "They might, but it'll all be lies. Stalling for time."

"So this isn't over."

James put his arm around her as the two looked up into the dark of the night and the vast expanse of space.

"No," he said, sadly. "I'm afraid this was just the beginning."

About the Authors

Graham Brown grew up in Connecticut and Pennsylvania, went to college in Arizona and fell in love with the desert and the blue skies. He's lived in the Southwest ever since. His first three novels, *Black Rain, Black Sun* and *The Eden Prophecy* were published by Bantam-Dell. Since 2010 he's been lucky enough to work with Clive Cussler on the NUMA FILES. *Devil's Gate, The Storm* and *Zero Hour* were all NYT bestsellers, with *The Storm* debuting at #1.

You can get in touch with Graham via facebook at https://www.facebook.com/GrahamBrownAuthor, on twitter via @AuthorGB or the old fashioned way - as of a few years ago – though his website at www.grahambrownthrillers.com.

Spencer J. Andrews is from Pennsylvania, where he attended Penn State University and The Carnegie School of Film and Media. He is the co-author of the *Shadows* trilogy of novels and *The Gods of War*, a dystopian yet hopeful tale of endless war, future slavery and the terra-forming of Mars as humanity's last attempt to save itself.

In addition to being an author, Spencer J. Andrews is a screenwriter and independent filmmaker. His love for the creative arts spans many disciplines including painting and music.

You can get in touch with Andrew via Facebook at www.facebook.com/spencerj.andrews, or on Twitter via @SpencerJAndrews

MORE FROM
GRAHAM BROWN
and
SPENCER J. ANDREWS

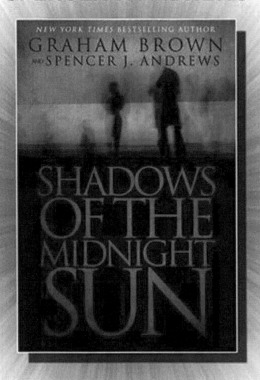

www.StealthBooks.Com

The first book in the Shadows Trilogy.
Watch for Book Two: Shadows of the Dark Star in August 2014

CUTTING-EDGE NAVAL THRILLERS BY JEFF EDWARDS

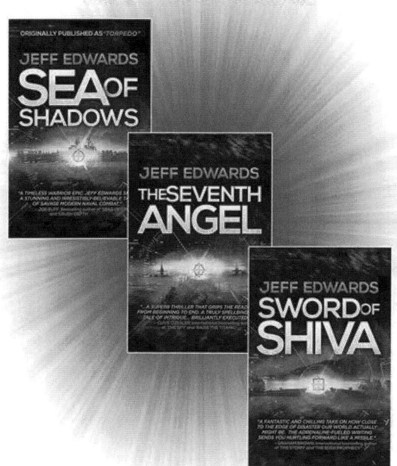

www.StealthBooks.Com

HIGH COMBAT IN HIGH SPACE
THOMAS A. MAYS

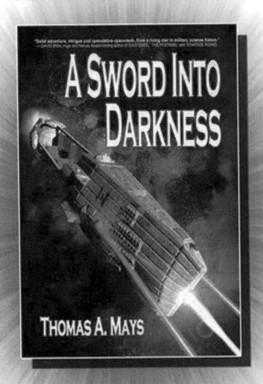

The Human Race is about to make its stand...

www.StealthBooks.Com

WHITE-HOT SUBMARINE WARFARE
BY
JOHN R. MONTEITH

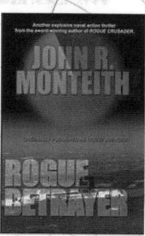

www.StealthBooks.Com

Made in the USA
San Bernardino, CA
06 August 2014